PRAISE FOR GEOFF NICHOLSON

"An offbeat master of black comedy."

— *Publishers Weekly*

"Critics have compared Geoff Nicholson to Evelyn Waugh, Georges Perec and Will Self... Nicholson is incomparable. He doesn't just give you what you want, he gives you what you never even knew existed."

— *The Independent*

"Read him—and laugh yourself sick,"

— *Time Out*

"A very funny, subversive writer."

— *The Times*

"An excitingly inventive novelist."

— *GQ*

"Nicholson's writing is rife with deadpan wit, a style that brings warmth to his characters and a chill to his obsessions."

— *Arena*

THE MIRANDA

A NOVEL

GEOFF NICHOLSON

The Unnamed Press
Los Angeles, CA

The Unnamed Press
P.O. Box 411272
Los Angeles, CA 90041

Published in North America by The Unnamed Press.

1 3 5 7 9 10 8 6 4 2

ISBN: 978-1-944700-36-2

Library of Congress Control Number: 2017952791

This book is distributed by Publishers Group West

Cover design & typeset by Jaya Nicely

On the battlefield, in the torture chamber, on a sinking ship,
the issues that you are fighting for are always forgotten,
because the body swells up until it fills the universe, and even
when you are not paralysed by fright or screaming with pain,
life is a moment-to-moment struggle against hunger or cold
or sleeplessness, against a sour stomach or an aching tooth.

— GEORGE ORWELL, *1984*

In the name of Hypocrites, doctors have invented the most
exquisite form of torture ever known to man: survival.

— EDWARD EVERETT HALE

That's what's the deal we're dealing in . . .

— FRANK ZAPPA, "THE TORTURE NEVER STOPS"

THE MIRANDA

ONE

How did it work? Well, it never worked exactly the same way twice—that was the nature of the process—but it always started out in an office in an unmarked government building, an outpost in the edgelands; an institutional room, though not quite as anonymous as it might have been: a bright, ground-floor office with a lot of windows and a view of a suspiciously empty parking lot. There'd be a map of the world on one wall, and maybe a calendar illustrated with bright, clear, artless photographs of dogs or sports cars, and a whiteboard on which somebody had drawn a not-so-bad sketch of Felix the Cat.

The encounter would be one-on-one, just me and the "volunteer," a term I never liked, but it was the one we used, and I definitely thought it was preferable to "subject," with its overtones both of lab rat and regal underling. All the volunteers I dealt with were men; it got far too complicated with women. There'd be two chairs in the room, but no desk: this wasn't supposed to look like an interview. Neither I nor the volunteer was armed.

The volunteer walked into the room and looked at me with suspicion and very possibly contempt. No surprises there. I was an unknown quantity. He had never seen me before, but he immediately knew he didn't like the look of me, could see right away that I wasn't one of his own kind, and of course he was perfectly right about that, and that was the point. Probably he didn't like the way I spoke or dressed, or the way I carried myself. Maybe I looked too soft, maybe I looked too professorial, or maybe there was some kind of pheromone I was exuding that alienated him. But that was OK. That was only to be expected. In any case, these were things that would soon be the volunteer's problem rather than mine.

I began talking immediately, as soon as the volunteer stepped into the room, without preamble, without introducing myself. And again, I didn't have a set speech, but I usually said something like, "One day you'll be on a job and you'll find yourself in difficulties. You may be in the capital of some failing state that's buckling under the strains of insurrection and corruption, or maybe you'll be in what looks like a cradle of civilization. We currently imagine that some crazed fundamentalist ideologues will be involved, but these things change constantly. I'm old enough to remember when Maoists rebels were the latest thing."

I might allow myself a smile at that point.

"Be that as it may, wherever you are, whatever the circumstances, however it happens, there'll be a fight, a skirmish, perhaps an ambush, and you'll be on the losing side. You'll survive but you'll be captured."

Now the suspicion and contempt turned to anger. I'd insulted him. This was a strong, confident, competent young man who believed he knew exactly what he was doing, who believed he was in control, who thought that terrible things could never happen to him.

"Of course," I said, and I sat down at that point, and the volunteer would always do the same, "you might think you'd rather fight to the death than be captured, but strangely enough your enemy may not give you that choice. You will wonder whether your captors intend to kill you, and the answer to that is: possibly but not necessarily. Although we're only concerned with the second of those cases.

"In that first phase of captivity you will ask yourself why don't they just do it and get it over with. And the answer to that may be because they want something from you: a name, a set of coordinates, a password, a piece of gossip. But in addition, though hardly separable, they may keep you alive simply because they want to have the pleasure of torturing you."

The mention of torture focused any straying attention.

"We can argue," I said, "and governments and politicians and lawyers and military strategists argue constantly, about definitions of torture, about its effectiveness and morality, but when you find yourself in a concrete bunker, naked, bound, wet, hungry, with electrical wires attached to your genitals, these arguments will seem a little academic."

At this point the volunteer always said something to the effect of "How the fuck would *you* know?"

And I replied, "Because I've been there," of course being deliberately vague about what "there" meant in this context.

The volunteer scrutinized me. Did I look like a man who'd been tortured? How exactly does a man who's been tortured *look*?

While he was thinking about that I said, "Torture affects people in a surprisingly varied number of ways. It can turn strong men and women into cowards, and it can make weak men and women suddenly very heroic. It's hard to know which kind you are, and nobody can be sure until it happens, but by the time you're in that concrete bunker, folded into a 'stress position,' it's a little late to start finding out. So that's why we're here today. I'm here to help you learn a little more about yourself."

The volunteer still wasn't sure what I meant. He might think I was going to regale him with war stories, with my own tales of survival and empowerment, or perhaps he thought I was going to give him a few psychological tips on how to focus the mind, how to endure and transcend. But no, that's not how it worked.

I got up from my seat, stole a glance into the parking lot, where there was now a large white car: it was always white for some reason, anonymous and unthreatening, except perhaps for the tinted windows. I couldn't see the men inside, but they could see me, and I knew they were watching me as I walked across the room and stopped when I came to the whiteboard. I took a sponge and erased the drawing of Felix the Cat, which was a signal visible to those inside the car.

Shortly thereafter, three men in nonstandard uniforms, with hoods and masks, entered the room, and there was a struggle, an unfair and unequal fight that went on for as long as necessary, between the men and the volunteer—I stayed well out of it—but it always ended the same way, with the volunteer subdued, tied, blindfolded, and unconscious. Then I could start my real work.

TWO

Naturally the senior members of the Team already knew a certain amount about the volunteers—their aptitudes, their temperaments, family situations, their sexual preferences if any—and somebody in authority undoubtedly knew their names, but I never did, any more than the volunteers knew mine. It was thought to be better that way.

When the volunteer came back to consciousness, in darkness, naked, bound, wet, hungry, with electrical wires attached to his genitals, in a concrete bunker (which in fact was simply the basement of the unmarked government building), if he was smart he accepted that this was part of the procedure, a necessary part of the training, something that would make him stronger, more capable. To reinforce this idea, as soon as he was alert, I told him there were rules to this game. I said I was one of the good guys. I said I was on his side. And I told him there was to be a safe word, one of his own choosing. If and when he said that word, the process would end, it would all be over, the mission would be aborted, and he'd be free. I told him there was no shame in that.

Of course we all know that this safe word business is often part of a certain kind of sexual role-playing, and this in itself perhaps quelled some of the volunteer's anxieties, reassured him that this was indeed just a game. Usually he'd pick what he thought was an inventive or clever or funny safe word, but you know, the safe words were never as inventive or clever or funny as all that.

Torture is a classic form, an ancient calling. I understand from my sources on the Team that there are scientists and technologists out there who are working on new, exotic, probably computer-aided forms of torture, but I never met one of those people. We wouldn't have had much to say to each other. For me it wasn't about science and technology; it was more like beating on an old tribal drum, raising the spirits, becoming part of the tradition.

I won't go into precise details of what I did. For one thing, I'm not allowed to, but the fact is I don't believe I did anything to the volunteers that would surprise you. I was going to say I did everything you might imagine, but that couldn't possibly be true. Any of us, even the most innocent and vanilla, can easily imagine forms of torture that are far, far beyond anything that I did, that I was *allowed* to do, to the volunteers. I stayed within limits. I was constrained by law and decency and to an extent by my own inherent squeamishness. I was, and remained, one of the good guys. But if you were to think of sensory and sleep deprivation, bright light and loud noise, electric shocks, simple physical assault—the punch to the gut, the blow to the head, the belt around the neck, the dog whip—then you'd be on the right lines. And at every stage I said to the volunteer, "Believe me, you'll be grateful for this one day."

At some point—sometimes sooner, sometimes very much later—the volunteer inevitably broke and said the safe word. He said "Shakespeare" or "Corvette" or "word" or "goiter," and sure, this

was a kind of defeat, but more often than not the volunteer believed it didn't really matter, because this was only a simulation,
only a game. You could always see the relief in his face, a kind of
relaxation, sometimes even a look of triumph as he said his precious safe word.

But the relief never lasted long. I was there to make sure of that.
The volunteer said the safe word and *absolutely nothing* happened,
nothing changed, nothing ended. I continued with the process,
with my job. The volunteer would complain, of course. I suppose
he couldn't help it. He felt angry or self-righteous or betrayed.
He said this was not what he'd signed up for, this was breaking a
promise, breaking the rules, this was not the way the good guys
conducted themselves. He might say this was a violation of his
human rights, a war crime, a crime anyway. And I'd say, "You're
probably right," and then continue with the process.

This went on for a considerable time. There was no script at this
point, no handbook. There were many variables, and ultimately it
all depended on the individual. But even the dumbest of the volunteers eventually worked out that there was nothing he could do,
nothing he could give me, no name, no set of coordinates, no password, no piece of gossip, no promise or threat that could make
any difference. He had nothing of value, nothing that I wanted.
He perceived that this was torture for its own sake, for the sheer
hell of it. He decided that I was as bad as anybody on the other
side, a monster and a psychopath; that I'd gone rogue, gone off
mission, turned into some bargain-basement Kurtz. Of course he
was wrong about that, but I was happy for him to believe it, and
it concentrated his mind wonderfully. It also, of course, gave him
a genuine, practical insight into the nature of torture and into the
nature of himself.

Eventually we would have been together for several days, at least a hundred hours, usually more, and the volunteer would have seen nobody but me. His world began and ended with me. By now, if I was doing it right, and I always was, the volunteer had some intuition of endless, unassuagable pain, which it seems to me is crucial to any vision of hell, theological or otherwise. The volunteer had been forced to confront and accept his own weakness and powerlessness, which was absolute. Now we were getting somewhere. The volunteer was able to recognize himself in ways he never had before. My job was almost done.

And then, inevitably, inescapably, without fail, a moment would arrive and the volunteer broke again, but in a brand-new, more profound way than he had before. He didn't just give in, he succumbed, he surrendered, he *submitted*. It was always a perfect, exquisite moment: physical, mental, no doubt partly sexual, perhaps spiritual, if you believe in that stuff. I looked into the volunteer's eyes and I could see that he was simultaneously there and not there. It had happened. He was ready. He had reached the place where he had always been destined to arrive. He understood. He knew in every cell of his body. He was, you might say, enlightened. I'd done what I set out to do. Then I administered an injection, and the volunteer passed out, not for the first time, and when consciousness returned I was gone. He would never see me again.

As the volunteer stirred back to life, he was no longer bound, naked, wet, and the rest, certainly in no concrete bunker. He was traveling fast in an unmarked SUV with a couple of other men he'd never seen before—not friends, not colleagues, but recognizably members of his own tribe. They were taking him home. There would be no debriefing, no discussion. If the volunteer tried to talk to the men in the vehicle about what had happened, they'd ignore him. The men would behave as though nothing had happened, because in several important senses nothing really had.

Am I making this sound a lot more casual than it was? Perhaps. It was certainly hard work for me, both physically and emotionally, and it wasn't the kind of job you could leave behind at the end of the shift when you went home to your wife, though god knows I tried to. On the other hand, in some respects it was a job like any other, with a job description, a salary, terms and conditions, and, ultimately in my case, when I quit because I couldn't stand it any longer, a less than generous golden handshake. Banal stuff for sure.

And yet the satisfactions were beyond anything most people will ever know in their work. The volunteers were all good men, and they became even better with my help. I made them bigger, stronger, wiser versions of themselves. Most of them, anyway. I never doubted there would be failures. And one thing of which I was absolutely certain, had known right from the very beginning: sooner or later the failures would come back to haunt me.

THREE

It seems very long ago that I was employed by the Team, though we know that time is elastic, and in reality it was no time at all. It was the kind of work that anybody would grow weary of sooner or later, the kind of work a man might choose to put behind him and try to forget, if he had any choice. I have no data on the Team's staff turnover, but common sense suggests this was not a career that encouraged a lifetime of service. Certainly my immediate superior, the person I reported to, Christine Vargas, didn't seem remotely surprised when I told her I was quitting. She remained as calm, as quiet, as steely as ever.

"What are you going to do now?" she asked.

"I think I might do some walking."

It was a reasonable enough reply. I'd always been a walker, right from when I was a kid. I didn't like sports—I didn't care about competition—but I could walk forever. Sometimes I walked with my dad; sometimes I walked alone. Sometimes I walked in order to get places; sometimes I walked for the hell of it. When I grew up, when I became a serious person, I sometimes walked very seriously, as a hiker, a trekker. Sometimes I took two- or three-day solo hikes into and out of the wilderness. Sometimes I walked coastal paths and mountain trails; sometimes I was an urban explorer. But sometimes there was nothing very serious about it at all: I just strolled or sauntered or meandered. Pretty much any kind of walking was fine by me.

The benefits of walking are well known, for both mental and physical health, and sure, I was always happy enough to receive those benefits. In my line of work I needed all the health improvement, and all the distraction, I could get. But I didn't walk to keep "fit," and I was certainly never one of those spiritual or sacramental walkers. I never saw anything very holy about it. I didn't walk to find myself or lose myself, at least not if I could help it. It started as a habit and maybe at some point it became a kind of addiction, but if you have to have an addiction (and it seems that a great many people do), then I think walking is one of the better ones. I walked because I *liked* it. I walked because I wanted to. I walked because I walked. This went on for a very long part of my life. And then certain bad things happened, which I'll tell you about sooner or later, and at that point I stopped walking.

After these bad things happened, and after I quit my job, and after my wife, Carole, and I divorced (another story that I'll have to tell), I didn't feel much like walking anymore. It got to the stage where I never walked at all. I didn't feel like moving from point A to point B. I scarcely felt like stepping foot outside the front door. And when I was first getting "back on my feet" (as Carole insisted on putting it), I lived in a motel in a neighborhood so unpleasant and so potentially dangerous that only those with a death wish would have walked the streets if they didn't have to. But the fact was, at that point in my life, I wouldn't have gone walking even if it had been the safest, prettiest, most pedestrian-friendly neighborhood in the world.

In retrospect I can see that I deliberately chose a horrible place to live. If I'd moved into somewhere that was more or less bearable, I might have stayed there the rest of my life through sheer inertia. The appalling state of the motel guaranteed that I would have to move on sooner rather than later, though god knows some of my neighbors in the adjoining rooms looked like they were there for the long haul. The psychologist in me knew that most of them were troubled rather than plain bad, but the way these troubles manifested themselves was, of course, another motivation for me to get out of there.

And so, in due course, I spent a certain amount of time with realtors, looking at properties. My budget was, let's say, modest. My early retirement package was less than heroic, and although my wife hadn't taken me for every penny I had, she'd nevertheless taken me for plenty. She seemed to feel just a little guilty about this, but she also seemed to be somehow pleased with her own sense of guilt, that it was an indication of her finer feelings, that she wasn't all bad, but it did nothing for me. I've always thought that guilt is one of the least useful of human emotions.

I wanted a house. It didn't have to be big, it didn't have to be in a "good" area, it didn't have to be in great condition, but it did have to be on its own patch of land. It had to feel secure, it had to be secluded, and, given my price range, I knew it had to be a couple of hours upstate from the Big Smoke. There were quite a few options but I kept rejecting them, looking for the one that spoke to me. I knew I'd eventually find what I needed, because eventually everybody always does, one way or another. And I did.

It was a small house, one story—some would call it a bungalow—neat, symmetrical, solid, made of pale redbrick, the kind of place the wise little pig would have chosen. There was a glassed-in porch at the front of the house, dilapidated but solid enough to create a kind of airlock between the world at large and my own front door.

The house sat in the middle of a more or less square 1.25-acre plot of land, on the very edge of a village, in a kind of scattered rural suburbia. I'm sure some people would have thought it was in the middle of nowhere, but I was delighted to be in the middle of nowhere. The previous owner of the house had used it only as a vacation and weekend home, and not often, so I could move in right away.

A quiet rural road ran along the front of the property, so the house bordered only three other plots, had only three immediate neighbors: one at either side and one over the back fence. That was plenty. I'm one of those people who believes that good fences make good neighbors, and personally I'd prefer to have good *electric* fences, and good razor wire, and possibly good man traps, but I hoped that wouldn't be necessary. I had no intention of befriending my neighbors, but I didn't want to make enemies of them either. Above all I didn't want them too close or too present.

People pick their homes for all kinds of reasons, many of them trivial, some of them downright irrational. People will buy a house just because they like the color of the kitchen tiles or because the bathroom has a bidet, and by these standards my choice was completely reasonable. I picked my house because of the yard.

It contained some fine oak trees, some less fine pines. There was a lichen-encrusted stone bench, left behind by the previous owner, featuring two lions carrying the seat on their backs. There had once been a vegetable garden, and its outlines were still visible but only just. In one corner was the concrete foundation where a greenhouse had once stood. These earlier forms were disappearing under ivy, nettles, and some rangy, flowering weeds that I didn't know the names of. I wouldn't be taming or improving the yard, just so long as the path was kept clear. It was this path, above all, that really clinched the deal for me.

This path ran in a perfect circle, more or less equidistant from the house at all points and not too close to any of the boundary fences. On maps or from above, the layout looked like a figure in a geometry textbook, or maybe a cattle brand, the square in the circle in the square.

While the realtor waited, I took a couple of thoughtful, exploratory strolls around the path as though I were inspecting the house from all angles, and although I did indeed take a perfunctory look at the state of the guttering, at the roof and window frames, at the columns supporting the porch, and so on, my attention was chiefly focused on the path itself, how it felt underfoot. Once I'd completed the first circuit I knew what I'd suspected just by looking at it: the path was about one hundred paces around, creating, as I would subsequently discover once I'd measured it precisely, a circuit of exactly one hundred yards. I didn't know whether I was surprised or not.

I'm tempted to say that when I saw the circular path, I became aware of all kinds of possibilities, of things I'd been thinking about for a long time, but in truth I really became aware of only one possibility. I saw a place where I could start walking again. And I saw something else as well, something more, something much bigger. I saw the start of a grand project. I saw the stage where I would act out a script that, in some form or other, I'd had in my head for my entire life. I knew exactly what I had to do. I would walk around the world, and I would do it without ever leaving my own yard.

FOUR

Nobody has ever *literally* walked around the world. Nobody could, since however you tried to do it, that would involve walking across, or on, many thousands of miles of open water. So "around the world" walkers—and there are plenty who call themselves that—always have to get inventive, even as they limit themselves: they walk in every country or in every state, or across every continent, or around every coastline. Some might consider this cheating.

But however you do it, an "around the world" walk, however metaphoric, obviously demands strength, stamina, determination, discipline, and the ability to survive in alien environments. You need to have plenty of time on your hands, and it helps a lot if you have an independent source of income. Oddly enough, to my considerable surprise, in some form or another I had all the above, although I wasn't a big fan of alien environments. That was why I intended to walk around the world in my own backyard.

Let me tell you how it worked. There's a certain amount of math involved, but don't worry, it's simple stuff really. The first thing to know is that Earth is not genuinely spherical. Its shape is what's called an ellipsoid, like a ball that's been slightly squashed from the top. Earth's circumference at the equator is 24,901 miles, whereas the circumference through the poles is 24,860 miles—a fairly minor difference given the large distances involved, but it seems to me that if you don't want to be accused of trying to make life easy for yourself, then when you decide to walk around the world, it's probably best to cover a full 25,000 miles, a nice round figure that leaves no room for doubt or nitpicking. And let's face it, a lot of people in the history of the world must have walked at least that distance, often in a single country or a single city. The kind of thing I was planning to do was by no means unheard of.

A mile contains 1,760 yards, so 25,000 miles contain 44 million of them. If your garden, by some chance, happened to contain a circular path that was exactly 100 yards long, you would need to walk around it 440,000 times in order to cover a distance equal to the circumference of Earth at the equator. To put it another way, you would need to make 17.6 circuits of your garden path in order to cover a mile. Repeat that 25,000 times and the job would be done. And that was exactly what I intended to do. That was my plan, my grand project.

Thought of in these easy, step-by-step terms, the grand project didn't even sound all that grand. A mile is nothing. Any damn fool can walk a mile. Even a quite leisurely walker is likely to move at 3 miles per hour. I usually walked much faster than that. To cover 3 miles I'd have to walk around my path 52.8 times. That may seem like a big number in one sense, but an hour's walk is nothing. Do it for 8 hours a day and you'll easily have covered almost 25 miles. And that was the pace I set myself. I could probably have done a higher daily mileage, but why be a show-off? Plus, 25,000 divided by 25 comes out to a very convenient 1,000: I would have to walk 25 miles a day for a thousand days. How satisfying is that?

It occurred to me that a certain kind of person might even be able to consider this as a job, to treat it as nine-to-five employment, five days a week, with time off for weekends and vacations, sick days and personal days. But I didn't want it to feel like a job; I wanted it to feel like a grand obsession, which of course it was. I didn't want days off. I didn't want vacations. I wanted to walk every single day: that seemed vitally important. Naturally there might be the occasional day when I had trouble getting in the full eight hours—illness, bad weather, unavoidable interruptions— but there was plenty of wiggle room in the other sixteen hours of the day. I could walk all night if I needed to make up lost time and distance.

Now, since a year contains 365 days, a rate of 25 miles per day adds up to an annual total of 9,125 miles. In other words, my entire journey would take just 95 days less than 3 years. In more or less 2.75 years I would have walked around the world. I was never the kind of person who takes anything for granted. I always knew the world was full of shocks, both natural and unnatural—bolts from the blue, heart attacks, strokes, snipers' bullets—and I knew I was getting older, but even so I reckoned I still had, at the very least, 2.75 good years in me.

Could I walk 25 miles in a day? Yes. I absolutely could. I'd done it often enough in the past to know it was easily possible, well within my limits. I also knew exactly how it felt to walk 25 miles in a day. It felt pretty damn good. Did I think I could walk 25 miles on each of every one of a thousand consecutive days? Well, yes, I *thought* I could, otherwise I wouldn't have taken on the project. But did I absolutely *know* that I could? Well, no, obviously not. It was the kind of undertaking you can't possibly be certain about until you've tried it. You do it in order to discover whether you *can* do it.

I knew for sure that it wouldn't be easy, that there'd be bad days as well as good, days when there were problems: practical, physical, possibly psychological, maybe philosophical. Some of these I could easily anticipate, but I knew there'd be surprises, new challenges and difficulties that had as yet never even crossed my mind.

But I didn't fear these things, and in the larger sense I didn't fear failure either. I wanted to succeed, of course. I wanted to walk around the world in my own special way. But if I failed then I failed, and I could see no great shame in failing. I did, of course, expect that somewhere along the line I might have a visitor or two from my past. I didn't relish that, obviously, but I would deal with it when the time came. I would have no choice. They'd find me ready; they'd find me walking.

FIVE

My worldly goods, such as they were—my share of the marital chattels—had been in storage in the city, and I arranged that on the day I took possession of my new house, movers would make the transfer from the storage unit. This, the day I moved in, I considered to be Day Zero, the day before I started my grand project, and a day on which I didn't plan to do any "real" walking. The movers were a friendly but rough bunch, and I'd have felt like an idiot striding determinedly in circles around the path while they worked unloading the truck, so I held back.

The guys were even friendly enough as they complained about the weight of many of the boxes I was making them carry. "What have you got in here anyway?" one of them asked. "Guns and ammo?"

Before I could answer, one of the others had given an answer based perhaps on experience, or perhaps he thought I looked somehow "bookish," and he said, "It's books, isn't it?"

"Yes, that kind of thing," I said, and the men all nodded in what looked like sympathy.

That I didn't have any bookcases might have been an extra cause for sympathy. The bookshelves in the marital home, where my ex-wife, Carole, still lived, were fitted to the walls and I'd seen no point trying to take them with me. The thought that they remained there in the old house, empty, to remind Carole of my absence, gave me a significant, if not especially noble, pleasure.

After the movers had gone, I did a couple of exploratory circuits of the garden path, just to get the feel of it, but no more than that. I was saving my energy for the next morning, which would be the start of Day 1. I couldn't even be bothered to do any unpacking.

On Day 1 I got up early, stoked myself with coffee and protein, and I started walking. There was no drama, no ceremony, no fanfare. It was a cool, bright spring day. There was no likelihood of rain and conditions were good, a fine day to start a project, though I'd have started walking however bad conditions were.

As Lao Tzu might have said, a journey of twenty-five thousand miles begins with a single step. And I'd done rather more than that, walked thirty circuits, taken at a good, steady pace, which meant I'd covered three thousand yards, less than two miles, when I realized I was being watched by a young boy whose head had appeared over the garden fence shared with the neighbors on the west side of the house. I've never been very good at estimating the ages of children, but I guessed he was ten or eleven years old, and in order to peer over the fence he must have been standing on a box or a rock. His pale, fleshy, hesitantly cheerful face looked out at me with both curiosity and suspicion.

"How you doing?" he asked, sounding, or at least trying to sound, grown up and casual.

"Doing good," I said, which I thought was the right answer.

"Doing some walking?"

"You got it," I said.

My instinct was to keep walking and ignore the boy, but somehow he looked like a kid all too many people had already ignored. It wouldn't completely ruin my grand project if I stopped for just a couple of minutes to talk to the neighbor kid.

"What's your name?" I asked.

"Paul," he said. "They call me Small Paul because my dad's called Paul as well, and he's bigger than me, so he's Big Paul, and this way there's no confusion."

"Good to know you, Paul," I said. "I'm Joe."

"Are you saving the Earth?" Small Paul asked.

"What's that?"

"They teach us at school that walking's really good for the environment. You know, reducing your carbon footprint."

"Well," I said, "I think there might be an argument that by walking I'm actually using up quite a bit of oxygen and exhaling quite a bit of carbon dioxide, so that might be bad for the environment. I'd certainly be producing less greenhouse gas if I just sat on my couch and did nothing."

This made the boy think, but only for a moment. "At least you're not using your car," he said.

"That's true. And I'm not showering or shaving very often either," I said. This was my attempt at boyish good humor, but it fell flat.

"And it's good exercise too," said Small Paul. "Exercise is really important."

He didn't sound either convinced or convincing. I couldn't really see his body, but his face suggested he was a plump, unathletic little thing.

"Walking *is* good exercise," I said, "but that's not why I'm doing it."

Now he looked confused, which I imagined was not a rare experience for him.

"So is it for charity?" he said. "You know, to find a cure for cancer or Alzheimer's or whatever?"

"No, Paul, I really don't believe that walking around my path will result in any kind of medical breakthrough."

"So you're not, like, sponsored—that's when you get a bunch of people to sign up and they pay you money for every mile you walk."

"I know what sponsored means," I said.

"Oh, yes, sorry."

Saying sorry seemed not to be a rare experience for him either.

"I'm not sponsored," I said. "I'm walking for my own selfish purposes."

This was another attempt at humor, and another failure.

"Well, you know," Small Paul said, "it's good to try and make a difference."

It sounded like something he'd heard somebody say. I thought about it for a second, and then I invoked chaos theory.

"Look, Paul," I said, "they say the world can be changed by the beating of a butterfly's wings, so I'm sure it can be transformed out of all recognition by a man who goes for a long walk around his own yard."

"Wow. I never thought about that," said Paul.

"Well, you think about it," I said.

"I will," he said, though I wasn't sure he would.

"But I'm not walking to change the world," I said.

I was now ready to walk on, but another face appeared over the garden fence.

"Is he bothering you?" this new arrival asked.

I knew this had to be the boy's father, Big Paul. There was a distinct family resemblance, the same soft features, but the dad's came in a larger size and were scuffed and creased with age. I could see a little more of him than I had of his son, and although he too appeared plump, he also looked solid and muscled, and he was wearing a camouflage T-shirt that showed off thick, sinewy arms.

The effect was spoiled, however, since in the palm of one hand he was holding a tiny dog, a ball of soft, tremulous white fluff. He seemed to be doing his best to pretend the creature wasn't there, so I didn't mention it either.

"No," I said, "the boy's not bothering me, just distracting me a little."

"Well, if he starts to get annoying, tell him to fuck off. Or words to that effect."

Small Paul looked crestfallen, as though he'd frequently been told to fuck off in precisely those words.

"OK," I said, though I didn't mean it. I didn't have the greatest affection for children, since I still have very clear memories of being one, but in general I think it's probably best not to tell them to fuck off.

It was at this point that Big Paul and I introduced ourselves.

"I'm Joe."

"They call me Big Paul. I like to think of myself as the eyes and ears of the community."

"Is that right?"

"Yeah, I work in security." Naturally I assumed this meant he was a bouncer, and maybe he sensed this, because he added, rather grandly, "Yeah, I'm in charge of security up at the new outlet mall. I have a lot of people under me."

This amused him more than was reasonable. When he stopped snickering he said, "So if you ever have any kind of trouble, you should come to me."

I already knew perfectly well that in no circumstances, regardless of how much trouble I got myself into, would I ever turn to Big Paul for help, but I saw no reason to tell him that.

"Well," he said, putting a less than fatherly arm around Small Paul's neck, "his mother's got to get him to school. And make sure he goes inside. Can't trust the little bastard to get there by himself on the school bus."

Small Paul smiled sheepishly. He seemed to think this was something to be proud of. Maybe it was.

However, there was still the matter of the tiny white dog. Big Paul seemed to have forgotten all about it, but now he became acutely aware of it again, as though it were a piece of litter that had somehow become stuck to his hand. He peeled it off and handed it over to his son, who didn't appear to want it much either.

"Anyhow, enjoy your day," said the senior Paul. "If you can."

I said that if I could, I would, and I continued walking.

SIX

A surprising number of people came and went at my new house in those first few days after I moved in, after I'd started walking. They were people I didn't know, didn't want to, and, in most cases, never would: the cable guy, a couple of meter readers, the realtor, who said he came because he wanted to make sure I was "comfortable" in my new home, and he left a stack of business cards and leaflets that he encouraged me to give to loved ones, neighbors, or just anybody I knew who was thinking of buying or selling or renting a place to live. I didn't say I wouldn't. A deliveryman came with a fruit basket sent to me by my ex-wife: I was pleased enough to get some fresh fruit. I didn't let any of these people interrupt my walking for longer than necessary, and with the exception of the realtor, who evidently had time on his hands, they were all keen to be on their way and get to their next call.

On Day 3 I met another of my neighbors, the one who lived on the east side of my house. I was walking around my path and I became aware that someone was out in the yard next door, a woman with a cell phone apparently taking pictures of some new spring growth in her flower beds. She was an older woman but not old, I'd have said, although if I'm no good at guessing the ages of children, I'm even worse at guessing the ages of women. She was large, frizzy-haired, round-faced, oval-bodied, wearing a multi-colored smock and a lot of heavy wooden jewelry: a woman who probably liked to think she was vibrant and larger than life.

I didn't intend to do more than say a quick, perfunctory hello, which I did, but my neighbor wanted more than that. A little while later, having gone into her house, she reemerged and came up to the fence, and I saw she was holding a tray with a mug of something and a slice of sponge cake on it. I didn't take much notice, since I didn't immediately think it had anything to do with me, but I did another circuit of the path, and when I came around again she was still standing at the fence, waiting for me. I wasn't sure what she was up to, but then she held out the tray and said with great seriousness, "This is for you," so I felt I ought to stop and exchange a few words with her.

She handed the tray over the fence, and I took it from her. The cake appeared to be homemade, as for that matter did the plate and the cup and the tray. We introduced ourselves, and my neighbor told me her name was Wendy Gershwin (no relation) and that I could call her Wendy. I hoped I wouldn't have much occasion to.

"I'll save the cake for later," I said, "and I'll let the tea cool down a little before I drink it."

"Hey, you won't break my heart if you throw it to the squirrels," Wendy Gershwin said.

"I won't throw it to the squirrels," I said. "I appreciate it. Really."

It was true to an extent; I did appreciate the gesture, and I definitely didn't want to insult the woman, much less break her heart. I wanted to be civil, but I didn't want to be actively, positively *friendly* toward her. I didn't want to make any assumptions about her, didn't want to deal in stereotypes, but I was well aware that larger than life, middle-aged women can be very chatty. They tend to have a lot of time on their hands, and admittedly, in many ways I had a lot of time on my hands too, but I wanted to fill my time with walking, not with chatting over the garden fence.

"If I were you," Wendy Gershwin said, "I'd reinforce that back fence of yours."

"Yes?"

"I'd build a big wall, as high and as thick as you can make it."

I was determined not to ask her why, although the notion of a high, impregnable wall suited me well enough.

"That property back there," she said, "it's empty right now."

It was true that I hadn't seen any signs of life over the back fence, but I hadn't thought too much about it. It was early days. If I'd considered it at all, I'd have thought maybe the inhabitants were away, or it was a vacation home, or maybe they were just very quiet people.

"But it won't stay empty long," Wendy Gershwin said. "It never does. They rent it out to all kinds of riffraff."

"Riffraff?" I said.

"Lowlifes, scum, trash, *all* kinds of riffraff. It's empty now because they had to evict the last bunch. But I'm sure they'll soon find some brand-new riffraff to rent it out to."

I was perfectly willing to believe her, although I'd have thought Big Paul, in his role as eyes and ears of the community, might have mentioned something about trouble with the previous neighbors. Maybe he didn't want to alarm me. Or maybe his neighborly prejudices, and his ideas of trouble, were different from those of Wendy Gershwin. One woman's riffraff is another man's colorful, arty Bohemian, although I imagined Wendy Gershwin would be rather more enamored than Big Paul when it came to colorful, arty Bohemians.

In due course I would come to see that Wendy Gershwin's notions of riffraff were in fact largely the same as my own. The new tenants who moved into the house beyond the back fence would indeed prove to be quite a handful. But that was all some way ahead of me on Day 3.

"I like a quiet life," Wendy Gershwin said.

"Me too," I agreed.

"My niece and I just want to be left alone to get on with our art."

She gestured toward her house, and I saw a sullen, willowy, gawky teenager standing in the doorway, glowering out at us, but she scuttled inside as soon as I looked at her.

"She's a fragile soul," said my neighbor.

I suspected that Wendy Gershwin wanted me to ask a few questions about her niece and her art, so obviously I didn't. I sipped some tea, forgot about the cake, and walked on.

SEVEN

Of course, as soon as I moved into my new house, I had one regular, more or less daily visitor: the mailman. He was a black man, tall, quiet, self-contained, very straight-backed, and he had a head of bouncing dreadlocks that somehow, surprisingly, seemed to go very well with his postal uniform. For the first few days he pulled up in his truck, put the mail into the mailbox outside the gate, and went on his way. I didn't always see him, but when I did, he'd nod seriously, unsmiling, his duty done, and then go on his way. I liked that.

In fact, no words were exchanged between us until Day 10, when he got out of the truck, stood at the gate, some of my mail in his hand, and called to me, "Mr. Johnson, I presume," which wasn't much of presumption given that my name was on the mail.

I left the path, walked over to the gate, and took the mail from him. That would have been enough for me, but clearly he wanted something more. In other circumstances I might have ignored him and kept on walking, or told him that if he wanted to talk he'd have to walk along with me, but I reckoned that a mailman has to follow some pretty strict rules about where he's allowed to go and when, and in any case, I thought he probably did enough walking in his job not to want to do any extra.

"You just moved in," he said.

It didn't sound like a question, and he obviously knew the answer.

"That's right," I said.

"Well, it's good to put a face to a name. I like to know the names and faces of all the people on my route," he said. "And I like them to know mine: Darrell."

I wouldn't have guessed that many mailmen had that attitude about names and faces, but then I didn't know many mailmen. I looked at the two envelopes I was now holding, one white, one buff. Neither looked like anything important.

"Probably junk mail," the mailman said.

"Probably," I agreed, though in fact I've never particularly objected to getting junk mail.

"Junk is mostly what keeps me in business," said the mailman. "That and delivering stuff that's been ordered online."

"I can believe it," I said.

I didn't think we had much more to say to each other, but the mailman didn't leave. He looked me up and down and said cautiously, "You're doing some walking."

"Yes," I said. I thought it was best to keep things simple.

"Are you a military man by any chance?"

"No," I said, "strictly civilian."

"My mistake. I thought maybe I saw something in the way you carried yourself."

I couldn't imagine where he was getting that from. Nobody had ever previously accused me of having a military bearing.

"I've known a few servicemen," I said, "but I never felt the urge to become one of them."

"Very wise," said the mailman.

I was well aware that a lot of ex-servicemen joined the postal service, and I figured Darrell might be one of them, otherwise why would he have asked if I was?

"Yeah, I was in the army for a while," he volunteered. "Very short while."

"Doesn't suit everybody, I'm sure," I said. "I know it wouldn't suit me."

He looked me over, as if considering whether I might, despite my denials, have the makings of a soldier after all. If he arrived at a conclusion, he kept it to himself.

"I liked the discipline," he said. "I liked the camaraderie, and I liked the idea of being in foreign countries. I didn't even mind the killing too much. It was the *marching* I couldn't take. I should probably have figured that out before I enlisted."

"Probably," I agreed.

"I got out with a general discharge. There are worse things to come home with."

"I'm sure," I said.

"And now I'm a mailman. I have my truck of course, but there's still plenty of walking. I can live with that, just so long as there's no marching."

"Good," I said. I was more than ready to end this encounter.

He gave me another long, searching look, as though now trying to decide whether he could trust me. This time he evidently found what he was looking for. He said, "'No one saves us but ourselves. No one can and no one may. We ourselves must walk the path.'"

This was, I happened to know, a quotation attributed to the Buddha, but I didn't say anything. I didn't want to look like a know-it-all. The mailman didn't reveal his source. Maybe he wanted me to think he'd made it up himself.

"That's very true," I said.

The mailman nodded gravely. He'd delivered the mail, and then he'd delivered an uplifting spiritual message. His work was done.

"I'll be getting on with my appointed round," he said.

"So will I," I said.

EIGHT

Shared enthusiasms always make for strange bedfellows, fellows you definitely wouldn't want to get in bed with. This is especially true of walkers. They come in all shapes and sizes, with all kinds of personalities, motives, and ideologies: the Buddha certainly, as my mailman seemed to know, and Jesus of course, and Moses obviously, and all the Muslims walking around the Kaaba in Mecca, and Mao on his Long March, and Grandma Gatewood on the Appalachian Trail, to name just a few.

To be honest, I didn't think I had a lot in common with any of these characters. The truth was (and if apologies are in order then I'm perfectly willing to make them) I thought I had much more in common with Albert Speer, chief architect of the Third Reich, confidant of Adolf Hitler, and eventually his Minister for Armaments and War Production.

Did I regard Albert Speer as a role model? No, I did not. As an inspiration? Well, no, of course not, he was a Nazi. But he did seem, in certain ways, to be a fellow traveler. In September 1954, Speer decided to walk from Berlin to Heidelberg, a distance of 345 miles, though he thought of it metrically as 555 kilometers. Since he was incarcerated in Spandau Prison at the time, after his prosecution and conviction at the Nuremberg Trials, and since he re-mained there until 1966, his walk had to be a theoretical or, as we might now say, a virtual one.

Speer paced out a walking path in the prison garden—a gar-den he himself had designed, and a plot considerably bigger than my yard. His course was 270 meters long, which is near enough 300 yards, so nearly triple the length of my own. Then he began a journey that would require him to make just over 2,296 circuits of that course. In some, though not all, ways his project was less ambitious than mine. He set himself the task of walking just sev-en kilometers a day—not very ambitious at all—but ultimately he did keep walking for a full twelve years, which still strikes me as very impressive indeed. I didn't see myself walking for nearly that long. Once I'd walked around the world I intended to stop and find some new obsession.

Speer made detailed records of his walking, marking off the days, noting the distances covered, along with daily, weekly, and overall totals and averages. Rudolf Hess, Hitler's deputy in the Nazi Party, who was also an inmate of Spandau, helped Speer keep count. I would have no equivalent of Hess, but clearly re-cord-keeping was important.

I didn't care about proving to anyone that I'd covered the dis-tance, but if I didn't keep accurate records I'd never know how far I'd walked, nor how far I still had to go. I wouldn't even know when I'd finished. My perfectly simple recording method consist-ed of making many, many hash marks, arranged in groups of five, like five-bar gates, on the pages of a series of small, unmatching notebooks I happened to have.

I thought of using Moleskine journals, as a very small nod to-ward Bruce Chatwin, who used those to record his travels, but

I decided against it. I thought it would seem pretentious or precious, and to be honest, I thought that nobody in his right mind would want Bruce Chatwin as a role model. The notebooks I had were small enough to fit into any of my pockets, and although I had enough to be going on with, clearly I'd need to acquire plenty more along the way.

In my notebooks, each individual hash mark indicated 1 circuit of the path, 100 hundred yards. I filled each page with 50 groups of 5 hash marks, for a total of 250, so each filled page showed that I'd walked 25,000 yards, call it 14.2 miles. So each day I would fill just over 1.75 pages. Then I'd start a new page the next day.

I knew that eventually I'd have quite a few of these notebooks, depending on what kind I used and how many pages were in each. But I didn't want to fetishize the books themselves or the recording process: both were just a means to an end. As each one was filled, I would put it safely in the footlocker (not quite a piece of junk, but definitely not an antique) that sat in front of the couch in my living room, doing service as a coffee table. The notebooks wouldn't be hidden exactly, but nobody need see them.

In truth I don't know where Speer stored the records of his walking, but I do know that he completed his "journey" to Heidelberg on March 19, 1955, his fiftieth birthday, as it happened. Pleased with what he'd accomplished, he then decided he might as well keep going and make another imaginary walking trip, this time to Munich and beyond. Again Hess tried to be helpful and suggested that Speer could walk all the way to Asia if he wanted to. Speer liked the idea but fretted that any route he chose would involve walking through some dreaded communist countries. He couldn't face that, not even in his imagination.

Speer's walk is an interesting case. As his feet trod the path in the Spandau Prison garden, his mind took him to places in the real world outside the prison, the places he'd have gone to if he'd actually been walking in that world. He even persuaded the prison library to buy him maps and travel guides so he could imagine his journey more accurately.

I wasn't sure whether this was a good idea. In one way, sure, there was pleasure to be had in imagining yourself to be walking in places you'd never been and had only seen in books. But it seemed to me that a lot of frustration must go with it too. Speer could imagine himself anywhere he liked, but the moment he stopped imagining, which is to say the moment he stopped walking, he was back in the garden, back in the prison yard, in the place he'd never left. That surely must have made things worse. For me it was different. I didn't regard my own yard as a prison, though I'm sure some people might have thought it was. More than that, I was content to walk in the here and now. I didn't need my mind to transport me to some faraway place or time.

According to Speer's published diary, he and Hess had some discussions about whether his walking was inherently sane. Speer at first claimed it wasn't and wrote, "I insisted on my claim to have a screw loose." This is a translation obviously, but still a strange thing for anybody to insist on, I'd have thought, unless he calculated that symptoms of insanity might speed up his release. Hess, however, wasn't buying it. "That just happens to be your pastime," he said, quite reasonably it seems to me, and this is surely one of the very rarest moments in history when a person is tempted to side with Rudolf Hess rather than Albert Speer.

By September 18, 1956, Speer had come around to Hess's point of view and didn't think his walking was so crazy after all. In fact he saw it as a sign of sanity. He wrote in his diary on that day, "I have walked 3,326 kilometers; counting the winter that makes a daily average of 9.1 kilometers. As long as I continue my tramping, I shall remain on an even keel."

Apart from the walking, I've never had any desire to emulate Albert Speer in any possible way. Equally it never occurred to me that walking would be the means of either proving or disproving my sanity. I've always been well aware, both personally and professionally, that trying to prove your sanity to other people is a fool's game. Proving it to yourself strikes me as even more of a problem. And proving it to your ex-wife may turn out to be just about impossible.

NINE

My cell phone was not a very smart one, but I didn't need or want it to be. I didn't use it for e-mail, or to listen to music or podcasts, or to do online banking; I didn't use it as a pedometer or map or GPS. I used it only for phone calls, and I knew there wouldn't be many of those. But the best thing about my cell phone, about any cell phone I guess, is that you can talk to the person on the other end and you don't have to interrupt your walking.

On Day 14 I got a phone call from Carole. I wasn't entirely surprised. She called me every now and then to make sure I was "all right," whatever that meant. I found this understandable, even welcome on occasions. It was good to know that, for better or worse, she still cared about me, and the truth was I still cared about her too, even though I was the one who'd insisted on the divorce. She had been angry and wounded at the time, often tearful, occasionally threatening savage revenge.

But she had, in some sense, come to accept it: you can't keep insisting that you want to stay married to somebody who doesn't want to stay married to you. She had consoled herself by believing that I was in the middle of some deep personal crisis, and I was happy enough to let her believe that. So she called me every now and again, to keep the lines of communication open, to make sure

I was "all right," and to assure me that she was all right too. She had apparently given me two weeks to settle into the new house, and now it was time to talk.

I answered the call and kept on walking.

"How are you?" Carole asked, a little too earnestly for my tastes.

I could picture her leaning against the counter in the kitchen— what had once been *our* kitchen, a place where we'd talked and eaten and drunk, and sometimes argued, and once in a while had sex. Now it was *her* kitchen. Try as I might, I couldn't stop myself from feeling a small, sharp pang of loss.

"I'm all right," I said.

"You got the basket of fruit?"

"Yes. Thanks."

"You're settled into the new house?"

"Not really. Not yet."

"It takes a while."

"For sure."

"So how are you filling your time?"

I had no reason to lie to her. "I'm doing a lot of walking," I said.

"Really?" she said. "Really?"

I wasn't surprised that she sounded surprised. Obviously she knew I'd once been an enthusiastic walker, but she also knew that at a certain point, for reasons she didn't understand, I'd stopped walking completely. The fact that I was walking again might possibly be taken as an indication that I was better than just "all right," though naturally, at that point, she knew nothing about my decision to walk around the world.

"I only walk in my own backyard," I said.

"Well, you have to start somewhere," said Carole.

"And end somewhere too," I said.

"Are you walking alone or with other people?"

The way she said it suggested that she thought solitary walking was evidence of psychological disturbance. Tell that to Rousseau. But I didn't mention Rousseau. She knew I had long been a solitary walker, and although she accepted it, she didn't really *get* it. Carole was enthusiastic about "exercise" (that strange word). She worked out in the gym, went swimming, rode a bike, but she had never been much of a walker. Some people just aren't. When we were married I did all my serious walking alone. I suppose I could say that had something to do with why we split up, and it wouldn't be a complete lie.

"I've been walking with Albert Speer," I said, admittedly not all that helpfully. My ex-wife wasn't a student of twentieth-century history.

"I don't know him, do I?" she said. "Is he a new friend?"

"He's not a real friend," I said.

There must have been something wrong with the way I said that. Carole was instantly suspicious.

"He's not an *imaginary* friend is he, for Christ's sake?"

"No," I said. Just how crazy did she think I was? "He was perfectly real. But he died thirty some years ago."

There was some equally dead air at the other end of the phone. Maybe Carole thought I was walking with ghosts, but then maybe I was; maybe we all are.

"He was a high-ranking Nazi," I said, "but he was a 'good Nazi.' Even the Allies said that."

"Are you mocking me, Joe?"

I didn't think I was, but I also knew I wasn't the best judge of these things.

In retrospect I can see it may have been stupid and unnecessarily provocative to tell my ex-wife that I was walking with a dead Nazi. Possibly she imagined I was striding around in jackboots, with swastikas painted on my cheeks. I could perhaps have told her instead that I was walking with, or in the spirit and tradition of, some of the world's greatest travelers, adventurers, writers, artists, saints, sages, and nomads. I could have said that I was walking with Thoreau and Whitman, Blake and Coleridge, Dorothy and William Wordsworth; with explorers like Oates and Amundsen, like Speke and Burton; with Paul the Hermit and John Bunyan, James Joyce, Emma Sharp, Guy Debord, et al. I could have said I was the spiritual descendant of a whole gang of pedestrians, pilgrims, fire walkers, moon walkers, tightrope walkers, labyrinth walkers, flâneurs flaneurs, psychogeographers, and so on. It would all have been more or less true, but I'm not sure that Carole would have found it a whole lot less troubling than talk of Albert Speer.

"I'm not mocking you," I said, trying to sound all sweet reason, and then, in as sincere and unironic a way as possible, I told her what I was doing. It was, obviously, the first time I'd told anybody about my grand project, and I didn't have my explanation down pat, but I told her what I've told you, about the ellipsoidal nature of Earth, the problems of *literally* walking around it, and how I intended to walk twenty-five miles a day for a thousand days. The explanation didn't take me very long, and I wasn't nearly as articulate as I'd have liked to be, but I got the job done.

"You're walking around the world," Carole said when I'd finished.

"Yes."

"Without leaving your own yard."

"Yes."

"Why?"

I considered a number of smart replies, "because it's not there" among them, but in the end I said, "I don't think I need a reason."

She was wise enough not to argue about that.

"You don't think this is a little . . . eccentric?"

"Sure," I said, "but not crazy."

"I never said you were crazy. I never said that. But don't you think it would be better if you walked with other people, you know, *actual* people? Rather than imaginary Nazis? You could join a hiking club or something: make friends, have a social life, maybe meet a new woman."

Did she not know me at all? Well, no, in many ways I'd made sure that she didn't.

"I have so very many reasons for not wanting to join a hiking club," I said, but I didn't feel the need to explain what they were.

There was a long silence, which enabled me to cover a full circuit of my path.

"Look, Joe," my ex said at last, "don't be afraid to ask for help."

I said I wasn't. She probably didn't believe me. She was probably right not to.

TEN

Of course I did things other than walk, but not many, and not with much enthusiasm. I tried to put my house in order, do some unpacking, but my heart wasn't in it, and it didn't seem like a priority, and of course I didn't have any shelves to put my books on even if I unpacked them. Otherwise my spare time was spent reading or watching a little basic cable. That was enough. I had decided to live without the Internet—not a Luddite decision, but rather that, like any sane person, I knew the Internet was full of snoopers and eavesdroppers and betrayers. I didn't want anyone peering over my shoulder, scrutinizing my habits and needs, virtually or otherwise. I didn't want to leave a trail, didn't want persons unknown to know too much about me, not even my tastes in cat videos or pornography.

I didn't go out in the evenings. I didn't want to go to a bar or a restaurant or the movies, and besides, those things weren't exactly abundant in the area. It did occur to me that I might be turning into a sad, lonely shut-in, but the fact was that after walking twenty-five miles in a day, I was usually pretty tired, if also profoundly content, and I didn't want to do much of anything, although I certainly did plenty of sleeping.

And of course I had to feed myself. I had to get groceries. The nearest place to buy food was a mile and a half away, not exactly a long way, a five-minute drive. A mile and a half was even walking distance, a mere nothing for a man who was planning to cover twenty-five thousand miles, but in fact I was already feeling resentful at having to do any walking anywhere except in my own yard. Walking through the aisles in the store, walking across the parking lot, even walking from my own front door to my car and back again seemed like a waste of time and energy since they weren't part of the grand project.

The supermarket, on the far edge of the village, was named Nature's Cornucopia, a name that said more about its ambitions than its reality. In its dreams this was an "alternative" enterprise, and sure, it had hand-painted signs over the various sections, and it sold organic this, artisanal that, and heirloom the other, and the people who worked there seemed to be some kind of collective, maybe even a cult. The place ensured that a man wouldn't starve, but once you'd been inside for a while you noticed a rising feline stink, you saw that some of the produce was so natural that it had begun the all too natural processes of decay, and you also became aware that basic items like bread and milk and breakfast cereal were ridiculously expensive.

There was a big-name, corporate supermarket about fifteen miles down the highway, where things were no doubt fresher and cheaper, but a fifteen-mile drive struck me as an intolerable distraction. Online shopping was, of course, not an option.

I'd first gone to Nature's Cornucopia on Day 8, done a week's shopping and hated the process. I gritted my teeth and went again on Day 15, and the hatred grew. I shopped there again on Day 22 and found it all completely intolerable, and I felt I might go insane if I ever had to go back in there. But as I said, life sometimes brings you what you need, or think you do.

As I was escaping from the store with my load of overpriced, not very fresh groceries on Day 22, I saw it had a community noticeboard. Well, it would, wouldn't it? And there were postcards and flyers offering all kinds of services—computer repair, tax preparation, pet sitting, massage, personal training—but nobody was offering anything as simple and useful as grocery shopping.

I was disappointed, but then as I walked out to my car, and as I was putting my groceries into the trunk, I noticed somebody slipping flyers under the windshield wipers of the cars in the parking lot. It was a youngish woman, thin but by no means waifish, energetic, serious looking, determined, displaying elements of miscellaneous fashionability, from punk to Goth to rock chick to hippie: a leather jacket, tiger-print leggings, hair yanked up in a top knot and dyed an improbable purple black.

As she came alongside my car, I took a flyer directly from her. The paper was canary yellow, and the font was big and strident:

NEED HELP?
CLERICAL? DOMESTIC? LIGHT MANUAL?
BASIC HOUSE MAINTENANCE?
SIMPLE GARDENING? CAR WASH?
HEY, THAT'S WHAT I DO!!!
(PRETTY MUCH ANYTHING LEGAL)
MIRANDA

And then there was a phone number. I was a little surprised that she stood there while I read the flyer, and when I'd finished I saw she was staring at me with big, eager, persuasive eyes. She had the kind of face that told you she was interestingly troubled. I saw no harm in that. Which of us isn't troubled? But so few of us are interesting. She also looked like quite a tough cookie, and I didn't mind that. If she'd appeared more harmless I might have been more suspicious.

"Does 'anything' include grocery shopping?" I asked.

"Sure. That's legal, isn't it?"

"It certainly is."

"Any more questions, give me a call," she said.

"Are you Miranda?"

"Yeah. You think maybe I'm fronting for a consortium?"

I said, "No, I didn't think that."

When I got home I called the number and spoke to her again, and I asked if she could come over to discuss work. She said she could probably fit me in the next afternoon. I said that would probably be fine. I guess neither of us wanted to appear too eager.

Next day she arrived in a noisy red truck, and she was now wearing black vinyl pants and a T-shirt for a rock band I'd never heard of. She had a couple of tattoos visible, one on each arm, an orchid and a martini glass. I thought this probably wasn't the way many people would have presented themselves for a job interview, but once we started talking it wasn't clear whether I was interviewing her or she was interviewing me. I could work with that. I know how to charm people when I need to, and I thought I was a good judge of character. Well, no doubt everybody thinks that.

During the interview Miranda walked with me while I did circuits of the path. This wasn't meant to be any kind of test: I could happily have employed somebody who didn't care about walking, although I couldn't have employed somebody who found it absurd. Miranda didn't. She was perfectly willing to walk along with me.

By the time we'd completed a handful of circuits, she'd already told me a lot more about herself than I needed to know, about having made some bad choices in life, involving men and recreational drugs mostly, she said, but she was trying to put all that behind her, and now she was getting her life in order, planning to go to college, and she calculated that some regular but occasional and not too demanding work was what she needed to stay "straight" and get a little money together before enrollment. I wasn't especially interested in knowing these things, but I was glad she wasn't trying to be mysterious.

"What are you going to study?" I asked, keeping up my end of the bargain.

"Bartending," she said.

In general I think education is a good thing, at least for those who want it. And I didn't intend to appear snobbish or disapproving at the mention of bartending college, but maybe I failed in that.

"Actually *mixology*," Miranda said. "Handcrafted cocktails. That's what they call them these days."

"Fine," I said.

"Yes, it is fine. And I know what you're thinking, that in the old days you'd just walk into a bar and ask if they needed any help, and they'd take you on, and then you could learn on the job. But these days you need a college degree for *everything*. Or at least a diploma."

"I understand that," I said.

I'd already decided I wanted to take her on, and I told her so somewhere toward the end of our twentieth circuit. Then we did

a few more as I told her what I needed her to do: basically go grocery shopping for me so that I didn't have to leave my yard.

"Why don't you want to leave your yard?" she asked, and I
appreciated her directness, even if I could have done without it.

"Because if I leave my yard I won't be able to do my walking,"
I said.

"You must really like walking."

"More than like," I said.

"Walking's good," she said.

"Yes," I agreed.

"I should probably do more of it."

"Only if you want to," I said.

"I hear it's real good for keeping depression at bay."

"I've heard that as well," I said. "And I know it's true. But that's
not why I walk."

"So why *do* you?"

The directness paid off again, and slightly to my surprise I
found myself telling her all about my grand walking project, much
as I'd recently told Carole, though a little more eloquently now,
since I was doing it for the second time, and I didn't mention Albert Speer.

"That's really cool," she said when I'd finished, and her enthusiasm sounded genuine enough. "So maybe you'll need me to do
more than just grocery shopping. Maybe you'll want me to go to
the hardware store once in a while."

"It could happen," I said.

"And you'll probably need somebody to go to the post office
for you sometimes, or take your boots in to be repaired. And what
if the washer or furnace breaks down? You'll need somebody to
make phone calls and deal with the repairmen when they come,

and keep an eye on them and keep them in line when they get things wrong. I can do all that."

I didn't doubt that she could. "Sure," I said. "Why not."

"And if you need your car taken in for an oil change or a lube job. I'm there for you."

She seemed to have understood my situation very well; perhaps she understood it better than I did.

"But no cooking," she said. "And no cleaning. I'm not going to be a maid."

"I don't want a maid," I said.

"I'm pleased to hear it. A man really doesn't need a maid."

"Then it sounds like we're in business."

We discussed money: not a lot but enough, and paid in cash, on the nail, off the books.

"OK then," she said. "So what's my job title?"

It was a question that surprised me. I scarcely thought this arrangement constituted a job, so why would it need a title?

"You know," she said, "so I'll have something to put on my résumé."

Well OK, I could see that a woman who had made bad choices and was putting her life in order might need to pad her résumé where she could, but I had no suggestions.

"How about assistant?" she suggested.

I didn't argue. Why would I have? I said, "Sure. That's fine by me."

"Fantastic," she said with an enthusiasm that amazed me. "Let's make a shopping list."

ELEVEN

The pace of walking and the pace of thinking fit very comfortably together, it seems to me, and I realize I'm by no means the first person to have noticed this. I know that some people say they do their best thinking while running or swimming or working out—my ex-wife had been known to say that—but those activities have always driven thoughts right out of my head. And for sure there are times when a man *wants* to have thoughts driven out of his head, but in general, and certainly in my own yard, I did some of my best thinking while walking.

I've never claimed to be a "thinker" per se, and I don't claim to be any kind of philosopher, but I did sometimes think about the "big questions" as I walked: God and death, free will and pre-destination, war and peace, crime and punishment, occasionally about love and sex. I'll spare you the results of these ruminations. I'm sure I never came to any very original conclusions. I'm sure I thought what many millions of people have thought before me, which in itself was something to think about. How many people in the entire history of the world have ever had a genuinely original thought? Friedrich Nietzsche said, "All truly great thoughts are conceived while walking," to which I would only add, "And a lot of not so great ones are conceived then as well."

"Hey, you!"

My thoughts, such as they were, were interrupted by yet another head popping up over my neighbor's fence, the one I'd come to think of as Big Paul's. A young woman looked at me. The face appeared drained and taut, but she was trying to be outgoing and engaging: a difficult trick to pull off. The eyes were heavy, the hair was straw blonde, the tanned shoulders were bare, and there was an e-cigarette in the corner of her mouth, and you'd have to say she just looked a little trashy, though it's not a word I like to use about people. A moment later Small Paul's head appeared beside the woman.

"OK," she said, "all right, so the kid was telling the truth."

"Yes?"

"I'm Small Paul's mother," she said. "Big Paul's wife."

"Oh, OK," I said.

She didn't look much like the classical idea of a mother, but I'd learned long ago that mothers come in all varieties. For that matter she didn't look like the kind of woman who'd be married to Big Paul: but again, I'd learned not to make judgments about people's choice of partner.

"You can call me Renée," she said. "You can call me any time. Just joking."

I introduced myself. Small Paul stood silently, awkwardly, beside his mother.

"Small Paul said you were walking in circles, and I see he wasn't lying. That makes a change."

I didn't want to get into the intricacies of Small Paul's lying habits, so I said, "Yes, I'm walking."

I hoped that might be enough of an answer to get rid of her, though I didn't honestly expect it to be.

"He says you're trying to save the Earth."

"He's wrong about that," I said. "I mean, I'd be happy to save the Earth if I could, but I have enough trouble trying to save myself."

She smiled at me. It was a smile that wasn't nearly as warm and powerful as she imagined it was.

"He also tells me you collect butterflies," she said.

Small Paul looked thoroughly embarrassed.

"No, I don't know where he got that idea," I said. "I only mentioned butterflies in relation to chaos theory."

Small Paul now looked more than embarrassed. He seemed to be in agony, but his mother was impressed for some reason.

"He gets ideas everywhere," she said. "Sometimes I wish he'd get a few less."

We both let that one go. Renée peered over the fence with renewed interest, looking me over, looking around my yard, with a strange mixture of curiosity and mild disapproval.

"I suppose it's a good yard for walking in," she said. "Nice round path, and plenty of privacy. You could walk naked in there if you wanted to. Nobody would see you."

I wasn't sure this was actually true.

"Unless, of course, they stood on a chair and looked over like I'm doing now. Just joking."

The joke was lost on me.

"Are you a single man, Joe?" Renée asked.

"Yes," I said.

"I didn't really have to ask. I can tell."

I never doubted that my single or divorced status would be apparent to anybody who was interested, though I didn't imagine many were.

"You're a lucky man, Joe."

"I don't think luck had much to do with it," I said.

"I guess married people always envy single people, but let me tell you there are days when I sure could enjoy being a merry widow."

"Yes?"

"Just joking," she added belatedly, though this time she hardly sounded as though she was joking at all. After a pause she said, "Big Paul isn't easy to live with."

"Who is?"

"I've got a favor to ask," she said.

I groaned inwardly and I may have groaned outwardly as well. I have never been very good at doing favors.

"Feel free to say no," she said.

"I will."

"It's this pet of ours," and she signaled to Small Paul, who reached down below the level of the fence and came up displaying the small white dog that I'd already seen when I first met Big Paul. It was now wearing a red leather collar spangled with rhinestones.

"He's part Havanese, part Maltese," Renée said.

Now that I could get a better look, I might have thought he was also part, or perhaps largely, a failed genetic experiment, but I kept that to myself.

"He's called Hopeless," she said. "Small Paul picked the name."

The boy's agony hadn't eased in the slightest. His mother pulled back some fluff on the dog's head to reveal its face: shiny black eyes, something that sniffled and drooled and made a noise that didn't quite sound canine.

"Not much of a hound," she said, "but he still needs a lot of exercising."

I found that hard to believe.

"And Big Paul refuses to take him out for a walk. He says the dog makes him look like a sissy. And I said to him, 'Well, Paul, you're the one who works in *security*, but it seems to me that if you were a bit more *secure* in your own masculinity, you wouldn't be so afraid of looking like a sissy.' He didn't like that, as you can imagine."

I could, and I could also see that it was best to stay well out of that little marital debate.

I said, "Can't the boy take the dog for a walk?"

"Oh please," said Renée. "Look at him. He looks like a sissy walking down the street even when he *isn't* dragging a powder puff of a dog with him."

I had never seen Small Paul walking down the street, but this sounded very plausible, if not exactly the kind of thing a boy wants to hear from his mother.

"So I was thinking about *you*," Renée said. "You walk all the time, don't you?"

I couldn't and didn't deny it.

"And I'm sure you're totally secure in your masculinity, but that wouldn't matter anyway. Nobody'd ever have to see you. I was thinking that Hopeless could tag along with you while you're walking in circles in your yard. Couldn't he? Eh? Feel free to say no."

"No."

"If you think it's too much to ask, just say so."

"I think it's too much to ask," I said.

After a pause that I suspected she thought was pregnant, she said, "Mmm, you're no pushover, are you, Joe?"

"No," I said.

She looked suddenly sad, though it seemed a very performed kind of sadness.

"How about Wendy Gershwin?" I said. "Maybe she'd like to walk him."

Renée made a noise of deep, damp, throaty contempt. "Wendy Gershwin is going to be way too busy with her *art*."

I couldn't tell whether it was Wendy Gershwin herself or simply art that Renée held in contempt.

"Or maybe her niece could walk your dog."

"Niece, my ass," said Renée.

I preferred not to know what she meant by that. I wasn't so foolish, at a time like that, to bring up Jacques Lacan, the French post-Freudian psychiatrist, psychoanalyst, and deconstructor. But if I had, I'd have referred to what he said about love, neighbors, and Jesus. He took Jesus's line "Love thy neighbor as thyself" and pointed out that most people actually hate themselves, so naturally they also hate their neighbors. I always had a lot of time for Lacan.

"No, Joe," said Renée, "you were my only hope. But it's OK. I like it that you're no pushover. I like a challenge. I can see I'm going to have a lot of fun changing your mind."

I didn't think that sounded like any fun whatsoever. She looked down at Hopeless, and for a moment I thought she was going to hurl the little critter at me, but she didn't. She placed the dog on her bare shoulder as though it were a parrot, or perhaps an epaulet, and then she looked at me through half-closed eyes, a look that I suspected was meant to be kittenish or even vixenish. I looked back with what I knew to be a neutral expression.

"Ah well, I hear that some new people are going to be moving into the house over your back fence," she said. "Maybe one of them will want to be a dog walker."

"Just so long as they're not riffraff," I said.

She laughed, but I wasn't sure what at, and then, before she and her dog and her son disappeared behind the fence again, she said, "Oh, and when you decide to start walking naked, give me a call."

I wondered if she'd say "Just joking" again, but I wasn't altogether surprised when she didn't.

TWELVE

I suppose there must be some people who buy a dog just so they'll have an excuse to go walking. They exercise themselves as they exercise the dog. The idea of getting somebody else to exercise your dog has always struck me as just plain wrong, not that I know a whole lot about dogs. All the time I was growing up I really wanted a dog, but my father put his foot down and wouldn't allow it. He said I wasn't responsible enough to take care of a dog. Maybe he was right, but I don't think so. Walking it certainly wouldn't have been a problem. My father and I walked all the time.

I know from my practice and from the literature that a lot of people believe that when fathers and sons walk together, it creates a deep, primary bond, and I'm sure that's largely true. Not in my own case, however. Certainly there were many times as I was growing up when I went walking with my father, but I wouldn't read too much into it. I suspect he had some mixed motives. Partly, it now seems to me, he simply wanted to get away from his wife, my mother. More creditably, I think he felt he ought to try to be a good father to his son, felt he ought to do something with his boy, but he didn't have a clue what. He had no more interest in sports than I did. He'd never dream of taking me to see a movie. If he'd ever set foot inside a museum or art gallery he kept the fact very, very well hidden.

So we went out walking together, not in any very organized way. We just walked to get some fresh air, in the so-called great outdoors, in the so-called wide-open spaces, in parks, woods, hills, forests—all the places that are supposed to be good for you, possibly even good for the soul, if you think you have one. Consequently my father and I spent a lot of time together, but we never got close, never formed much of a bond, primary or otherwise. We definitely never talked about anything important. Sometimes, for long periods, we didn't say anything at all. I think my father found that very appealing, a way of avoiding noise, and also, I can now see, a way of avoiding intimacy. A lot of the time we might both just as well have been walking alone, although if I'd been walking by myself I'd surely have walked more slowly and over much shorter distances.

My father demanded that we cover what seemed to me at the time huge distances, and I still have the clearest memories of being out of breath, sweating, my lungs and legs aching. I wasn't especially wimpy or unfit; it was simply that I was trying to keep up with a grown man, and that's hard for any kid.

Naturally I did a lot of complaining. Sometimes my father tried to encourage me, sometimes he mocked me, sometimes he just ignored me. I can't say that I learned not to complain, but I did learn that complaining wouldn't do me any good. Maybe my father was trying to make a man of me, and of course I wouldn't say that he failed, but the strange thing is that, with a few pitiful exceptions, men are made one way or another regardless of what their fathers do for and to them.

Did these weekend excursions with my father instill in me a love of walking and solitude? In fact, I believe they did, though it's easy to imagine they might have had the completely opposite effect. Sometimes, though not often, I think about my father when I'm walking, but it's never a clear or uncomplicated thought.

My father had been in the army, and I know he saw action, but that's as much information as I have. I have no idea what he really did or what was done to him. He never told me. He never told anyone as far as I know, not even, and perhaps least of all, my mother. Given that he was smart, articulate, and more or less middle class, I'm sure he had plenty of other options. He was a volunteer; he *wanted* to go to war. I find that the real and unsolvable mystery.

I'm assuming nothing good happened to him out there, though I'm working only with circumstantial evidence. He survived, but he was fucked up by it, as it seems most are to a greater or lesser degree. He'd left the service before I was born and worked the rest of his life in various management jobs for a furniture wholesaler and distributor. It didn't make him happy. The person I saw as I was growing up was a miserable man: stressed, quick to anger, emotionally closed down, anhedonic. And I don't doubt that, much as I've fought against it, I've inherited some of those deeply unlovable traits.

My father died of lung cancer when he was in his late fifties. It was sudden and it made for a horrible end, but it didn't seem at all surprising. Today I'm sure that even most laymen would be able to recognize that my father suffered from some form of post-traumatic stress disorder. Would he have been better off if he'd seen a therapist, gone through some kind of talking cure? Well, yes, how could he not have been? And were my father's problems instrumental in my becoming, in what now seems like a different life, a psychologist and therapist? Again, surely they must have been, though if my training taught me anything, it's not to be too glib about connecting causes and effects.

I got into psychology initially because I was "interested" in it, whatever that means, but I was interested in plenty of other things too. Then I studied it at college, and when I started writing essays and taking exams and doing clinical work, it was obvious that I was "good" at it, whatever *that* means. I liked the subject. The teachers liked me. I liked the theory. I liked reading Lacan, Laplanche, Leclaire—I even wrote a thesis on error and discourse—but at the same time, I found it hard to see how I was ever going to apply most of that stuff. Fortunately I also liked the problem-solving aspect of the subject: looking for clues, solving mysteries, coming up with solutions, then coming up with alternative or *contradictory* solutions. It took me a good while longer to develop an interest in living, breathing, suffering people. But I got there eventually.

Like the majority of contemporary psychotherapists, I ended up believing in and practicing cognitive behavioral therapy—because it worked. If you have a fear of spiders, we don't need to put you on a leather couch for ten years and get you to describe your dreams about your mother. We just need to find a way of desensitizing you to spiders.

People exaggerate the extent to which therapy is a luxury of the self-absorbed, self-indulgent rich, but it's true enough that down in the ghetto, an appointment with a therapist isn't high on the list of priorities. I made a good living from my profession as a private, licensed psychotherapist, and of course most of my patients weren't living anywhere near the poverty line. But I tried to ease my conscience a little by doing pro bono work with troubled youth, the homeless, addicts of one kind or another, kids with eating disorders, the occasional "reformed" gang member, and so on.

I didn't usually go in for treating ex-servicemen because that seemed to require a skill set that was *way* outside my area of expertise, but when one of them came to see me at the office, a guy called Robert Ardiles, I didn't turn him away. I had assumed, not entirely unreasonably, that any member of the military (past or present) would look at me and decide I was some kind of wimp who didn't know the first thing about war or combat—and he'd have been essentially right. I also assumed that the military had its own specialists for this kind of thing. And Robert Ardiles said sure it did, but he also said, "I'd rather shoot myself than go and see one of those military-industrial mind butchers." I made a note of that phrase.

So I did what I could for him. I did what anybody else in my position would have done: the usual stuff. I tried to get him to relax. I tried to get him to talk. I tried to identify "unhealthy behavioral problems"—he told me he had plenty of those. I tried to identify "problematic thought patterns," and again he had no shortage. I suggested he try to take pleasure in small things, to get out in the sunlight and increase his melatonin levels, to get more exercise, to get a cat or a dog, to maybe do something artistic, like drawing or taking pictures, or to go for long walks. He listened and he didn't argue, but I had the sense that very little of what I said was doing any good.

It wasn't till the sixth session that he was able to tell me about the time he'd been captured and tortured. If I'd felt out of my depth before, I now felt as though I were drowning, as though we were both sinking together. In that session I listened and said very little, and then I went away and did some research. There's plenty of material out there about living with the memory of torture, and there's more of it all the time, though there's nothing resembling a guaranteed quick fix, or a guaranteed fix of any kind. Again, I did what I could. I didn't doubt, and didn't deny, that there were people who could have done a better job than me, people with more skill and experience, but I played the hand I was given, dealt with the problem—and the person—in front of me, and at least I felt reasonably sure I was doing no harm.

The first indication that I might actually be doing some good came when Robert Ardiles asked if a friend of his could also come and see me, another guy who'd been through the same stuff that he had. I'd helped him, so maybe I could help his friend. Guys like that have a way of finding each other, no doubt. I said sure, of course I'd see him.

From then on one patient led to another, and over the next couple of years I saw a total of ten torture survivors—a drop in the ocean, for sure. Every time a new one arrived, I was completely up front and said that I wasn't a specialist, that I was feeling my way just as he was. Maybe they liked that I wasn't coming across like some know-it-all doctor who thought he had all the answers. In any case, for one reason or another, they all kept coming back.

For me it was a steep learning curve, but I did gradually develop some genuine expertise. And, call me a cynic or a mercenary, I could see that this might be a growth area: it wasn't just combat troops who got captured and tortured; it was an ever-growing number of civilians, like activists, reporters, refugees, sometimes even children. There was no doubt that a man, a psychologist, could carve out a niche, a career, for himself in this area. Was it wrong of me to think that? Probably. But in the end it didn't matter much. I never got very far with this brilliant career plan.

I think I did a pretty good job with nine out of ten of my torture patients. The last one was a guy called Dan Moslowski, a big, angry, sad ruin of a man. We had just two sessions and he said maybe a total of twenty words in all. Mostly he sat there in my office looking morose and quietly threatening, staring at me as though he was trying to decide whether he could be bothered to beat me up. Apparently he couldn't.

The day after Dan Moslowski's second appointment I got a call from Robert Ardiles telling me that Moslowski had killed himself. I couldn't say that I was altogether surprised, but neither did I feel any particular sense of responsibility. I didn't see what I could have done any differently because I hadn't really done anything at all. The guy hadn't given me the chance.

THIRTEEN

I was still thinking about Dan Moslowski's suicide a few days later when a blonde woman arrived unannounced at my office, at the end of the day, as I was getting ready to leave. She was young, lean, blonde and severe looking, cold and awkward, with an unchanging expression of mild disdain on her face. She wore a dark gray pantsuit and had a military Rolex on her wrist. She said her name was Christine Vargas, but of course that meant nothing to me then. She said she wanted to talk about Dan Moslowski, and she looked like a woman who, one way or another, probably got to talk about the things she wanted to talk about.

I thought at first she might be a family member, then I thought she might be a cop, then a lawyer. Whatever she was, professional ethics might have limited what I could tell her, but in this case it was irrelevant: there was nothing to tell. I knew next to nothing about Dan Moslowski.

I was trying to explain this to her when she took out her wallet and flashed an ID card at me. It looked official enough, and must have meant something to somebody, but she made sure I didn't have time to read it properly. Then she said, "You've been treating ex-military personnel for PTSD, is that right, Mr. Johnson?"

I didn't feel I had any need to apologize for the fact. Even so, I said, "I've been treating *people*."

"No need to be defensive," she said. "We know you're a good man."

I wondered who the "we" referred to in that sentence, and I wondered even more where they'd gotten their information about my goodness. Also, and you don't need to be a psychotherapist to realize this, few things make a man more defensive than being told there's no need to be defensive.

"Let me tell you what we know about Dan Moslowski," Christine Vargas said.

"OK."

It wouldn't have taken much for her to know more about him than I did.

"He wasn't military, you know?" she said.

"No? He said he was."

"Sure. But I imagine you're used to patients not telling you the absolute truth about themselves."

"Of course."

"We can only speculate about why he made that claim," she said. "Possibly he thought you only treated ex-military."

"I made it very clear that wasn't the case."

"Then maybe he wished he *had* been ex-military. Maybe he thought that would've been better for him in some way, made him more resilient, better able to cope."

"Maybe," I said.

It didn't sound implausible or impossible, but this "speculation" had already come to feel both intrusive and absurd. My acquaintance with Dan Moslowski didn't run to more than a couple of unproductive hours, and now I was discussing his psychological makeup with somebody I didn't know at all.

"He was out there as a private contractor," Christine Vargas said. "There are a lot of them out there. He worked for a company that provides electronic optical equipment and the data collection software that goes with it. A computer nerd basically. It's work that some people think should only be done by the military, but that's a whole different conversation."

"For sure," I said. "And either way, soldier or computer nerd, military or civilian, I'm still sorry I couldn't help him."

"Of course you are, Mr. Johnson," she said. She looked at me sympathetically, but I didn't feel I was the one who needed sympathy. "The problem as I see it," she continued, "is that Mr. Moslowski came to you too late."

It seemed to me that was the least of his problems, but maybe she had a point.

"But it's not just that he should have sought help earlier. Maybe he should have been provided with psychological help *before* it was needed. Prevention is better than cure, yes? Or is that an outmoded concept?"

I didn't think an answer was required.

"What I'm saying, Mr. Johnson, is that maybe Dan Moslowski should have been provided with help before he went out there, before he started the job, long before he was abducted and tortured. What if he'd come to you before he went? What if your treatment had been preventative?"

"There's no way of knowing, is there?"

"But don't you think you might have been able to help him, in advance?"

"It's impossible to say."

"But I think we can make an educated guess."

"I don't understand what you're saying."

"I'm saying I'd like you to join the Team."

In retrospect I realized that I never quite said yes or no, never definitively agreed to anything, never said I was joining any team, but after that conversation with Christine Vargas, she began sending me high-ranking civilian contractors before they went on postings in and around war zones. I suppose it was assumed that low-ranking contractors wouldn't be captured and tortured, that they'd simply be killed, or the powers that be thought they weren't worth saving.

Again, there's a significant quantity of literature about how people can prepare themselves prior to being tortured and about what they can do to endure it while it's going on. I read as much as I could find. And as ever, in practical terms, I did what I could, but at that point it was very basic stuff, just talking—not a talking *cure*, obviously, more a kind of theoretical "talking preparation," and it all proved to be a complete waste of time.

The men, and at that stage the occasional woman, without exception thought I was a jerk. They didn't bother to hide it. They thought I was talking bullshit. I wasn't. By then I really did know what I was talking about, and I could genuinely have been some help, but I couldn't convince the volunteers that anything I said was worth a damn. Above all, I couldn't make the situation *real* for them. Sure they knew that torture happened, that it happens all the time. They knew it was bad, they knew it was a horror, but they couldn't *imagine* it, or at least their powers of imagination were too feeble.

They thought I was wasting their time, and I got to the point where I knew I was definitely wasting my own. I called Christine Vargas and told her I'd had enough, I was quitting. I asked her not to send me any more volunteers. She said she understood. She said she'd been expecting this. Then she said there were other options for us to consider, and so there were.

By a combination of trial and error and mission creep, via a series of meetings with Christine Vargas and her colleagues who were, or said they were, doctors and psychologists, and who were in any case definitely part of the Team, my way of working changed out of all recognition. We, or more precisely they, decided we would make the possibilities of torture more real for the volunteers, give them a "taste" (a terrible word, and not mine) of what they might actually face.

Before long we arrived at the methodology I described at the beginning of this narrative: an office in a government building, a ground-floor room, a view of an empty parking lot, a map of the world on one wall, a calendar, a drawing of Felix the Cat on the whiteboard. And I was there to help the volunteers, guide them through the process, to be of practical help. I was there to be their hands-on, benevolent, in-house torturer.

There were times, *many* times, when I suspected that this was the outcome—the only outcome—that Christine Vargas and her colleagues had envisaged from the very start. I suppose I could have declined to be involved. There was no gun held to my head, no obvious attempt at coercion; the money was good but it wasn't *corruptingly* good. I could have said no, but I didn't. I was seduced by the idea that I was doing some good, or at least that's what I told myself most of the time.

Oh, and there's one small but vital thing that I should mention. Before I began the work, I had to go through what the volunteers would have to go through. I had to have done to me what I was going to do to them in the concrete bunker: the stress positions, the sensory deprivation, the belief that I had fallen into the hands of a sadistic madman. All that. Yes, I was a torture victim, a torture survivor. I knew exactly what I was talking about. That which doesn't kill us fucks us up for life—right, Herr Nietzsche? Right, Dad?

Was any of this ethical? Was it moral? I'm no longer sure. I don't have a stable answer to those questions. But as far as I knew, as far as anybody knew, it *worked*. Naturally there was no experiment by which one could absolutely test the method; there could never be a meaningful control group, and of course in a great many cases it was preparation and training that was never needed. But I did have one or two definite "successes" that I knew about, contractors who were indeed captured and tortured who lived to tell the tale and came back still mentally in one piece. And if they didn't exactly send me letters of thanks, I nevertheless heard through the appropriate channels that they were, in some way or other, in some sense of the word, grateful.

Of course nobody gets into the business of psychotherapy in order to be thanked, but it's certainly better than some of the alternatives. I was doing what I could, and if I knew that it worked in some cases, I never doubted for a moment that other outcomes were entirely possible, were in fact downright inevitable, though for a long time I had no idea what the consequences would be.

FOURTEEN

In general I'm not one of those people who worries too much about things that haven't happened yet. Worrying about what *might* happen strikes me as a waste of time, because absolutely anything might happen and absolutely anything might not. You can't be prepared for an infinite number of events and outcomes. The skill, as I see it, is not trying to foresee every possible situation in advance, because that's impossible, but rather to be confident that you can handle any situation as and when—and if—it arises. Should your confidence turn out to be misplaced, well, at least it stopped you from worrying in advance.

So inevitably, Wendy Gershwin's early warning about the succession of previous bad neighbors who'd lived in the house beyond the back fence hadn't concerned me all that much. And Renée's announcement that new people would be moving in didn't worry me much either. Bad neighbors are everywhere. The trick is to deal with them appropriately at the right time in the right way, to let them know, as soon as possible, that you're tolerant but no pushover, and if problems arise, you deliver the punishment that fits the crime. I believe this applies as much to nation-states as it does to people with adjoining properties. Essentially, I thought I had nothing to fear from the new riffraff.

Even without building a thick, high wall, as Wendy Gersh-win had suggested, I felt reasonably well separated from any rear neighbors. The wooden fence between us was substantial enough, and there were bushes and trees acting as a partial screen, though it was by no means an impenetrable barrier.

I hadn't spent much time peering in that direction, but occasionally, while walking, I'd looked through the branches and seen the outline of a small house, a basic box with what had once been white, now gray, wood siding, and there was a broad over-hanging roof and a deck, both of them sagging wearily. I could also see the driveway of the house and the outlines of a couple of decrepit cars, which had apparently been left behind by the evicted tenants.

The place clearly didn't look as though it belonged, or had recently been rented out, to anybody who was very house proud, but that in itself didn't bother me either. A house strikes me as a strange thing to be proud of, and I can easily understand that people might decide to direct their pride elsewhere. Still, it was clear that nobody who was very fussy about where they lived would ever rent this house, and so it proved when the new tenants moved in, on Day 26.

They arrived in several stages, in a number of trucks and in cars with troubled exhaust systems, and there was much coming and going, although as far as I could see they weren't bringing many possessions. I didn't put too much effort into getting a good look at them, but I could see and hear a number of loud, rough-looking young guys wandering and slouching around the property. Some of them were perhaps friends helping with the move rather than people moving in, though it was impossible to tell which were which, and all of them were yelling at each other, occasionally throwing things, and always on the brink of some playful or real violence.

In fact, over the next few days, evidence appeared that the new guys were practitioners of various martial arts. An old-school leather punching bag appeared, hanging from a tree branch, and they set up one of those rubberized torsos on a spring-loaded base that you can kick and punch to your heart's content and it always bounces back for more and (probably more important) never retaliates. There was much shadowboxing and sparring and the whirling of nunchucks. The boys' training regimen seemed undisciplined, though highly enthusiastic, and it required a lot of shouting.

Before long I also noticed that these new inhabitants had spray-painted the abandoned cars in the driveway with various tags, patterns, and symbols, and again, from what I could see, it appeared the work was more enthusiastic than skilled, though this was by no means my area of expertise. The boys played their music loud, and they owned a number of big, energetic, brutal dogs: about half a dozen of them, somewhere between mutts and monsters—nondescript, casually malicious things, the genetic opposites of poor little Hopeless. It struck me as unlikely that Renée would be able to persuade any of these boys to do her dog walking for her.

In general I think very little good ever comes from a floating population of loud, violent, rough-looking young men and half a dozen big, vicious dogs living together in a broken-down house, practicing martial arts and spraying graffiti, but I still didn't worry.

On the weekend after they moved in, the boys threw a party. It was loud, though I've heard louder. There was a barbecue or perhaps it was just a bonfire, and although there was even more shouting than usual, and maybe a little bit more fighting, it didn't sound as though there were very many people at the party, and I don't think I heard more than a couple of women's voices. The event may have had its wild moments, but there was nothing that kept me awake that night.

The morning after, however, which would have been Day 29, as I walked the first circuit of my path, I discovered a number of beer cans and a vodka bottle that had found their way into my garden, no doubt from the party. Naturally I threw them back over the fence. I heard the vodka bottle smash.

A little later that day, after I'd completed a few hundred circuits, I met my new neighbors. Four heads appeared over the back fence. These were heads bearing the faces of four fierce, angry-looking, possibly hungover young men. They had shaved heads and scattered tattoos that might once have identified them as "skinheads," but these days there's a whole different demographic that has shaved heads and tattoos. Even so, they didn't look like the kind of guys most people would want as neighbors. With the best will in the world you'd be inclined to think that sooner or later these boys were going to make trouble for somebody, possibly me, and they were definitely going to make trouble for themselves.

"Hey," one of them said, the oldest and heaviest, whose name, if his neck tattoo was to be believed, was Butch. "Have you been throwing broken bottles into our yard?"

I could have done that old "Are you talking to me?" routine, but I try to avoid old routines. I simply said, "No."

"I think you have," the guy said.

"No," I said again, "it wasn't broken when I threw it. It only broke when it hit the tree."

"Are you trying to be fucking funny?"

"No," I said, "I don't do funny."

And then one of the others lobbed a new, empty vodka bottle, unbroken, over the fence, imprecisely but definitely in my direction. I had to take a couple of hasty steps in order to catch it before it hit the ground, and as I grabbed it by its neck, I spun around and flipped it back, rising, spinning over the fence so that it hit a tree trunk just a couple of feet above the head of the guy who'd thrown it. Glass confetti trickled onto his shoulders. He was both angry and surprised, which was understandable, but he also seemed somehow insulted, which I thought he had no right to be.

"You're very lucky that didn't hit him," Butch said.

"No," I said. "If I'd wanted it to hit him, it would have hit him. Or hit you."

Butch laughed without being amused. I could see he had a problem with me. I hoped I could solve it for him.

"Look," I said. "I didn't ask to be your neighbor, and you didn't ask to be mine, but here we are. We have to live with it. We have to put up with each other."

I didn't want to sound fatherly because I figured these were boys who might have had some trouble with their fathers. And I didn't want to sound authoritative because they looked like boys who would definitely have some trouble with authority. I wanted to sound like a good neighbor, though the kind who could hit you in the face with a vodka bottle from thirty feet if he felt like it. In fact that was precisely the kind of neighbor I was, and the boys obviously had some inkling of it.

"How about this for a deal?" I said. "You don't throw anything my way, I won't throw anything yours. Or do you think I'm being totally unreasonable here?"

They couldn't bring themselves to say that I was or wasn't. This didn't surprise me really, since I suspected that their grasp of what constituted reasonableness might be patchy. None of them said anything at all, so after a decent pause I started walking again.

"Oy," Butch called after me. "Are you walking away? Are you turning your back on me?"

"Well, yes," I said, "though the latter is only a consequence of the former, obviously."

The four of them stared hard at me, unsure if I was a fool or a wiseass or a man asking for a beating, or possibly all the above.

"We'll see you again," Butch said.

"Only if you look over your fence," I said.

A couple of days later I happened to see Big Paul out in his garden and I asked him if he'd ever had any trouble with previous inhabitants of the riffraff house.

"Trouble?" he said. "I know how to handle trouble."

That seemed a useful skill for a man who worked in security, but it didn't answer my question.

"What about these new guys?" I said. "That was a pretty loud party they had over the weekend."

"Loud? You call that loud?"

Obviously I did or I wouldn't have said so, but I didn't want to argue with him about definitions of loudness.

"And what about all the martial arts business that goes on?" I asked.

"Martial arts," he said contemptuously. "Drop a bomb on 'em, see how their martial arts help with that."

We didn't seem to be getting very far with this conversation.

"A word to the wise," he said, all too confidentially, "all these dogs and martial arts and tattoos and shaved heads, they're just for show. These boys are *compensating*. You know what compensating is?"

"Yes," I said.

"Basically I reckon these guys are just a bunch of pantywaists."

"Really?" I said. Big Paul didn't look like the kind of man who'd use the term "pantywaist."

"Yes," he said. "And I don't think there's anything wrong with being a pantywaist, but I think there *is* something wrong with being a pantywaist and pretending to be a dangerous thug. That's just insecurity, if you ask me."

I wondered if his wife would have agreed with that. Personally I didn't think things were quite as clear-cut as Big Paul wanted them to be. Some people who look like dangerous thugs really are dangerous thugs. True, sometimes a man who owns a big truck and a big gun may be compensating for some penile inadequacy, but some men have big trucks, big guns, *and* big penises. I thought it best not to raise this issue with somebody who went by the name of Big Paul.

"So you don't think they're riffraff?" I said.

"Who said they were?"

"Wendy Gershwin," I offered. "She says it's only ever riffraff who live in that house back there."

"Wendy Gershwin gets a lot of things wrong," said Big Paul.

It was still way too early for me to have an opinion about that.

FIFTEEN

It was the very start of Day 31, an ordinary walking day, a good day. I'd been on my grand project for more than a month, and spring was edging toward summer. I'd covered 750 miles, filled a couple of notebooks with hash marks. But now, before I'd even completed one lap, my phone buzzed in my pocket. I fished it out and saw the call was from my ex-wife. I thought about not answering it, but only for a moment.

Carole, on the other end, said, "How's it going, honey?"

"Who is this?"

It wasn't a great joke.

"Carole. Your ex-wife. You remember me?"

That was probably a better joke. As before, I wasn't surprised that Carole was calling me, but I was very surprised that she was calling me "honey." I couldn't remember her ever using that term while we were married, although I'd forgotten, maybe even blotted out, a lot of things from that period. It was probably best that way.

"I've been thinking," Carole said. "I think I owe you an apology, for the other day, for the way I reacted."

"Really?" It seemed out of character.

"Yes," Carole said. "When you told me about your grand project, your walk around the world, well, I guess I sounded critical, skeptical. I thought it was . . . weird."

"You're entitled to think anything you like."

"But I was wrong to think it," she said. "And even more wrong to say it. I should have been more supportive."

I suppose a part of me was touched that she still wanted to "support" me, though I wasn't sure much good would come of it.

"I should have trusted you," she continued, "because obviously you're a smart guy and you know what you're doing. So I just want to say, I don't think it's weird. I think that you're right to trust your instincts. If you want to walk twenty-five thousand miles in your own backyard, then go ahead. It's not my or anybody else's business. You know what you need better than anybody else does."

All that was perfectly true, of course, and I didn't need Carole's confirmation, much less approval, but I wasn't going to reject it.

"Physician, heal thyself," she said.

"I was never a physician," I said, perhaps a little too insistently, and I knew it didn't really need saying. Again I had a mental picture of Carole making the call from what I still somehow thought of as "our" house. She had, of course, no picture (mental or otherwise) of where I lived, but it seemed she wanted to change that.

"I'd like to see your house," she said. "See where you live."

"Maybe I could send you some pictures," I said. I was lying. I didn't have any pictures, but even if I'd had some, I still wouldn't have sent them, but there was no need to make an issue of it.

"Have you done any gardening yet?" she asked.

"No. I've cut down some weeds that were growing over the path, but otherwise I'm letting nature take its course."

"Don't they say that gardening is good for relieving stress?"

"I know some people say that, but I think it would increase mine. I prefer walking. You know, trusting my instincts again."

"Of course," she said, all sweet reason. "Maybe you should employ some gardeners."

"I would no more let a strange man touch my garden than I'd let a strange man touch my wife. If I had one."

I thought that was a slightly better joke, and possibly one that might bring the conversation to a natural conclusion, but Carole wasn't ready to let go yet.

"I guess you probably miss your job," she said.

"No," I said. "I really don't."

"Are you sure?"

"As sure as I can be."

"Aren't you lonely? Walking all by yourself?"

"Let me tell you something about Carl Jung's walking habits," I said.

"Do you have to?" Now she sounded downright playful.

"Obviously I don't have to, but I'm going to unless you hang up."

She didn't hang up.

"After Jung's mother died in 1922," I said, "he bought a patch of land in Bollingen, on the shores of Lake Zurich, and he built a tower for himself, a place where he could sit and think and philosophize, but over time he extended it so that it became more like a proper home, and he also created a garden he could walk in.

"And sometimes when he walked in this garden he encountered a whole bunch of what he called spirit guides, and top dog among them was a spirit named Philemon. According to Jung's account, the two of them did a lot of walking together, having beautiful and meaningful conversations."

"You never were a Jungian, were you, Joe?"

"That's true enough," I said. Then I continued: "Of course Jung was the only person who could see or hear this Philemon character, and you might think the old boy was just talking to himself, but Jung insisted that Philemon had to be a separate entity from himself, because Philemon had his own thoughts and idea, and said things that had never crossed Jung's mind."

"So you're saying he wasn't lonely?"

"Yes, that's one of the things I'm saying," I said.

"Are you saying he wasn't nuts?"

"No, I'm not really saying that. I've always thought Jung was as crazy as a loon."

"Are you saying there are a lot of people in the world who are crazier than you?"

"I wasn't saying that either, but it's undoubtedly true."

"Do you think that should reassure me?" she said.

"Carole, honey," I said, using that word very deliberately, "we all need to find reassurance wherever we can."

"I'll talk to you again soon," she said, "when I'm feeling stronger," and at that point she didn't sound at all reassured. For some reason I preferred it that way.

SIXTEEN

Obviously you have to accept, as a basic principle, that if some-body else does your grocery shopping for you, then it's not going to be the same as doing it yourself. No, it's going to be *better*. Sometimes maybe that other person will buy a piece of meat that you might have rejected because it looked too fatty, or she'll buy a pineapple that's over- or underripe, or some apples that you think are too mealy, but I was willing to live with all that. An imperfect pineapple seemed a small price to pay for not having to go to the supermarket, for not having to interrupt the grand project. Miranda had a little trouble coming to terms with this.

My initial impression, once she started "assisting" me, was that she was trying way too hard. To a limited extent I could under-stand it. I could see that she wanted to do a good job, wanted to have something significant to put on her résumé, and obviously trying hard, even trying *too* hard, is not in itself such a terrible thing. But I do think there are serious limits to how good a job you can do, however hard you try, when that job consists largely of shopping for groceries at the supermarket fifteen miles down the highway.

Miranda and I spent a lot of time making shopping lists—far too much time, it seemed to me. And obviously I could see that lists needed to be made; I couldn't expect Miranda to read my mind, to intuit what I needed without asking. But even so, I thought she asked far too many questions.

In order to save time we did the list-making while I was walking. Miranda accompanied me around the circular path, and she interrogated me as we went. What percentage of fat did I want in my milk and yogurt? How did I feel about gluten? Did I want my tomatoes plum or beefsteak or vine ripened? Did I want my bacon cured or uncured, smoked or unsmoked; if cured, then with maple or honey, or if smoked, then with applewood or hickory? Did I want my eggs free range as opposed to cage-free, hormone-free as opposed to antibiotic-free, from chickens that were vegetarian or omnivores? In most cases I didn't have a very good answer for her. I wasn't trying to be evasive, and it wasn't that I didn't care: I just didn't care *enough.*

Still, at some point, the list always got made, and Miranda went off, bought the groceries, brought them back, got them out of her truck, and stashed them away in the fridge and the kitchen cupboards. She was doing a perfectly good job, and I was especially glad that she didn't ask me for help with the unloading and putting away.

I'm not wholly convinced by the notion that we are what we eat, because if my own groceries were anything to go by, I was a simple, straightforward, meat-and-potatoes, fad-free, essentially healthy kind of a man, which was only partly true. Drink was another matter. Of course I knew that Miranda must have some interest in alcohol—otherwise she wouldn't have wanted to become a bartender or mixologist or whatever—but my own interest in booze didn't extend much beyond the occasional six-pack or a cheap bottle of Merlot. I could tell that disappointed Miranda.

"Look," she said, as we walked around the circular path, post-list-making, on Day 33, "I wouldn't want you to think that I'm planning to be a truly great bartender—I'm not., but I don't want to have a chip on my shoulder about it. I just want to be able to make a great martini and a great old-fashioned and a great negroni and a great Killer Zombie."

"OK," I said. These sounded like perfectly realistic, realizable, if not especially lofty, goals.

"Because I know I'd feel inadequate if I *couldn't* make those things," she said.

"I can understand that," I said.

"But I know I'm not going to end up running the bar in some fancy-schmancy, five-star, *watering hole*. I think my greatness probably lies elsewhere."

"Greatness," I repeated. Now that seemed far less realistic and realizable.

"You see," Miranda said, "I think I might be able to *invent* something new: a brand-new cocktail. You know, like somebody had to invent the piña colada or the Rob Roy. There was a time when these things didn't exist."

This notion apparently filled her with quiet wonder.

She continued. "I'm looking to invent something simple and brilliant, something that seems totally obvious to everybody once it's been invented, but that nobody's ever thought of before. And then they'll name this cocktail after me."

"The Miranda," I said.

"That's right, Mr. J. That's exactly the idea. I'll join the ranks of the eponymous. But I'm not naive about it. I know how these things work. People will try to steal my idea. They'll try to take credit away from me, like there's a big debate about who was the original Margarita, or who was the Harvey in Harvey Wallbanger, but all the same, I seriously believe I can do this."

"Good for you," I said. "And what will be in this Miranda cocktail?"

"Well, that's still to be discovered. By trial and error."

"I see."

"And I know what you're thinking, Mr. J, you're thinking, 'Easier said than done,' but you know, *everything* in life is easier said than done."

I said nothing: it seemed easier.

"And that's where you come in, Mr. J."

I'd been pretty certain that I'd come into it somewhere.

"It'd be good to get in some practice before I go to bartending school, don't you think?" she said.

"Sure."

"Call it preliminary research."

"OK."

"So how about this for a deal? Every time I go shopping for you at the supermarket, I'll call in at the liquor store and buy a bottle or two of liquor, or liqueur. Then before long I'll have a full range of ingredients, and then I can really start experimenting."

"And I'd be paying for these?"

"Well, that's very generous of you, Mr. J. Thanks. Think of it like a subsidy to the arts. And of course I'd keep the booze here in your house. I wouldn't just take it home and drink it all by myself. You'd be totally involved. I'll make the drinks here, and you'll be my official taster, my judge, my mentor. How does that sound?"

Did it sound like I was going to be exploited? Yes, of course it did. Did I object to being exploited? Well, yes and no. As forms of exploitation went, this one seemed comparatively minor. The expense wasn't going to ruin me, and I did in some vague way want to help Miranda. I kind of liked her. More than that, I was starting to feel I'd been behaving way too negatively of late. I'd said no to Renée's dog-walking proposition. I'd been difficult with my ex-wife. I'd been downright vicious to the riffraff boys. I felt the basic urge to be *nice* to someone.

"OK," I said, "I'll be your guinea pig."

"Oh no, you're much more interesting than a guinea pig."

I wondered if that meant I was going to be a lab rat.

SEVENTEEN

I was well aware that I was living an unorthodox life at this point. How could I have thought otherwise? Like any psychologist I could argue about what is and isn't "normal," but I understood that walking twenty-five miles a day, every day, and not doing very much else, was unusual behavior in anyone's book. More than that, I didn't have so many of the things that so many people wanted, that so many people took for granted. I had no job, no friends, no girlfriend, no social life, no hobbies, no "interests" in the usual sense. But equally I didn't feel I was lacking anything.

I may not have been conspicuously, demonstrably happy, but I definitely wasn't unhappy. I was content with my life, taking pleasure in small things and in the much larger thing of walking around the world. Renée and the two Pauls and Wendy Gershwin and her niece didn't seem by any means the worst neighbors in the world, and I'm sure I appreciated them more for not seeing too much of them. The riffraff boys, of course, I did my best not to see, or even think about, but I concluded that their existence might possibly be a good thing, in that they reminded me I wasn't living in the best of all possible worlds. And I was always happy enough to see Darrell, the mailman.

On the morning of Day 36 I noticed that he'd stopped his truck right in front of my gate and had gotten out and was waiting for me, as he'd done that time when he first wanted to put the mail into my hand and put a face to a name. This time, however, he didn't have any mail in his hand. He beckoned for me to come over to the gate, and although this was an unwelcome interruption, I did what he wanted and walked over there.

Without preamble, he said, "Two Zen monks were walking from one monastery to another. Of course they were celibate; they weren't even supposed to *look* at women."

"OK," I said uncertainly.

"After they'd already walked a good long way, they came to a river, and they had to get to the other side. There was no bridge, no stepping-stones; they'd have to wade across, through the water.

"Of course a Zen monk wouldn't worry about getting wet, so there was no problem there, but then a woman came walking along the riverbank, and she also wanted to get to the other side, but she was far too refined to go walking through a river. So she asked the monks for help. Hey, stop me if you've heard it."

I didn't. I hadn't.

Darrell continued: "The first monk was happy to oblige. Without hesitation he picked up the woman, carried her in his arms across the river and put her down on the other side. She was delighted, thanked him big-time, and went on her way. But the second monk was furious with the first monk. They weren't supposed to look at women, and yet his companion had not only looked, he'd talked to, he'd touched, and he'd lifted and carried a woman.

"But the first monk was perfectly serene about it and said, 'Yes, I picked up the woman, walked across the river carrying her. But then I put her down, and now it's over. But you—*you're* still carrying her.'"

Darrell bowed and rippled his dreadlocks.

"Nice story," I said, and I more or less meant it, "although if I'd been the second monk I think I might've thrown the first one in the river for being such a smart-ass."

"You got that right," said Darrell gravely. "Knowing the difference between wisdom and smart-assery is definitely one of the steps on the path to enlightenment."

I don't believe the Buddha ever said that. I think Darrell just made it up on the spot: that was OK by me. But he hadn't finished.

"Are you at all familiar with the kaihogyo, Mr. Johnson?"

I wasn't. I didn't know whether it was a person or a place or an example of Japanese cuisine, but something told me that I'd know what it was before too long.

"Otherwise known as circling the mountain?" Darrell added, not all that helpfully.

"No, you're going to have to enlighten me," I said.

I think he was trying to look humble, but in fact he looked smug.

"Kaihogyo is a kind of spiritual training used by Buddhist monks on Mount Hiei, above Kyoto, in Japan."

"You don't say," I said.

"You see, the Buddha was a great walker," said Darrell. "The Lotus Sutra says he was the most loved creature ever to walk the earth."

"Is that right?" I said, for the sake of having something to say. It wasn't exactly news.

"Oh yeah, and he was also heavily into meditation, so he combined the two, turned his walking into a *form* of meditation: the walking Buddha—that's one of the four Buddha postures. So I was wondering if that's what you're doing: a kind of walking meditation."

I knew, of course, that there were certain practitioners who would tell you that psychotherapy and meditation are just different ways of arriving at the same ends: stress-reduction, self-knowledge, inner peace, however these things might be defined. And there are plenty of mindfulness-based therapies out there. Others will tell you meditation is a therapeutic "bubble," a New Age fad, and that in fact it can intensify problems in those who lack a "cohesive ego," as we psychologists sometimes like to put it. I really had no ax to grind in the debate. If meditation got you where you needed to go, then I wasn't going to stand in anybody's way.

"No, it's not really walking meditation," I said.

Darrell looked at me sadly but sympathetically. "You're not interested in trying to reach a higher state of consciousness?" he said.

"Well . . ." I said.

The truth is I've always been more than skeptical about this whole "higher consciousness" business. It's always struck me as a bit of a status thing, with elements of snobbery and spiritual class warfare about it: *Hey, my consciousness is higher than your consciousness.* But that didn't seem like the kind of thing to say to your mailman.

I said, "No, not at the moment."

Darrell obviously didn't want to push things, but he said, "So anyway, the deal is, with the kaihogyo, that novices sign up to become monks, and the first thing they have to do is walk around the mountain every day, twenty-five miles a day, for a hundred consecutive days. It's a kind of walking meditation. As a walker, I thought you'd be interested."

He wasn't completely wrong.

"OK," I said.

"I thought so. I guess it's a kind of boot camp that sorts out the spiritual men from the unspiritual boys."

"Or at least the walkers from the non-walkers," I said.

"But there's more to it," said Darrell.

I knew there would be.

"After they've done the hundred-day kaihogyo," he said, "and become basic monks, then they can apply to become super monks, if the top monks will let 'em. And that involves doing a thousand-day kaihogyo, although it only involves another nine hundred because the hundred they've already done count toward the total."

This, of course, sounded all too relevant to my grand project, and I wondered if Miranda had been talking to Darrell about me behind my back. I wondered why she'd do a thing like that.

"They're allowed seven years to complete it," Darrell said. "They don't walk every day because they have to do other things too—temple duties and fasting and learning calligraphy—but even so you couldn't call it leisurely."

"No, I wouldn't call it leisurely," I agreed.

"And there's even more. And this is the killer. While they're on the hundred-day kaihogyo they can drop out if they want to, like I dropped out of the army. But once they're on the thousand-day version, there's no dropping out. They either complete it or they have to commit suicide. One or the other. No half measures. There are graves all over the mountain belonging to those who didn't make it."

"That's a shame," I said, again for the sake of having something to say, though I wasn't actually sure how much of a shame it really was.

"Only forty-six men have completed the thousand-day kai-hogyo since 1885," Darrell said. "And three of those guys did it twice. Which is kind of showy, if you ask me."

"Yes," I said.

"Anyway," said Darrell, "I was wondering if maybe you were conducting your own kind of personal kaihogyo, Mr. Johnson, though I can see you're not circling a mountain."

"And I'm not doing temple duties and learning calligraphy," I said. "And I'm not going to kill myself if I fail."

"Well, that's great," said Darrell, "and I guess if it's not a kaih-ogyo, then that means you don't have to be bothered with all that Buddhist stuff about sobriety and chastity."

I considered what were about to become my cocktail-drink-ing habits, considered the state of my sex life, and concluded that maybe I was already halfway to becoming a monk. I found myself thinking about Carole and experiencing a strange pang of both loss and lust. I knew no good was going to come of that.

EIGHTEEN

"So, you won't walk with my dog, but you'll walk with your bitch."

The voice, of course, belonged to Renée, Small Paul's mother, Big Paul's wife, and Hopeless's owner. I wondered if she'd say she was "just joking," but she didn't. Instead she said, "Forgive me, I shouldn't have said that, but I'm really upset."

"I'm sorry to hear that," I said, though I couldn't see that I was in any way responsible.

"I've been watching you walk," she said, "*and* I've seen you walking with that girlfriend of yours."

"I don't have a girlfriend," I said.

"The one with the hair and the boots."

"Oh no, she's just my...assistant." It sounded absurd even to me.

"Well, that's one word for it," Renée said.

Could this really be what was upsetting her? I was relieved to find that it wasn't.

"It's Hopeless," she said. "He's gone missing. And if he'd walked with you it wouldn't have happened."

Ignoring the accusation, I said, "He probably didn't go far."

This was surely true—he didn't look like a dog for the long haul—but then he wouldn't have needed to go far before he was likely torn to pieces by a roaming coyote or raccoon or even a feral kitten.

"The two Pauls are out looking for him and putting up MISSING DOG signs. Me, I'm too upset to go out there."

I suppose a good neighbor would have offered to help with the search and the signs, but I didn't want to appear to be something I wasn't.

"You owe me one," she said.

Maybe I did, maybe I didn't, but I didn't say anything. Renée wiped her nose on a much-folded piece of kitchen towel.

"It's true," she said, "what you told Small Paul about chaos. Everything is chaos."

I couldn't really remember the details of what I'd said to Small Paul, but I knew it wasn't exactly that.

"Do you actually *know* about chaos theory?" Renée asked.

"A little," I said, trying not to sound too defensive or too knowledgeable. "I read a book about it once, a beginner's guide."

"Mmm. You're quite an intellectual, aren't you, Joe?"

I supposed there were some places where reading a beginner's guide to chaos theory, or reading anything at all, would mark you out as an "intellectual." These were obviously not places where being an intellectual counted for much, perhaps places where the term was an accusation rather than a compliment. I hoped Renée wasn't going to accuse me of anything else.

"I wouldn't go so far as to call myself an intellectual," I said.

"No? How far *would* you go?"

Now that didn't sound like an accusation. It sounded more like we were back to double entendres, maybe just single.

"Not very far at all," I said.

"Just like your walking," Renée said. "That's not taking you very far either, is it? No offense."

I had no intention of explaining my grand project to Renée. If nothing else, it would take some time, and I wanted to get back to my walking.

"It's taking me far enough," I said. "It's taking me where I want to go."

"Yeah, you're smart, aren't you?" she said.

Again, this could well have been another accusation, but I wasn't quite prepared to pretend I was an idiot, so I said, "Doesn't everybody think they're smart?"

"What about Small Paul?" said Renée. "Do you think he's smart?"

I'd only seen the kid only twice, spoken to him only once, and he hadn't struck me as a great brain, but it seemed wisest to say, "Sure, smart as a whip."

"That's right," said Renée. "You're very perceptive. Not everybody can see that in him. He's bright, he's downright *precocious*, but he's not doing well at school. So we're thinking about home-schooling."

I had a lot of sympathy with any kid who didn't do well at school.

"And you know," said Renée, "I'm smart too, but I'm not book smart. And frankly Big Paul is dumb as a pipe wrench, so there's no way we can teach him ourselves. So we're looking into other options. That's where you could come in."

I suddenly saw exactly what she had in mind, and the prospect didn't please me one bit. "I couldn't teach anybody anything," I said, which wasn't strictly, literally true, but I saw no reason for Renée to know that.

She smiled indulgently. "I know you're only joking, Joe. I like a man who makes me laugh."

And then she laughed, though it seemed a little forced, and it certainly had nothing to do with me.

"Look," she said, "here's the idea, and I'm not saying it's a very new or very brilliant idea, but see, sometimes when you're doing your walking, why don't you let Small Paul walk along with you, when your girlfriend's not here, obviously—"

"She's not my girlfriend."

"—and then as you walk you can share your wisdom with him."

"Like Aristotle?" I said, and I regretted it the moment it came out of my mouth.

"Say what?"

It was too late to take it back.

"The Peripatetic school," I said cautiously. "Greece, fourth century BCE. Aristotle would walk up and down in the Lyceum, and his acolytes would walk with him, and he'd talk and they'd absorb his teachings."

"Well, that sounds like a fabulous plan," Renée said. "And obviously it wouldn't be all the time and not every day, and it wouldn't have to be anything formal. You carry on with your walking and Small Paul pops up from time to time, and you walk together, and you talk about whatever's on your mind, chaos theory or whatever."

"I've pretty much told him everything I know about chaos theory," I said.

"Then just talk to him about . . . you know . . . anything. About walking why not? Or is that too boring?"

"Not boring at all," I said, and I knew I'd regret saying this too, but somehow I couldn't stop myself. "A discussion about walking can be turned into a discussion of just about anything: art, poetry, history, anatomy, geography, evolution..."

"Sounds perfect," said Renée.

I felt manipulated, of course, far more than I had by Miranda and her cocktails, and it wouldn't have been so very hard to say no to Renée. Despite her opinion, I didn't think I owed her anything, and certainly not as a result of refusing to walk Hopeless, but I did have some sympathy with Small Paul. From what little I'd seen of the kid, he definitely needed something he wasn't getting, and maybe homeschooling, or at least schooling in the yard of the house next door, might be a start.

"I'd be so grateful to you," said Renée. "You wouldn't mind me being grateful to you, would you, Joe?"

"No," I said, though I was already imagining many forms of gratitude that I definitely wouldn't appreciate.

"Just one thing," Renée said, "don't tell Big Paul about this, will you? He wouldn't understand. He'd feel threatened. This will be our little secret. OK?"

"You, me, and Small Paul?" Small Paul didn't strike me as the kind of kid who'd be much good at keeping secrets, but maybe I could teach him about that too.

"That's it," said Renée. "The unholy trinity."

It was another thing I didn't like the sound of, but Renée's head had already disappeared behind the fence before I could say anything else. I wondered if the two Pauls would manage to find that dog. I wondered if it wanted to be found.

NINETEEN

A few days later, on Day 40 in mid-morning, after I'd already been walking for a couple of hours, a very anxious-looking Small Paul sidled into my yard to begin his education with me. He looked well scrubbed and neatly dressed: his hair was brushed to within an inch of its short life, and he was wearing hiking boots that looked brand new. I'm sure some would have thought he looked "just adorable," but I wasn't so sure. I thought he had something of the baby-faced psychopath about him. He also had a huge backpack strapped to his shoulders, a thing so big and cumbersome that it was obviously going to hinder any attempt to walk.

From my point of view, it felt like a fine day for walking. The year was warming up. I felt fresh. My rhythm was good, and I didn't want to disrupt it, so I quickly helped Small Paul take off the stupid backpack and we placed it on the garden bench, where it could be supported by the stone lions. Small Paul was glad to be relieved of the burden, though his overall anxiety eased only slightly. He was obviously worried about what lay ahead of him. Still, the kid showed some character. He started walking alongside me. He may not have been a natural born pedestrian but he was game enough to try. Perhaps he feared I'd punish him if he didn't, although I suspected walking in itself might be punishment enough.

Small Paul's legs were obviously shorter than mine, and although I slackened the pace a little, he still struggled to keep up with me, having to take the occasional extra couple of rapid strides so as not to be left behind. I thought it better to pretend I didn't notice this.

"Have you found your dog yet?" I asked, to start the ball rolling.

"No," Small Paul said. "I don't think he's coming back."

That seemed very likely to be true.

"Maybe he's gone to a better place," I said.

Small Paul shrugged. The loss of the dog didn't seem to bother him much. I did my best to ask a few education-related questions as we walked. What were his favorite subjects at school: he didn't have any. Who were his favorite teachers: ditto. What was the last book he'd read: he couldn't remember. The conversation didn't exactly flow, partly because I didn't have much idea of how to talk to a young boy, but also because Small Paul was panting for breath. I hoped he'd get his second wind before long.

We'd completed maybe a dozen more circuits together before it became quite clear that no second wind was likely to arrive. Instead I saw that Small Paul was drenched in sweat and looking unsteady on his feet. I was carrying a canteen of water and I offered him a drink as we continued to walk. He swigged down the entire contents of the canteen and gamely carried on. At least he wasn't going to suffer dehydration, but I did start to worry that he might keel over from simple exhaustion. This was obviously not what was required either from homeschooling or the Peripatetic method. In fact I wondered if it might constitute child abuse.

"Why don't you sit down for a little while, Paul?" I said. "Take an early recess."

He didn't have to be asked twice, and he lowered himself onto the garden bench next to his backpack. I continued with my circuits. Before long I could see that Small Paul was sweating less, breathing normally, and looking as though he might fall asleep. That didn't seem very educational either.

"Ready for more?" I asked.

"Not really," he said. "I'll tell you as soon as I am."

I suspected this might be never. I did another circuit.

"Don't you have any books in that backpack of yours?" I asked. If he couldn't walk, he could at least sit and read.

He rooted around in the backpack and pulled out a copy of *People* magazine. I supposed it was better than nothing, but not much. In any case he didn't seem very interested in the magazine. Each time I completed a circuit and came around to the bench, he was staring off into space, although he did keep an eye on me each time I walked through his field of vision, as if he might learn something just from watching me in action. This did not make me feel comfortable.

I decided it wouldn't kill me to stop and talk to the kid for a couple of minutes, so I sat down on the bench beside him.

"Is this better than school?" I asked. I admit that a part of me wanted him to say no, so that he could go back to "real" school and I could be rid of him. I was destined to be disappointed.

"Anything's better than school," he said.

"You don't like learning stuff?"

"Learning's OK. It's everything else."

"Bullies?" I asked.

"Sure. The teachers are as bad as the other kids."

"Sounds like my old school," I said.

"Really?" This seemed to cheer him up just a little.

"But school isn't the only place there are bullies," I said.

"No?"

"There are bullies everywhere," I said. "Everybody gets bullied once in a while."

"Even you?"

"Sure. And you know the worst thing, Paul?"

"No."

"Most people do a bit of bullying themselves if they get the chance."

"Even you?"

"Even me, Paul. And even you one day, I expect."

For Small Paul this was a brand-new, if not, per-Nietzsche, "truly great" thought. It gave him considerable pleasure.

"Wow. I can't wait for that," he said.

I had the strangest feeling that despite all the odds, I might actually have taught him something. Whether I'd taught him anything worth knowing, I wasn't so sure.

"I need to start walking again," I said.

"OK, I'll just sit and watch."

"No," I said. "I think that won't work."

"My mom said you were going to teach me all about walking," said Small Paul.

I think we both knew that wasn't the deal, but I didn't want to argue with the kid.

"OK," I said, "so is there anything you particularly want to know about walking?"

"I don't know."

"Do you want to know about the savanna theory of bipedalism?"

"I don't think so," said Small Paul.

Well, I didn't think he would. "How about El Camino de Santiago?"

"I don't like the sound of that," he said.

"So how about the Bataan Death March?"

I think it was the mention of death rather than marching that piqued his interest.

"What's that?" he asked.

As it happened, I knew a certain amount about the Bataan Death March. If you're concerned with history and walking and torture, it's the kind of thing you're likely to take an interest in.

"American and Filipino prisoners dying in huge numbers while being corralled by Japanese soldiers," I said. "Some of the prisoners had their heads chopped off with samurai swords."

I may not have known much about education or small boys, but something told me I couldn't go far wrong with beheadings and samurai swords.

"Cool," said Small Paul, and he was as enthusiastic as I'd ever seen him.

"OK," I said. "Go home for now. Next time you come I'll try to teach you something about the Bataan Death March."

Aristotle might almost have been proud of me.

TWENTY

I wonder if Aristotle got along with his neighbors. I wonder how he, or Jung, or even the Buddha—perhaps especially the Buddha—would have handled living adjacent to riffraff. There were continuing hostilities between the riffraff boys and me, comparatively mild at first, if you can have mild hostilities. There were more parties, for instance, some louder than others, and sometimes it may not even have been a party, just the boys whooping it up, practicing their martial arts, and expressing themselves in their own special way. It wasn't something you'd want to live next door to, but neither was it something worth making too much fuss about. And what good would it do to make a fuss?

The barking of the dogs was a special, consistent, and very audible irritation, and even though I tend to believe there's no such thing as a bad dog, only bad riffraff, the dogs actually annoyed me at least as much as the boys themselves.

Beer cans and vodka bottles still found their way into my yard from time to time; more than you'd want, obviously, because you wouldn't want any at all, but at first there weren't so many. I threw them all back, of course. I assumed the boys were testing me, seeing if I was going to try to make them stop, determining just how much trouble I wanted for the sake of a few bottles and cans. The truth remained that I didn't want any trouble whatsoever, but if trouble was coming I knew I had to pick my battles. You don't start a scorched earth campaign over a few empty Bud Lights.

But then the boys became bolder, as I knew they inevitably would. They started throwing car parts, a bicycle frame, many, many empty aerosol cans, and even whole bags of garbage over the fence. Of course I threw these things back too, but I knew this wasn't any kind of solution. For one thing, I suspected that these guys weren't all that worried about living surrounded by a yard full of garbage.

And then one morning as I was gathering up a newly discovered bag of garbage, prior to throwing it back, the contents spilled out, and there, amid the coffee grounds and pizza boxes and cartons of Muscle Milk, I saw something that sparkled. It was a row of rhinestones on a red leather dog collar, the one, I had no doubt, that belonged (or *had* belonged) to Hopeless.

This was ominous enough in itself, but then I saw there were strands of hair, the remains of a backbone and what might have been ligaments or tendons attached to the leather of the collar. There were probably more canine remains in the bag too, but I preferred not to look, and what good would looking have done? It seemed that Hopeless had met his end in the yard of the riffraff house, in the jaws of one or more of the giant dogs.

I didn't immediately know what to do. Telling Small Paul or Renée what had happened to their dog would surely have done more harm than good, and although I might have told Big Paul, I didn't trust him to handle it very well, so obviously I had to take things into my own hands.

I waited and watched, did some reconnaissance, made a few observations regarding the boys and their dogs. The fence may have been substantial but it did have a few eyeholes, and I made an important discovery. I saw that during the daytime all six of the hounds roamed the boys' yard, but at night there was some kind of hierarchy and favoritism. Three of the dogs got to sleep inside the house; three of them remained outside, perhaps as guard dogs. Then, at some point in the late morning when the boys eventually got up—they evidently didn't have jobs to go to—they threw open the doors of the house. The three indoor dogs rushed out, and the three outdoor dogs rushed in. I could see real possibilities there.

When Miranda next came to make her shopping list—groceries, plus naval rum, vermouth, blue curacao, and cherry brandy—I asked her also to buy me a few pounds of cheap ground beef and half a dozen boxes of laxative, the kind that comes in powdered form.

"With stimulant?"

"Sure."

"And stool softener?"

"Why not?"

"Fast acting and reliable?"

"Don't they all claim to be that?"

"Gentle and soothing?"

"No, I really don't care about gentle and soothing," I said.

Miranda must have realized that these boxes were not for my personal use, but she didn't ask any questions, and obviously I saw no need to explain. Would this count as cruelty to animals? Maybe, but I reckoned it would be far crueler to the boys.

Once Miranda had returned with the shopping, made a cocktail involving curacao and cherry brandy—no, it wasn't good—then departed, I put the ground beef into a bowl, added the powdered laxative, and kneaded the ingredients together. I made a dozen or so tainted balls of meat. On the night of Day 46, after the riffraff house was dark and shut up for the night, I tossed six of the balls over the fence to the three outdoor dogs. Admittedly, I couldn't actually see them eating the stuff, but I could definitely hear the sounds of enthusiastic canine consumption, the kind that doesn't leave any evidence. I slept well that night, and the next morning I was up and out early, walking with a spring in my step.

It was a while before a couple of the boys got up and stepped outside the house to greet a brand-new day, though I imagined all their days were essentially very similar. The doors to the house were left open. The indoor dogs ran out. The outdoor dogs ran in. Surreptitiously, I now dropped the other six balls of meat over the fence. The three indoor dogs, now outdoors, found them soon enough and devoured them as excitedly and as completely as the other three had.

I couldn't really see what happened next, and I didn't stop walking in order to watch, but I heard plenty. Before long there was a lot of yelling from the boys, even more than usual, and yelling of a different kind, the sounds of outrage and disgust, and naturally all six dogs joined in the general noise and mayhem, and there may well have been some dog disciplining or even beating; certainly there was some unfamiliar canine yelping, and it all went on a lot longer than I thought was necessary. And, of course, I knew there'd be more to follow in the course of the day, once the laxative worked its way through the indoor dogs.

The riffraff boys obviously had their hands full, at least metaphorically, but the next day Butch's head appeared over the fence.

"You know anything about these dogs?" he demanded of me.

"*These* dogs? No. I don't know anything about *any* dogs."

"You know anything about diarrhea?"

"No more than the average person."

"These dogs of ours, they're shitting up a storm."

"Shit storms are never a good thing," I said. "Maybe it was something they ate."

"I'm fucking *sure* it was something they ate."

"Perhaps they were eating garbage. I see there's a lot of garbage scattered around your yard. You've got to be very careful when you have pets. Dogs will eat anything."

"So now you *do* know something about dogs."

"General knowledge," I said.

It was hard to see what Butch wanted or expected from this conversation with me. If I'd poisoned his dogs, I obviously wasn't going to say so. If I hadn't poisoned them, then there was nothing to say.

Nevertheless I said, "I'm sorry for your dogs."

It was by no means a complete lie, despite my part in their distress, but Butch wasn't very receptive to my sympathy.

"You think you're better than me, don't you?" he said, his tone even more demanding than before.

We both knew the answer to that one.

"What if I say no?" I answered.

"Then I wouldn't believe you."

"And if I said yes then that'll confirm your opinion that I'm some sort of arrogant snob. Which is what you think anyway."

He did me the honor of thinking about that for a moment.

"Did anybody ever tell you you're too smart for your own fucking good?" he said at last.

"Oh yes," I said. "But don't worry, Butch, that's not a problem you're ever going to have."

TWENTY-ONE

"So," said Miranda, when she next came to the house, "the laxatives worked?"

"They did a job, yes."

"OK," she said, "I guess I can live without knowing the details."

"Probably best that way," I agreed.

"You're an interesting man, Mr. J."

"I don't try to be interesting."

"Maybe that's why you are."

It sounded like flattery. I never liked or trusted that.

By now Miranda and I had established a method of working. She came to the house once a week, occasionally more than once if for some reason she needed to, and she walked with me for as many circuits as necessary until she'd made her list. You'd have thought the process should have got quicker, more streamlined, as time went on, but it somehow never did. There were always new questions that needed to be asked and answered. I learned to accept that. Maybe I even started to like it.

The list now always included some bottles of exotic booze, which she bought at my expense, brought back to the house, and then employed to made a couple of cocktails, one for her, one for me. We drank them together while I took my afternoon break from walking. We sat inside the covered porch, on a couple of frayed rattan chairs that the previous owners had left behind.

Miranda had acquired a vintage cocktail shaker, a chunky but stylish silver-plated, bomb-shaped thing, her idea being that this cocktail-drinking should be a civilized affair, not just a couple of lushes boozing it up in the middle of the afternoon. I preferred it that way too. Once we'd gotten about halfway into the drink she would ask me what I thought of it, and I'd offer what I laughingly called my "tasting notes," and she'd make a few actual notes on a scrap of paper. Then we'd finish the drinks, and she'd go on her way and I'd go back to walking, now with a little extra zip in my step.

Would I recommend this cocktail-drinking element to the serious, long-distance pedestrian? Not necessarily, but I would say, *Whatever works for you is fine.* The great Captain Barclay, who walked a mile in each of a thousand consecutive hours (if that sounds easy, just think about it, then try it), sustained himself with champagne and porter and the occasional roasted pheasant. Perhaps he was rather more what he ate and drank than I was.

Miranda was working her way through some "walking" cocktail recipes she'd found online—the Plank Walker, the Cloud Walker, the Dream Walker—all of these to be considered steps, or perhaps signposts, on the long road to the Miranda. On Day 49 we were drinking a cocktail known as Dead Man Walking—a cloying concoction made from absinthe and cinnamon schnapps that I'd have thought nobody would want to put his name to.

"I don't mean to pry," Miranda said mid-drink, "but did you used to be a teacher?"

I supposed she might have heard about Small Paul and me, though she certainly hadn't heard it from me.

"No," I said, "I may have taught one or two people one or two things in the course of my career, but I was never exactly a teacher."

"Well, I've already learned a few things from you."

I didn't necessarily take that as a compliment. "Yeah?"

"Sure. You've changed the way I think about walking," she said.

I had never intended to change anybody's way of thinking about anything.

"Is that good?" I asked. I could tell that wasn't the question Miranda wanted me to ask. She wanted me to ask what things she'd learned, or how her thinking had changed, but I didn't. I knew she'd tell me without being asked.

"Until I started working for you," she said, "I never really thought about walking. I mean I did it, obviously, but I didn't *think* about it, about how I did it or how other people did it."

Again I wondered what was good about that.

"But now," said Miranda, "any time I go into a drugstore, I see there's always a whole long aisle dedicated just to foot care. I never noticed that before, never even thought about it."

In truth I'd never given it all that much thought either.

"I see all these products," said Miranda, "the foot creams and the foot lotions, and the sprays and the powders and the balms, and the pumice and the corn removers and the callus removers and the wart removers, and the fungicides, and the arch supports and the heel cushions and the massaging gel insoles. It seems like a lot of people in this world must be in complete agony every time they take a step. And then there are all the people who need orthotics and who have plantar fasciitis or fallen arches or bunions or ingrown toenails. It's amazing that anybody's ever in any condition to do any walking whatsoever."

I could have pointed out that it's by no means just a matter of the feet. There are many other parts of the body that also affect, and sometimes hinder, the walking process. There are hordes of people who have trouble walking because of their bad ankles, or bad knees, or shin splints, or torn bursas or tendons, or hips that need replacing or backs that need surgery, not that back surgery ever really seems to work, but I decided not to labor the point.

"You don't get any of these problems, Mr. J?" Miranda asked.

"No," I said. "I'm not saying my feet don't hurt sometimes. I'm not saying I don't get a few blisters and calluses. If you walk twenty-five miles a day, every day, you're bound to get some aches and pains. But that's all part of the process, all part of the deal."

Miranda smiled at me with what might have been quiet admiration.

"Yep, it's a real learning experience," she said. "It's made me realize that if you've got trouble walking, then you've *really* got trouble."

"True enough," I said.

"Bad feet can be absolute torture."

"Oh sure," I said, "and torturers have always known to go for the feet."

"Yes?"

She sounded understandably surprised, and I wondered if maybe I shouldn't have said that. In my situation, with my history, I knew it might not be wise to bring up the subject of torture, but maybe it was the cocktail talking, or maybe it was because, for some reason, I trusted Miranda, and I found myself saying, "The bastinado, for instance. Well, that's just one of the names for it—simply beating the soles of the feet with a cane or a stick."

"Boy," said Miranda, "that's got to hurt."

"And there's foot roasting, which is pretty much what it sounds like, just exposing the soles of the feet to a raging open fire. And there's something called star kicking, where you wrap oiled string between the toes, like a fuse, and then you light it. And the victim kicks like hell, which is how it gets its name, of course. Countess Elizabeth Báthory is generally credited with the invention of that one."

"Aristos, huh?" said Miranda.

"Hungarian female aristo," I said.

"It just gets worse."

"Then there's the boot," I said, "sometimes called the Spanish boot or the Malay boot. There were a lot of variations on that one. Sometimes it was an actual, specially made metal boot that you heated in the fire till it was red hot, and then you jammed somebody's foot into it. But sometimes it was just an ordinary boot that you shoved wedges and stakes and hot oil into.

"And at different times people have used various kinds of foot press, which is basically a metal vise that slowly crushes the bones in the foot. Sometimes there'd be spikes or drills in it that pierced the flesh."

"I don't even like to have my feet tickled," said Miranda.

"And the great thing about foot torture," I said, "is that it's excruciating, and of course you probably don't walk so well afterward, and sometimes you can be crippled for life, but very few people ever *die* from it. And I guess that's important with a certain kind of torture."

Miranda was very thoughtful for a while, then said, "Yeah, I can see that. Like, if people think they're going to die, then why would they give up any information? If they trust you not to kill them, they might give you what you want."

"Maybe, but the thing is," I said, and now I suppose I was just showing off, which of course I knew was not a good thing, "torture has been pretty much ubiquitous throughout human history. Sure, nobody wanted to be on the receiving end of it, some people complained about it, and some possibly even thought it was morally wrong, but a vast number didn't. A lot of societies always seemed to have accepted that torture was just a regular part of life. If you went to jail, if you got captured by your enemies, then you expected to be tortured; that's just how it was. And if the circumstances were reversed you knew you'd have done to them what they were doing to you. People accepted it the way people today accept it when they get a parking ticket. They bitch about it, they resent it, they don't like it, but they can't honestly claim to be *surprised*."

"One of my mother's boyfriends used to have gout," Miranda said. "He'd be laid up for days at a time. He said he wouldn't wish it on his worst enemy. But that never made any sense to me. I wish all kinds of shit on my enemies, the worse the better. Gout would be the least of it."

"Who's your worst enemy?" I asked.

"My therapist used to say I was my *own* worst enemy."

She'd never mentioned having a therapist before, but it didn't surprise me.

"You tortured yourself?"

"Sure. It saved other people the trouble."

I saw that both our glasses were empty. We'd successfully killed the two Dead Man Walking cocktails. It was time for me to do some actual walking. I didn't feel in the least like a dead man.

TWENTY-TWO

Once in a while, naturally, inevitably, I thought about sex as I was walking—certainly nothing very original about that. Since my divorce from Carole, I'd been celibate; in fact I sometimes felt downright neutered. Divorce can do that to you, though of course, for some people, it can do the opposite. In general I think most people are much better off if they have a partner and a good sex life, but I hadn't taken any steps whatsoever to change things in that direction. It all seemed too much trouble. And how could it possibly have worked? Meeting women, dating (at however rudimentary a level), does tend to involve having to leave your own yard. I even occasionally found myself thinking about Carole.

The good thing is that thinking about sex really doesn't compromise your ability to walk. Back in the days when I worked nine to five in an office, I lived for the lunch hour, the time when I could get out and walk the streets and look at all the women who were also walking the streets on *their* lunch hour. I loved the way their bodies moved when they walked, the way their clothes moved against their bodies. In those circumstances it was difficult for me to walk and think about anything *other* than sex. You could argue, of course, that this was only imaginary sex, fantasy sex, not "real" sex, but I'd say only in the same way that you could argue I wasn't "really" walking around the world.

I found myself thinking about Marilyn Monroe's wiggle, which some people say was caused by high heels and weak ankles, but I think there was more to it than that. Marilyn Monroe looked sexy when she walked because she *wanted* to look sexy when she walked. That's why she wore the high heels that emphasized the weak ankles.

And I found myself thinking about the models in fashion shows, the ones who parade up and down on the runways and catwalks. They're sexy all right, and it's got a lot to do with the way they walk, but it's a very localized, very specialized form of walking. They strut and stomp; they stride out, hammer their feet and their heels down, scissor their legs across each other, and look as though they're really determined to get somewhere, but of course they never do get anywhere: just to the end of the runway, and then they stop, turn around, and stomp back the way they've come. Wouldn't it be better if fashion runways were circular and the models' walking was continuous? Maybe I'm prejudiced here.

Never for a moment did I imagine that I looked sexy as I walked around my path. That would have been a ridiculous thing to think. Any man who walks around thinking how sexy he looks is an idiot, though I suppose there's this whole "cruising" thing that some—maybe most—gay men do, which I suppose is a highly complicated form of walking. I know about it only by hearsay (he says, trying not to sound as though he's protesting too much), and frankly it sounds really difficult and time-consuming, and sometimes risky, and although I can see the appeal of going out for a walk and ending up having some spontaneous, anonymous sex with a stranger, on balance I'm really glad I don't have to do it. Well, I suppose nobody absolutely *has* to do it.

There are, it seems to me, several ways in which sex and walking resemble each other. First of all, they're both essentially very simple, repetitive activities that just about everybody does at one time or another. And yet despite being so ordinary and commonplace, they're both capable of great sophistication and elaboration. They can both be completely banal and meaningless, and yet they can also involve great passions and adventures.

Second, although both walking and sex can be sources of fantastic pleasure, there are also times when they can both feel like really hard work. There are times when you feel tired, when you're just not in the mood, when you'd prefer to just sit or lie there and do nothing. But in those circumstances I think it's always best to stir yourself, make the effort, get your head down and do what you've got to do.

Third, sex and walking are things that some people like to do alone, that some people like to do with just one other person, and that some people like to do in groups of various sizes. Some prefer the company of men while doing it, some prefer the company of women, some are prepared to do it with either. Some will do it only if certain very specific conditions are met. A few require special clothing and equipment. Others are eager to do it anywhere, any time, in any conditions, at the drop of a hat. A certain number, perhaps a surprisingly large number, really don't like to do it at all.

These thoughts of mine were interrupted by a voice calling to me from across the garden fence.

"Well, aren't you the hard taskmaster," the voice said.

It was Renée. Her hair was clean and soft and tied up in an elaborate bun, and she'd applied some shiny, blood-colored lipstick.

"Am I?" I said.

"Yeah. I hear you've been putting Small Paul through his paces."

Of course it was reasonable that a mother should be concerned about her son's education, though I didn't think I'd been especially hard on the kid.

"I hope you don't think I overdid it," I said.

"I'm all for it," said Renée. "Sweat some of that lard out of him."

Maybe it was tough love.

"Anyway, Small Paul says you're a very smart man."

I wasn't sure that Small Paul's opinions counted for much in these matters, but I saw no harm in him saying it.

"You know stuff, yes?"

"Some stuff," I agreed.

"You know anything about dreams, Joe?"

There was a time, not so long ago, when people imagined that psychologists, and certainly psychiatrists, spent their whole time listening to and interpreting their patients' dreams. I had come to share the notion that dreams are simply a form of emotional processing, but I wouldn't have fought about it, certainly not with Renée.

"I know a little," I said.

"I had a dream, actually a series of dreams. Can I tell you about them?"

For a moment I wondered if she'd somehow found out about my background in psychology and therapy (though I didn't see how she could have), and she now wanted a consultation. But whether she'd found out or not, I obviously didn't want to hear her dreams. Why would I? Nevertheless, I found myself saying, "I suppose so. If you're sure."

She was sure.

"I dreamed I was walking in your yard, on your path."

It sounded harmless enough.

"Was I there?" I asked.

"No, I don't think so, not unless you were watching me through the window. And I mean it was OK, I wasn't doing any harm, and I wasn't naked or anything. There was nothing dirty about it."

"OK then," I said.

"And I've looked it up online—there're quite a few sites that tell you what your dreams mean—but I'm still confused."

"Really?"

"The website said that a walking dream was about being powerful and in control and progressing toward your life goals."

"Well, that sounds like a good thing, doesn't it?" I said.

"But then I had the dream again, and this time I was walking a dog."

"Was it Hopeless?"

Yes, I knew how to play this game.

"Yes, that's right, at first it was. But then it turned into a big black mongrel and then—and maybe I shouldn't be telling you this—it turned into Big Paul. And he was on all fours, on a leash. And *he* was naked."

Now we were playing a different game altogether.

"And what did your website say about that?"

"Well, it said that walking a dog symbolizes loyalty and faithfulness. But then it said that being a dominatrix really indicated a feeling of powerlessness."

"It covered dreaming about being a dominatrix, did it?"

"Oh yes, and then it said that seeing a naked person in a dream means that you're trying to discover the naked truth about that person or the truth about your relationship with them, or maybe you're trying to see through this person."

"That all sounds pretty reasonable," I said, and it more or less did.

"But then—and this is the worst part—I had another version of the dream, and it wasn't Big Paul on the leash, it was you."

"I see."

I wasn't shocked; I wasn't even all that surprised. But I certainly didn't know what I was supposed to say or do about it.

"So now you know all there is to know," said Renée. "My dreams. My desires. I probably shouldn't have told you this. You'll think less of me."

"No, I won't. I don't."

"You're a good man, Joe."

I didn't think that listening to a neighbor's sex dreams, and not thinking any less of her for it, really scored very high on the scale of "goodness."

"I blame Big Paul," she said. "Even talking to you about this feels like a betrayal. But the truth is I *want* to betray him."

"Really?" I said.

"Because he's betrayed *me*. I'm sure you remember I told you he wasn't very secure in his manhood."

"I remember."

"Well, I was dead right about that. He was so insecure that he had to start fucking other people. Up at his job at the outlet mall, in the middle of the night, in the storeroom when they should be guarding the premises—they fall on each other like animals."

For some reason I pictured an orgy on Noah's ark, but that didn't seem to be a very helpful image. And I had no way of knowing if Big Paul was really doing what Renée claimed.

"What would Dr. Phil say about it, eh?" she asked, though I don't know if she really expected me to answer.

"Or Dr. Freud?" I suggested, and then I knew that was a mistake.

"How's that?"

I couldn't face having to explain Freudianism. I said, "I'm sure you don't need a doctor's opinion."

"Well, I definitely need *something*."

In my opinion, very few of us ever really needed Freud, though to be fair to the man he *was* something of a walker: a couple of hours every day after lunch. And he sometimes left the couch behind and conducted what we might call "walking cures." In 1907 he did his first training analysis on Max Eitingon in a series of evening walks. And in 1910 he walked for four hours with Gustav Mahler, who'd telegraphed him saying he needed an "urgent consultation." Mahler's marriage was breaking down—his wife, Alma, was having an affair with Walter Gropius—and Mahler feared he was about to have a mental breakdown.

Freud and Mahler walked in the city of Leiden, in Holland, and although we don't have a full account of what they talked about, we do know from one of Freud's assistants, who heard it from Freud himself, that Mahler recounted a life-changing incident from his childhood. His mother and father were having an angry argument in the family home, so the boy dashed out into the street, where he started walking and, after a while, encountered a man playing popular tunes on a hurdy-gurdy.

Young Mahler was completely captivated by the sound, to such an extent that he felt it ruined all his subsequent musical compositions. He was aiming for high, classical art but that encounter had somehow implanted the *wrong* kind of music in his brain—folk tunes, Jewish and military music, popular songs—and these low, vulgar things would insist on creeping in and taking over whenever he tried to write his own mighty, high-minded works. And of course he thought it was really all his father's fault for fighting with his mother and driving him out into the street where he had to hear those awful, *low* melodies.

I'd like to think that Freud told Mahler this was complete bullshit and he should pull himself together, but I know he didn't.

I said to Renée, changing the subject, though not out of all recognition, "Small Paul asked me to teach him about the Bataan Death March. Is that all right with you? It's kind of gory."

"Oh yeah, sure, whatever," said Renée.

Mothers and fathers: they have a lot to answer for.

TWENTY-THREE

One small thing I do know about sex: in general (and of course with exceptions) men, given half a chance, try to live out their fantasies, while women are content to let a fantasy remain a fantasy. I did hope that Renée would conform to her gender model. And then for reasons I didn't quite understand, but I'm sure had something to do with sex and longing and absence and fantasy, I called Carole. It seemed too long since she'd last called me.

Back in my old life as a decent, honest, middle-of-the-road psychotherapist—before I got into the whole torture-survival racket, before I started working for the Team—I was regularly forced to hear and think about other people's marriages. People paid good money so that they could come to me and tell me their problems. This, of course, made me do a lot of thinking about my own marriage and my own problems, about what makes a good marriage, what makes a bad one, why apparently "bad" ones often survive, why apparently "good" ones fail.

Only a fool would come to hard-and-fast conclusions about any of this, and only with the greatest reluctance would any self-respecting therapist claim to be an "expert" on the subject, and yet through experience and exposure you do inevitably gain a certain familiarity with marriage and its discontents, and I suppose that could be construed as wisdom.

Only a bigger fool would think that knowing what's good for other people's marriages would help you in any way whatsoever with your own. But I'll say this: I came to the conclusion a long time ago, certainly while Carole and I were still together, that more marriages are wrecked by telling the whole truth than are wrecked by telling a few lies. Nobody needs to know all your secrets, not even (perhaps least of all) your own spouse. If everybody knew exactly what their partner was thinking and feeling twenty-four hours a day, then most relationships would barely last twenty-four hours.

Of course Carole had always known that I was a psychotherapist, but as with most of the rest of the world, she had only the vaguest idea what that meant. That was OK by me. Why would she need to know more? At no point did I ever spill the sordid details of other people's psyches or marriages across the breakfast or dinner table. The question "How was your day?" never required me to give much detail. Confidentiality had something to do with it, but not much. I preferred to think of it as "not bringing your work home with you."

So when I changed my working pattern, when I began to work—on an ad hoc, freelance basis at first—for Christine Vargas and the Team, naturally I didn't hide it from Carole. I said I was doing some specialized work with a government agency, but I didn't give chapter and verse. Again, why would I? I'd never gone into detail about my work before, so why would I go into detail now?

True, I did start working some long, strange hours, and sometimes I had to be away for days at a time. And yes, I did tell a few direct lies about what I was doing, invented quite a few nonexistent conferences and morale-building weekend retreats. I thought it best not to say that I was away torturing volunteers for their own good. Carole knew I was up to something secret or at least secretive, but she didn't question me about it. She accepted a certain lack of transparency as part of the deal when you were married to somebody who was doing sensitive work for a government agency. I don't imagine it was very different from being married to somebody who works for the IRS: detailed questions about complex changes in capital gains law probably don't find their way into the general marital conversation.

I liked it that Carole didn't ask me questions. During the divorce proceedings that changed. There were all kinds of interrogations and disclosures, though no actual revelations. I didn't particularly want to lie, but mostly I did. I said, simply, that I wanted a divorce, and I didn't give any reasons beyond saying that I couldn't face being married anymore. I thought of inventing a mistress or a secret family or some horrible disease for myself, but I knew she wouldn't have believed me.

Carole did suggest that maybe we should have some counseling, but she already knew I would never go for that. She tried to be understanding. She knew that my work was at the bottom of it, though she didn't know how. She tried to change my mind. And then she realized that wasn't an option. She stopped trying. She acquiesced. What else could she do?

These days when we spoke, significantly or not, she felt free to ask me all kinds of questions.

"Why are you calling me?" she asked straightaway this time.

"Do I need a reason?"

"Yes. Usually. Are you lonely? Are you bored? Having trouble with your grand project?"

"No, everything's fine," I said.

"I wish I could believe that."

"Then believe it."

I knew that sounded aggressive, and I didn't want to sound that way, but I just couldn't help it.

"I was wondering why haven't you sent me those photographs of your house and yard?" she asked.

"I forgot," I said.

"You were otherwise occupied?"

"Well, yes."

She didn't find that a satisfactory answer, and I didn't blame her.

"It's not exactly a major commitment, is it, Joe?" she said. "You take a few pictures with your phone and send them to me. You can even do it while you're walking."

"I don't think my phone has a camera," I said.

"All phones have cameras these days."

"You're probably right, but I don't know how to use it."

"I don't believe that either."

For reasons I barely understood, it seemed important that she believe me.

"Is there some problem with where you live?" she asked. "Something you don't want me to see?"

"There's nothing much to see."

"Are you ashamed of it?"

"No."

"But you don't want me to see it?"

"Maybe you should come and see it for yourself." I was surprised when that proposition popped out.

"Do you mean that, Joe?"

I did. Somewhat to my own surprise, I really did. "I mean it," I said.

"OK then, when should I come?"

And then the awfulness, the impossibility of it, rolled back in. What I hadn't and couldn't tell Carole was that I'd needed to get divorced because I knew that somebody or other would be coming to try to kill me, and if I was married to her, then there was every possibility that they'd come and try to kill her too. I'd loved her enough to spare her that. Did I now love her any less? Or in a different way? I didn't think so.

Carole said, "If you're serious, Joe, then let's do it. Let's make it a date."

"OK," I said, "there are one or two things I need to deal with, but as soon as I've done that, then sure, I want you to come. We'll walk, we'll talk. Everything will be all right."

"I wish I could believe that," she said.

"You can. You should. Everything will be just fine."

I suddenly thought I sounded like the worst kind of delusional fantasist.

TWENTY-FOUR

It was the afternoon of Day 50. Miranda and I were sitting in the covered porch, on the rattan chairs, and I was thinking, perhaps unexpectedly, that I'd rather be there with my ex-wife. We were drinking Miranda's latest concoction, something that involved grapefruit juice, gin, mescal, rosemary twigs, and Kahlua. "The Thousand Miles cocktail," said Miranda. "Twenty-five of these and you're good to walk around the circumference of the world."

It tasted essentially rather bland to me, as though the various ingredients were canceling one another out. But perhaps it was deceptively strong, because when mailman Darrell appeared at the gate, Miranda raised her glass in his direction and called out in a loud, apparently friendly way, "Here's looking at you, kid."

"Just wanted to make sure you were home," Darrell said to me. "You wait right there."

Neither Miranda nor I had any intention of going anywhere, so we waited as Darrell went back to his truck and returned, coming up to the house carrying a big, more or less coffin-shaped package that stood about four feet tall. I didn't like the look of it. I wasn't expecting anything that could possibly be that size or shape or size, and in my experience no good ever comes from big, unexpected packages.

It seemed likely that Darrell needed a signature as proof of delivery. If so, I wasn't prepared to give one. He'd have to take the thing away again. I hope that didn't annoy him too much. At least the box, large as it was, didn't look especially heavy. Darrell was finding it perfectly easy to stand there holding it in his arms, which he continued to do.

"Is that really for me?" I asked dubiously.

Darrell ignored the question and said, "Look, Mr. Johnson, I know you're not a Buddhist, and I know you're not involved in walking meditation per se, but you are walking, and I can tell that you're a meditative kind of guy, so I do wonder if you might embody Buddhist principles without knowing it."

"I suppose I might," I said, though I wasn't sure that was actually possible.

"And the whole thing about meditative walking," Darrell continued, "is that you don't have to make an effort. In fact you *shouldn't* make an effort. The Buddha said his practice was nonpractice, the attainment of nonattainment."

"I see," I said, and I wasn't sure if I did or not.

"When you walk you experience the body in action, yes?"

"Sure," I said. There was no denying that.

"And sometimes," Darrell said, "you experience both movement and the *awareness* of movement."

"I guess."

Miranda sat beside me through all this, sipping her cocktail, exuding hostile skepticism toward Darrell.

"But if you're doing it absolutely right," said Darrell, "if you're doing it the Buddha's way, then both of those things—walking and the awareness of walking—arise and disappear in the very same instant."

Now I wasn't sure in the least. I was particularly unsure that there was an "absolutely right" way to walk. No doubt I looked suitably uncomprehending and maybe a little awkward. I assumed this was how Small Paul must often feel. Darrell sensed my discomfort, and he said, "It's OK, I'm on your side," and he finally handed over the package that he'd been holding all this time.

I took it. I felt I had no choice. It was even lighter than I'd expected. I looked at the packaging. Other than having been given to me by a mailman, there was no sign that it had come through the usual postal channels. There weren't any stamps on it, it hadn't been franked, and there was no label with my name or address on it. There was certainly no indication of the sender. It was just a large, plain cardboard box, folded shut but not taped or sealed, which at least made it easier to open, though I still wasn't sure I actually wanted to open it.

"Go ahead," Darrell said warmly, "there's nothing in there that'll bite."

I set the box on the ground, lifted the lid, and looked inside. There, in a bed of packing peanuts, was a figure, or I suppose statue, of a man, somewhat less than life size, and in the circumstances it didn't come as a complete surprise to discover that it was a statue of the Buddha, made of some kind of lightweight wood, brightly painted and varnished. With Miranda's help I lifted him out of the box and set him down on the wooden floor of the porch. It was the lean, walking version of the Buddha rather than the fat, jolly seated character we're more familiar with. This Buddha was in midstep, wearing an off-the-shoulder robe and some kind of pointed headdress that I assumed there had to be a proper name for. The left hand was raised.

"It's for you," Darrell said. "From me."

"Really?" I said.

"Really?" said Miranda.

"Really. It's not precious. It's just a replica, a knockoff, made of lacquered bamboo, Burmese-style."

"And it's hollow?" said Miranda.

"Sure. If it was solid neither of us could lift it."

"Is it for the garden?" I asked.

"No. You have to keep it inside, or the elements will play havoc with the lacquer."

Miranda ran her fingertips over the smooth surface of the Buddha, tapped on the bamboo with her knuckles, then shrugged extravagantly to show how unimpressed she was.

I wasn't accustomed to receiving gifts from strangers, even less from mailmen, and it didn't seem quite appropriate, but then I knew very little about the ways of Buddhists. True, I didn't know for sure whether Darrell was an actual Buddhist, but he talked a good game, and if he *was* a Buddhist, then it seemed possible that giving somebody a statue of the Buddha was standard practice, no big deal, the equivalent of Christians leaving a Gideon's Bible in a motel room. That made it seem less of a big deal, though still extraordinarily generous.

"It's very kind of you. I appreciate it," I said, and I meant it. "But are you sure?"

Obviously he was sure.

"Scholars differ," said Darrell, "but it's thought that the walking posture probably refers to the Buddha walking up and down the golden bridge in the third week after his enlightenment. So if you're trying to walk toward enlightenment this could be an inspiration to you."

Well, which of us would be so foolish as to say he didn't want to walk toward enlightenment?

"The raised hand symbolizes peace and freedom from fear," Darrell said.

"Who wouldn't want peace and freedom from fear?" I said.

"It'll help you walk the path of serenity," said Darrell.

Miranda snorted in an exaggerated way.

"OK," I said. "I'll see how it goes."

Miranda snorted again.

I'm not the kind of man who'd usually compare himself with the Buddha, but when I thought about it later it seemed to me that he, or at least Darrell, probably had a point about movement and the awareness of movement. There were days when walking around the path in my yard was simply very pleasurable for me, when it seemed very easy, when I did twenty-five miles with amazingly little effort. Then again, of course, there were other days when it felt much harder, when it felt like work, sometimes like very hard work indeed, even with a cocktail inside me. There were days when I had various aches and pains, in my bones and muscles, when walking simply *hurt*. Well, who would expect anything else?

No two days were ever exactly alike, and there was no telling in advance, before I started walking, what kind of day it was going to be. Sometimes the walking started out very easy and got more difficult as the day went on. Some days, surprisingly (although obviously it soon ceased to surprise me) the reverse applied, and the walking would actually get easier the more I did of it—something to do with rhythm or the circulation of the blood or the loosening of the joints. Or something.

I accepted these variables as essential to the process, and I never complained. Who would I have complained to? And in any case, the walking had to be done regardless of whether it was a source of pleasure or pain. I took the good days and the bad days in my stride, all part of the grand project. If that was a Buddhist principle, then so be it.

As for what was going on in my mind, well, sometimes, as discussed, I tried to do some more or less serious thinking, although often I was far less serious and I just daydreamed, and not only about sex. Both of these kinds of thought, arguably, were simply ways of distracting myself, and distraction was usually welcome. But then on other days I tried to avoid thought altogether, and I simply concentrated on the walking, focused on putting one foot in front of the other. That was good too.

And there were other days still, and perhaps these were the best days of all, when it seemed that I was neither thinking nor not thinking. And I imagine that's what the Buddha, and Darrell, might have meant: that there were times when the walking seemed to be *nothing*. And it wasn't simply a matter of being able to do it easily, of finding distraction, of my being on automatic pilot; it wasn't even that my mind was blank. No, there were simply days when I wasn't a man walking, rather I was a man who had *become one* with the walk.

And now, thanks to Darrell, at the end of a day like that I could go into my house, sit down on the couch, rest my feet on the footlocker, where the notebooks were kept, and read a good book or watch some bad TV, and occasionally I'd look up at the statue of the Buddha who was looking down at me, and I'd remember what Darrell had said about it helping me walk the path of serenity. At times like that I might well find my thoughts interrupted by the sound of music and yelling and hysterical barking that drifted over the fence from the riffraff house.

Nah, I said to myself, I wasn't quite ready for serenity yet.

TWENTY-FIVE

I wouldn't have claimed to know Miranda at all, but even so, I didn't think she was the jealous type, and I didn't seriously think there was anything in my life for her to be jealous about, certainly not my dealings with Darrell the mailman. And yet after she saw that Darrell had given me that statue of the Buddha, she became oddly, needlessly resentful. I thought it best just to let it go and say nothing about it. Talking cures are fine, but sometimes things cure themselves without talking. Not in this case, however. The next time Miranda came to the house to make a list and do the shopping, she was uncharacteristically moody, bristling with vague grievance. She went to the supermarket, came back, put away the groceries, and placed a couple of new bottles of booze on the kitchen counter: crème de noisettes and Drambuie.

"You know," she said unhappily, "that kitchen counter's getting pretty cluttered with booze."

She was right, of course: the counter was crowded with liquor bottles, although I hadn't particularly noticed, and that was because I didn't really care. But I could tell she had something in mind.

"We don't want everybody thinking you're a boozehound, do we?" she said.

I didn't care about that either, and there was definitely not going to be anybody looking around my kitchen and judging my
drinking habits, but I didn't argue.

"You wait here," Miranda said, and she went out to her van.

I didn't exactly wait. I walked another circuit of the path and
then another, before Miranda returned. When she did, she was
maneuvering, with some difficulty, a large globe of the world,
maybe three feet across, the ornate, freestanding kind, with a
wooden base and a carved spindle, and as Miranda demonstrated
once she'd set it down on the path, thereby blocking my way, it
wasn't a solid globe, but the kind that opens up to reveal itself
as a cocktail cabinet, a place to store or stash or conceal bottles of
alcohol. A dusty smell of pencil shavings and yeast emanated from
the interior.

"This is for you," she said. "From me. Better than a damn Buddha, right?"

I didn't immediately know what to say. I wasn't sure that one
was better than the other, and to be honest I didn't really need
either of them, but I didn't want to appear ungrateful or antago-
nistic, so I said, "Thanks. That's very thoughtful."

"And neat," Miranda added. "But more than that, it's a globe of
the world, right? So as you clock up the miles on your walk, I can
mark the distance on the globe."

"You really don't need to do that," I said.

"It wouldn't be your 'real' route," she said, "because if it was
real I'd have to draw thousands and thousands of tiny little con-
centric circles all in exactly the same spot. No, I'll mark a *theoretical*
route, as though you were walking around the equator, charting
your progress mile by mile."

She looked closely at the equator on the globe, traced it with her index finger.

"And maybe I could match my cocktails to the journey. So when you're crossing Brazil I'll make a version of the caipirinha, and when you're in Indonesia I'll do something with *moke*, and when you're crossing the Congo, well, I'll think of something. They'll be inspirations for me, for the Miranda."

It seemed to me there were a couple of obvious problems with this scheme. The first was one of scale. On a globe that's three feet across, a distance of twenty-five miles would be nothing at all, too small to see, too small even to mark in any meaningful way. I was also well aware that for most of its length the equator passes over water, so the notion of cocktails based on the local geography seemed completely impractical. Is there such a thing as a seawater cocktail? But I didn't want to be negative, and I didn't want to argue about it.

"OK then," I said tentatively.

"And we'll see what happens first," said Miranda, "whether you complete your journey or I invent my Miranda cocktail."

"Sounds reasonable," I said, though of course I didn't think it sounded reasonable at all.

"And I'll make you a cocktail right now," said Miranda.

I didn't refuse, and probably it would have made no difference if I had. Miranda made a concoction that tasted of rum, sherry, and aniseed, though I couldn't have sworn those were the actual ingredients. It was just about drinkable, but we both agreed that it wasn't good enough to be called a Miranda.

Then she said, "Oh, and another thing: the word on the street is that the boys are planning to make a move."

"The riffraff boys?"

"Who else?"

I let that one go. I had only the vaguest idea of what the riffraff boys might try to do, either as a group or individually, but Miranda had that covered too.

"They're going to wait till night, climb into your yard, and then spray dirty words all over your house."

"Sounds possible," I said.

"No," Miranda said meaningfully. "It's not just a possibility, that's *exactly* what they're going to do. Trust me."

For no very good reason, I did.

TWENTY-SIX

It came as no surprise, obviously, to hear that the riffraff boys were planning something. The ball, and the dog feces, was still very much in their court. Despite my professional experience, I didn't doubt that Miranda knew the hearts of boys far better than I did, though I did wonder on which street the word of the boys' future activities was being talked about, and how Miranda came to be on that street, and who exactly she'd been talking to.

Still, I did trust her, and I prepared myself for the next step. Each evening, after I'd completed my walking for the day, I went into my house and spent some time sitting, waiting, keeping both ears open for unusual offstage noises.

They came soon enough. On the night of Day 54 I heard the sound I'd been waiting for, something stirring over by the back fence, and I stepped quietly out into the yard. Now more than ever I was pleased that the yard was so densely overgrown. I was pretty sure I couldn't be seen, but even so, once I'd gotten into position, I stood as still as a statue of the Buddha.

Just two of the boys were visible, and they were in the process of climbing over the fence. They wore hoodies and bandannas to hide their faces, an unnecessary precaution, it seemed to me. Who exactly were they hiding from? I was the only person who possibly could see them. How could I not have known who they were? As Miranda had predicted, they were carrying cans of spray paint. I didn't know precisely which of my walls they were planning to tag, nor what words, messages, designs, or symbols they intended to put there, but I was content not to find out.

There's been a fair amount of research recently into the nature of concussion. The received wisdom used to be that if you could remember the blow that knocked you unconscious, then by definition you couldn't be suffering from concussion. Not remembering was considered to be the deciding factor. If you came to and you were on the ground and you didn't know how you got there, then yes, that was diagnostic evidence that you were concussed. These days that notion is discredited. It's accepted that you can have concussion from a simple fall or a simple bang on the head that leaves you conscious and that you can remember completely.

I can't say with any certainty what the two riffraff boys later did or didn't remember. They might well have been able to recall climbing the fence and lowering themselves into the bushes on my side, but after that I'm pretty sure they would have no idea, either metaphorically or literally, what had hit them.

The words "killing machine" are much overused. When I did my training with the Team, the term became a standing joke between the trainees and the instructor, who was a small, grizzled, dangerously harmless-looking man who went by the name of Duncan, though we never knew whether that was his first or last name, and maybe it wasn't his real name at all. He said, more than once, "A gun is a killing machine, a tank is a killing machine, a bomb is a killing machine. You're a human being: never forget that."

I never did. And in truth I had absolutely no desire to kill my riffraff neighbors. I just wanted to hurt them, and no, I didn't think of myself as a "hurting machine" either. I didn't want to fight them. I didn't even want to punish them particularly. I simply wanted to knock them unconscious.

Duncan wasn't a bad teacher, though it seemed to me he relied too heavily on mnemonics and sets of initials, not all of which have stayed with me. But I do recall him telling us that if you wanted to knock somebody out cold you needed SAP—surprise, accuracy, and power. I certainly had surprise on my side: the two riffraff boys didn't know I was there in the yard, and I had confidence in my own accuracy and power—that was what the training had given me.

I hit the first boy under the chin, a simple uppercut: very straight, very brutal, all the force going directly upward with a minimum of lateral movement. Some authorities say this targets the submental nerve that runs directly under the chin, though it isn't altogether clear how that knocks anybody out. It may just be a matter of rotational force. The chin is a long way from the head's center of gravity, so when it's hit, the brain revolves violently inside the skull and that results in a blackout and concussion.

The boy fell to the ground and his bandanna slipped away. It was Butch. He groaned a little but he certainly didn't yell or cry out, and by the time his companion was aware that anything had happened I'd hit him too, an equally accurate blow directly to the temple, which involves much the same process as far as the brain is concerned, and exactly the same result.

The two boys lay in a tangle of weeds and creepers, looking harmless now, even peaceful, but I hadn't finished with them. I took each of their hands in turn, not being sure whether they were left- or right-handed, and grabbed each forefinger and pressed it back, one after another, determinedly rather than viciously, until

I heard the thin break of bones, the cracking of the proximal phalanx. Operating a spray can would be tricky for them in the immediate future, though my intention was symbolic as much as
practical.

I then needed to manhandle the two bodies, pick them up and
throw them back over the fence. That wasn't especially easy, but in
the current circumstances, the work involved seemed quite enjoyable and definitely well worth the effort.

The boys would come around sometime later, back on their
own side of the fence, and have no idea how they got there or
what had happened to them on their adventure. Nor for that matter would they be able to work out how they'd both managed to
break the index fingers of both their hands. They would no doubt,
in time, do their best to come up with an explanation for what had
happened, perhaps blame it on their own clumsiness, on being too
drunk or having ingested something that was way stronger than
they were used to. But maybe no great explanation was required:
freak accidents happened all the time.

It might possibly, for a second, cross their minds that karma
was somehow involved, if they'd ever heard of karma. And it
might conceivably occur to them that their pedestrian neighbor
was somehow protected by some mysterious kind of providence,
but even if they did think those things, I expected they'd dismiss
the thoughts pretty damn quickly. They would surely not entertain the possibility that their pedestrian neighbor had been lurking
in the darkness, waiting for them, and that he was the one who'd
knocked them unconscious and broken their fingers and tossed
them back over the fence like two bags of garbage.

For my part, I felt good, exhilarated, invigorated, and quite a
number of other positive things too. There's nothing like an explo-

sion of precise, well-regulated, well-justified violence for making a man feel better about himself. I slept very well that night.

I realized, of course, that this would still not be the end of the story, that there would be further developments and escalations, that concussions and broken hands were not the final solution, but then, what is? I accepted that there might well be more garbage, perhaps another raid on my house, perhaps new and more original attempts to torment me. It didn't matter. I would be ready, and I would not be needing any luck, although I would gratefully accept any that came my way. I told myself it was all good practice for a similar, though hardly identical, kind of day that I knew was coming.

TWENTY-SEVEN

The next time Miranda came to the house we didn't discuss the riffraff boys or their concussions or their broken hands. I thought it was best to pretend ignorance so that I could then, if I needed to, plead innocence. Besides, I imagined there wasn't any need to say anything. I assumed the word would have gotten to her, and her street, without any help from me.

After we'd made our list and Miranda had gone off to the store, Small Paul arrived unexpectedly to continue his education. I couldn't really complain. On balance I thought it was better to have him come occasionally, more or less at random, than to have him come on a regular timetable.

As before, he was wearing his giant backpack and now carrying a bottle of vitaminwater. He began to take off the backpack but I told him to keep it on. In fact I dropped a few rocks into it. Then I took the water bottle from him, unscrewed the cap, and poured the contents into the weeds. He looked understandably confused and resentful. His education was about to take a small but significant leap forward.

"I thought you wanted to know about the Bataan Death March," I said.

"Yeah, but—"

"OK then, let's start marching."

I set off at a brisker pace than usual and Small Paul set off with me, still game though considerably flustered.

"One of the things to remember about the Bataan Death March," I said, "is that although it was appalling, although vast numbers died, it really wasn't all that long a walk."

"How long was it?" Small Paul asked between deep breaths.

"Sixty miles on foot," I said, "from Mariveles to San Fernando, up the western side of Manila, then a train ride to Capas, and then another walk of nine miles or so to the prisoner of war camp. A few selected prisoners even went all the way by truck."

"Somebody would be able to do that in a few days," said Small Paul. I think he was trying to suck up.

"The prisoners usually did it in five days," I said. "So it wasn't the walking—or marching—in itself that killed them. It was the *conditions* in which they had to walk."

Small Paul clenched and unclenched his shoulders under the backpack, but he didn't complain. Good for him.

"Bad conditions?" he said.

"Oh yes. Not much food or water, terrible heat..."

It was a warm day, though certainly not as hot as I imagined Manila to be, and Small Paul was already red-faced and breathing hard. I pretended not to notice.

"I know how they felt," he said.

"Do you really?" I said. "Would you like to stop?"

"Maybe."

"Well, if you were on the Bataan Death March you wouldn't be allowed to stop. If you were on the Bataan Death March you'd be pushed onward by Japanese guards who'd shoot you or bayonet you if you stopped walking or even slowed down and fell behind. They say there were even certain Japanese soldiers on horseback who beheaded some of the marchers with samurai swords."

"Yeah, you told me that," Small Paul said, and he still sounded enthusiastic but now somewhat troubled. "Kind of cool," he said uncertainly.

"I think they weren't doing it to be cool," I said.

"Why *were* they doing it?"

I increased my pace a little, so that the boy had to increase his too if he wanted to hear my answer.

"One explanation given," I said, "is that the Japanese military at the time were into that whole death before dishonor thing. If a soldier surrendered, any soldier on either side, he was considered beneath contempt, barely human. So killing him didn't matter much."

"That's *not* cool," said Small Paul, flipping a wave of sweat from his forehead.

"You have a fine moral sense, Paul," I said, "but I've never thought that explanation holds much water, because if the Japanese honestly thought their captives were inhuman, then why not just kill them straightaway, why not exterminate them like vermin where they stood? If you find them so contemptible, then why give yourself the trouble of marching them all the way to the prison camp?"

"So why do you think they did it?"

"Because they *liked* doing it," I said. "Remember we talked about bullying? Some people enjoy bullying. They just do. And a lot of people enjoy hurting other people, inflicting pain, reveling in their own cruelty."

"Do they?"

"They do, Paul, believe me. Especially when their government or their commanding officer or their code of honor says they can."

"Oh," said Small Paul.

"Then again, afterward, when they were called to account, the Japanese said they *did* treat the prisoners humanely, but that the American and Filipino soldiers waited so long to surrender that most of them were in terrible shape already and were half dead even before they started the march, so it was all their own fault."

"So how many did they kill?"

The prospect of a big, definite number clearly excited him.

"Nobody really knows how many began the walk," I said. "Maybe seventy-five thousand. And maybe fifteen hundred of them were Americans. And nobody really knows how many died along the way, maybe six hundred Americans, maybe ten thousand Filipinos, but there's always going to be somebody who has a reason to argue the numbers were higher or lower."

"Really?" said Small Paul.

"Really," I said. "One thing we do know, a lot of the Filipinos just disappeared along the way, wandered off and got absorbed into the local villages. They just walked away. The Japanese couldn't tell one Filipino from another. They could tell the Americans, though; there was no way they could slip away."

"These guys who did the killing," said Small Paul, "were they Buddhists like Darrell?"

"You've been talking to Darrell?"

"Little bit," he said, and he sounded vaguely ashamed. I wondered why.

"I guess some of them called themselves Buddhists," I said. "I don't imagine they were much like Darrell."

By now Small Paul was drenched in sweat, head down, limping, looking (in the strictly metaphorical sense) dead on his feet. I was surprised he'd lasted even this long, but he still kept going.

"So walking was a form of torture," he said.

"You could say that."

"Is that what you're doing to me now?"

"No," I said. "I'm not torturing you. But I'm educating you, making the Bataan Death March more real for you. You can stop any time you want."

"Can I?"

"Yes."

"You won't shoot me?"

"No."

"You won't cut my head off with a samurai sword?"

"I don't own a samurai sword."

Small Paul came to a halt and stepped off the path. I continued walking. The boy was still in the same place after I'd completed another circuit, and still there after another. The next time I came around he'd moved and was lying on his back in the weeds. It was OK. I knew he was only pretending to be dead, but he did it very convincingly.

"You haven't killed him, have you?"

It was Miranda, at the gate, returning with bags of groceries.

"No," I said.

"And he hasn't killed himself?"

"No."

"I guess you're in the clear then."

I felt a certain amount of explaining was required, and I was probably a little embarrassed to admit that, even if only in some vague sense, I was serious about educating Small Paul.

"I was telling him about the Bataan Death March," I said. "I was doing it while we walked together."

"What are you up to?" Miranda said archly. "Are you auditioning to be his new daddy?"

Maybe the word was out on the street about Renée and Big Paul's marital difficulties.

"No, I'm not doing that," I said.

"Good," said Miranda, then thoughtfully, "You know, I bet they even have cocktail bars in Bataan these days. I wonder what their specialties are."

TWENTY-EIGHT

In midafternoon of Day 62, two young men appeared at my garden gate, both very "presentable," very clean, if not exactly clean-cut. One was Asian—Korean I'd have guessed—and he had a Prince Valiant haircut that might well have been hiding a receding hairline. The other looked Eastern European: dark, heavy, with a beard that was even darker and heavier than he was, a beard that could have been edging either toward or away from hipsterdom. Both wore freshly ironed, pale short-sleeved shirts. They looked so healthy and harmless that I obviously knew not to trust them, not that it would have made much difference whether I'd trusted them or not.

I thought they might be selling something—religion possibly—though the look didn't completely fit that bill. The bearded one was laden down with a bulky shoulder bag, and I could see that it contained not scriptures, but a bunch of equipment: a couple of cameras, a digital recorder, even a good old-fashioned reporter's notebook. The other traveled more lightly and was the one who did most of the talking.

"Hello, Mr. Johnson," he said brightly, far too brightly, and I wondered how he even knew my name. "I'm Dee. And this is Yuri. We were wondering if we can talk to you."

"I wonder if you can," I said.

"We're from the paper," he said.

"What paper's that?"

"The local paper. The *Informer*."

If I'd thought about it, and I hadn't, I would probably have assumed there might be some kind of local newspaper, but I'd never seen a copy, and I hadn't looked for one, and I hadn't felt any lack of it.

"Are you sure the *Informer*'s a good name for a paper?" I asked. "Have you considered changing it? Maybe to the *Snitch*."

The irony and the insult were lost on him.

"Not our department," said Dee. "We're not exactly involved in executive decisions around there."

"What *are* you involved in?"

"We're interns."

"You mean you're not getting paid."

"That's true, for sure, but we do get credit for it in our college journalism course."

He was so much more cheerful than I'd have been in his position.

"Look, Dee," I said, "you probably mean well, but I don't really have a lot of time for journalists. Actually I don't have any."

He drooped and looked dolefully at his companion. Perhaps they'd encountered this response before, and perhaps drooping was Dee's way of gaining sympathy.

"Please," he said, with surprising intensity, "we're not some sleazy rag, we're a good, honest local paper—sports scores, police blotter, human interest—the backbone of this country."

I thought that was overstating the case.

"And what?" I said. "They send you interns out, door-to-door selling subscriptions?"

"No way," he said, and he wanted me to know he was offended. "I'm a *reporter*. Yuri's a photojournalist. We want to do a feature on you."

"You think I'm human interest?"

"Well, aren't you?"

"I'm human. Does that make me interesting?"

"Not necessarily," said Dee. "But in your case I think it does."

"Are you sure?"

"I guess we'll find out in the course of the interview, but I'd think that a man who's happy walking around and around his own yard would be of interest to our readers. That's the kind of stuff local papers live for."

I thought about challenging him on what made him think I was happy, but I decided to keep it simple. "How do you even know about me?" I asked.

"It's a small world. Word gets around."

"No, I'm not buying that."

"We have a friend in common."

"I don't have any friends," I said.

"But that's not true," Dee said. "There's Miranda."

I could hear a little uncertainty in his voice, as he suddenly wondered whether invoking Miranda's name was going to help or hinder his cause. In fact, it wouldn't have made much difference either way, but I didn't want him to know that. I was happy for him to remain uncertain.

"So, would it be OK if we interviewed you now?" he said.

"No, it wouldn't."

"And would it be OK if I took a few pictures?" said Yuri, speaking for the first time, and he took a substantial camera out of his bag so he might photograph me.

"No, that would be even less OK," I said.

"What if we came into your yard and walked with you for a while?"

"What if I smashed the camera over your head?"

Yuri held his ground, though he did lower his camera. "I don't think you'd do that," he said.

I smiled and replied, "But you're not sure, are you?"

He stroked his beard into impeccable smoothness, and no, he wasn't sure at all.

"Maybe we could e-mail you some questions," Dee said.

"That would be a waste of your time."

"Or," and I could suddenly see a bit of steel in him, "I could just make up a lot of inaccurate stuff, and you might like that even less."

I nodded earnestly to confirm that, indeed, I wouldn't like that one little bit. "And you're not afraid that if you do that, I'll come hunt you down like a dog?" I asked.

Maybe he was afraid of that or maybe he wasn't, but the pair of them drooped even further, in tandem, and then, reluctantly, with an exaggerated air of sadness and defeat, they went on their way, and I went back to my walking. I thought it was over.

However, just a few days later Darrell delivered a copy of the new issue of the *Informer*—a sixteen-page tabloid with a lot of real estate ads and reports of local burglaries—and there I was on an inside page next to a report on girls' basketball. Dee had evidently decided to risk my hunting him down, and Yuri had somehow managed to take my picture without me knowing about it. I didn't think it was a very good picture since it made me look hulking and brutish, which in general I don't believe I am, and it was under a headline that read "Hey, I'm Walking Here," the all too familiar line from *Midnight Cowboy*, delivered by Dustin Hoffman as Ratso Rizzo, a character I've never much resembled.

Beneath the headline and photograph was an article by Dee, purporting to be an interview, that was an extraordinary amalgam of fabrication and truth. I assumed the fabrications were all Dee's own work, though there was nothing wildly fanciful there, just a lot of obvious and erroneous stuff that said I was walking to improve my health, both physical and mental; walking to reduce my carbon footprint; walking as an opportunity to do some thinking, as a kind of walking meditation. Clearly I'm not a man who believes in always telling the truth, so I couldn't really get too upset about the inaccuracies; it was the accuracies I had more trouble with.

Dee wrote, quite correctly, that I was walking a distance equivalent to the circumference of Earth in my own yard, on my own path, a task that would take me exactly one thousand days. From the tone of the article he seemed to find this both heroic and absurd.

Obviously none of this accurate information had come from me, and unless it had come from my ex-wife, which was inconceivable, the only other person it could possibly have come from, the only other person to whom I'd explained myself, was Miranda. She was evidently an informer for the *Informer*.

I found myself unreasonably angry. I tried not to feel that way, told myself this was just an article in a shitty little local newspaper, a complete irrelevance, nothing worth getting even remotely upset about. And yet I *was* upset. *More* than upset. And far more upset with Miranda than with the two guys from the paper.

I'd never told Miranda there was anything secret about what I was doing, never said that she had to keep the information to herself, and yet I had somehow assumed she knew me well enough, was considerate enough, wise enough, not to go blabbing about me to other people. Of course I knew it was absurd to make such an assumption, and I knew it was even more absurd to feel *betrayed*. And yet that was exactly how I did feel. I could see I'd have to do something about that.

TWENTY-NINE

When Miranda next came to the house to make her damned shopping list, I was ready to do some straight talking, to flush these feelings of anger and betrayal out of my system. Better out than in, as we psychotherapists seldom put it. I think she must have been expecting this, because she played it very skillfully indeed. As soon as she arrived, before I could say or do anything, she demonstrated that she was feeling, or was pretending to feel, even more angry and betrayed than I was, and also very sorrowful.

"I'm sorry," she said with rising passion. "I'm so very fucking sorry. I'm desolate. And I'm so mad. I'm apoplectic. I want to kill both of them. They screwed me. I told them those things about you in strictest confidence."

I wasn't going to let her get away with it *that* easily. "Why were you telling them anything about me at all?"

"I was drunk, OK?" she said. "I was in a bar. I'd had a few too many cocktails. One thing led to another. They asked me what I did. I told them I worked for you. I told them about you. I was just trying to make myself sound interesting, trying to impress them."

"Like padding your résumé?"

"Kind of."

"And did it work? Were they impressed?"

"I guess so, otherwise they wouldn't have come to interview you."

"Couldn't you have invented something *really* interesting about yourself?" I said. "Pretended you were an astronaut or something?"

"They wouldn't have believed me. They're a couple of little shits, but they're not stupid. Not *that* stupid, anyway."

I gave one of those noncommittal, stick-in-the-mud grunts. I felt like a curmudgeon and an old bore. Saying how angry and betrayed I felt now seemed beside the point. Miranda meanwhile looked as remorseful as a wet, beaten puppy.

"Can I make it up to you?" she said.

"I don't know," I said. "Can you?"

"I could make you a cocktail. Would that do any good?"

I didn't think it would, but what good would it do to refuse the offer? "It probably wouldn't do any harm," I said.

"OK, let's call it the Truth and Reconciliation," she said.

I didn't think that was a great name for a drink, and when it was presented, I didn't think it was a great drink. I had no idea what was in it, and I didn't really care. Miranda and I sat on the porch and drank, and neither of us was happy.

"I know it's not good enough," Miranda said, and I didn't know whether she meant the drink, her behavior, or her apology, or something much larger than that.

She started to cry. That was the last thing I wanted. That was no good at all. I wanted her to be sorry—of course I did, I wanted her to feel terrible—but I didn't want some weeping woman sitting next to me on my own porch. And I absolutely didn't want to have to comfort her. The cocktail shaker had been full to the brim: enough for two cocktails each, which on a normal afternoon would be one too many for both of us, but this no longer felt like a normal afternoon. Miranda swiftly finished her first drink, poured herself another, and for a while she sat sobbing and sipping alternately, and I did my best to do nothing.

"I'm such a fucking waste of space," she said. "Why can't I ever do anything right?"

I wasn't made of stone. I cracked. I crumbled. I put a hand on her shoulder. I thought it was no big deal. I thought it might have been considered avuncular, even fatherly, though I knew that wasn't necessarily a good thing. She put her own hand on mine and moved closer to me. She turned her face upward, and I saw thick tears gathering in the corners of her eyes, and then— oh god—I kissed her on the forehead, and then—oh god, far, far worse—I found myself kissing her on the mouth, and then she was kissing me back.

"Oh yeah, let's fuck," she said.

And then I leaped up and darted away as though I'd been rammed with a cattle prod. Miranda seemed surprised.

"What's wrong?" she said.

"Now it's my turn to be sorry," I said.

"What are you sorry about?"

"You said you've made some bad choices. Having sex with me would be a *really* bad choice," I said.

"It wouldn't be the worst choice I've made."

"I don't need to know about that. Look, for one thing, I'm still in love with my wife." Then I corrected myself. "Ex-wife." Either way, I was very surprised to have said those words.

"So? I don't care. I don't mind fucking somebody who's in love with somebody else."

I didn't know where to go with that one, so I said, "No. Just no."

She sagged, looked sadder than ever, and said, "What are you so afraid of, Mr. J?"

I didn't tell her. At that time I couldn't have told anybody. Now I can.

THIRTY

I need to tell you about a man named Sylvester. I don't know if that was his real name, but it was good enough for his and my purposes. Before I can tell you about him I need to tell you some other things. Primarily I need to tell you about my habit of walking in the Black Kettle State Forest. It was one of my indulgences, one of my favorite places for walking, one of my favorite places, period. It was hard to get to, and once you were there it wasn't the most beautiful or dramatic or satisfying territory for walking. The views weren't especially "picturesque," and most of the trails involved some seriously punishing ascents. Consequently it wasn't popular with other hikers. You could walk all day and never see anybody else, which was of course why I went there. I went there often. I went to clear my head. My head needed a lot of clearing in the days when I worked with the volunteers and the Team.

Carole and I were still married at that time, of course. I wouldn't have said our marriage was a very happy one, but happiness isn't everything. We didn't yell at each other, certainly didn't hit each other. We certainly didn't hate each other, but that's a long way from being happy. I would have willingly admitted that I was the cause of all the problems. I could possibly have tried to weasel out of the situation and blamed my job rather than myself, but I didn't do that. I took full responsibility. I was difficult, broody and introverted, and probably depressed and sometimes very angry, but I didn't do any of the obviously bad things. I didn't drink too much; I didn't seek pharmaceutical or extramarital solutions. I gritted my teeth, hung in there, and hoped for the best. And that's what I was doing when I went away on weekends to do some serious walking: getting out of the house, giving both Carole and myself room to breathe. That's what I told myself, anyway.

My walking plan that final weekend, what I've come to think of as "the Sylvester weekend," was very simple, and I'd done similar things often enough before that it had become familiar. I'd set off very early on Saturday morning, drive my Jeep way out to the forest, take a minor road off the main road, take a dirt road off that minor road, take another dirt road off that one, drive for fifteen miles or so off road, find a place to leave the car, and then I'd put on my backpack and start walking. I'd walk for five or six hours, and I'd be lucky to cover more than ten miles: it was pretty hard to walk at more than a couple of miles an hour in that terrain.

When the time came, as the sun started to set, I'd look for a place to spend the night. I liked to find a broad, sheltered place, a ledge wide enough to sleep on without any danger of rolling off, a lofty place from which the world seemed cold and thin and very far away. I'd settle there, stare out across the fading, darkening space, a void that seemed peaceful but by no means wholly benign. I'd feel thrillingly, contentedly alone. I didn't scare easily in those days.

My "camping" was absolutely basic: no tent, no stove, no foam pad, no pillow—it was too much trouble to carry all that stuff. I just took a thin sleeping bag, food, water, half a bottle of wine transferred to a plastic bottle, a flashlight, and a very slim paper-back book. I didn't even take a change of clothes. When it got dark I'd eat, drink, read, look up at the stars, and eventually fall asleep. It wasn't the most intrepid or exciting or uplifting way to spend an evening, but it beat the hell out of staying home and arguing with Carole.

I always slept well in the forest, but the nights were short. I'd wake early on Sunday morning as soon as it got light, then I'd get up, pull myself together, and make the return journey. The walk would be a little easier this time, mostly downhill, so I'd take a different, longer route so that the journey time would be about the same in both directions. I wasn't trying to impress anyone, wasn't trying to prove anything to anybody, least of all to myself; I just did it because I wanted to do it.

But on the occasion I'm talking about, the Sylvester weekend, the time when everything changed, it didn't happen like that. The first part—the drive, the walk, the ascent, bedding down for the night—that was all business as usual, but this time it wasn't the daylight that woke me. On that morning I was shocked into consciousness just before dawn by a sharp, dense pain at the base of my spine: somebody was kicking me.

I was instantly awake and alert and angry, ready for flight or a damn good fight, and I scrambled out of my sleeping bag, dragged myself across the ground, and grabbed the flashlight, the nearest thing I had to a weapon. I still didn't really know what was happening, but I looked up and saw a man: a short, broad, weighty, slow-moving man dressed in camouflage hunting gear, though this definitely wasn't hunting country. And the gun he was carrying wasn't the kind that anybody would use for hunting. I'm no expert on guns, and I prefer to keep it that way, but this didn't look like the most serious of weapons; it was a chunky, light matte-black pistol, the kind they sell for "self-defense." The man's collar was turned up and his cap was pulled down, thin eyes peering out from shadow. The effect managed to be both sinister and absurd.

It crossed my mind that this guy might be a survivalist or a bootlegger or an illegal marijuana grower, and that I'd strayed into his territory, but again, this wasn't survivalist or bootlegging or marijuana-growing territory as far as I knew. Maybe he was just a lunatic, but he was a lunatic with a gun, which he was now aiming at my chest. I dropped the flashlight, raised my hands up where he could see them, and he let me get to my feet.

"What do you want?" I said.

It seemed a reasonable question, and at that point I was hoping this might be something as simple as a robbery. I wasn't carrying much that anybody would want, but I was happy for him to take everything I had if that meant he went on his way. However, other explanations for this assault were already forming in the grubby corners of my imagination.

The guy took off his cap and showed himself, a moment of inconsequential revelation as far as I was concerned.

"I want you to recognize me," he said.

But I didn't recognize him, not at first, not for a while. That was natural enough. Context is everything, and in this situation it was just another hard, angry, scowling face. I'd seen plenty like that. And if it's any justification, the fact was we weren't supposed to remember the volunteers as individuals. There would have been a file, of course, but I would never have known his name. And even when it clicked and I realized how we knew each other, it remained an unknown face. I reckoned he must have changed out of all recognition. He must have gone soft, put on a lot of weight: we never had volunteers who looked quite that doughy. And, of course, I still wasn't able to remember anything specific about him, about how he'd behaved during his training, whether he was a tough guy or a wimp, whether he was good at taking punishment, whether he'd cried like a little girl. None of that mattered as far as I was concerned. The process was nonjudgmental. There was nothing personal about it.

"Don't tell me you're *surprised*," he said.

"Not completely," I agreed.

It was true. I couldn't have said that I'd been anticipating this moment exactly, and I certainly hadn't spent any time worrying about it, nor had I rehearsed how I would react or what I would say if and when it happened. I knew the reaction would have to be spontaneous. I didn't imagine that anything I'd planned in advance would be of any use in the moment. But yes, it had regularly crossed my mind that one of the volunteers might one day wish to reopen negotiations with me.

"My name's Sylvester," he said. "Not that that means anything to you."

"Of course not. That was the whole point—"

He shut me up. He didn't want an explanation.

"I'm not here so you can justify yourself," he said. "I know that what you did was legal, government approved, maybe well-intentioned, considered necessary; maybe it was even for my own good."

"That was the theory," I said. "And you did volunteer for it."

"Yeah. I did that. I did it willingly. I took the training. I wanted the training. I believed in it. I was a sucker. Because when it came down to it, the fucking training didn't fucking work."

"No?" I said. I could have said that the training didn't come with guarantees, but I thought it better not to.

"No," he said, and he was now frighteningly calm, and it sounded as though *he* wanted to do the explaining. I didn't try to stop him. "We were out there, thirty miles outside the capital. I was with a civilian aid agency, government contract, military backing. They called it the Ministry for Rural Rehabilitation and Development.

"We had some half-assed, fuckwit scheme for turning local farmers away from opium, setting them up to grow grapes—not good eating grapes, but good enough to make raisins. Yeah. That was the brilliant idea. It happened. You can look it up."

"I believe you," I said.

"At first the locals just resented us, then they hated us, then they tried to fuck with us. Things went missing, things got stolen. There were arguments about lines of credit, warehousing, who paid for transportation to the packing plant. The elders decided it was all a cover for the CIA, and they weren't completely wrong about that, but it had nothing to do with me. I was just a stooge like everybody else. So some young 'tribal leader' who probably had ambitions to be a 'warlord' decided to make a name for himself by capturing a few of us."

"Who's 'us'?" I asked.

"Nobody you know. Nobody you need to know. This is just between you and me."

I hoped I could believe that.

"We went out to some blighted industrial zone to argue with a group of local mechanics about the price of truck maintenance. I knew it was bullshit but I didn't know what kind. It was a setup. There was a roadblock. They stopped us, kidnapped us, took us up-country, and then, just like you told me they would, they started on us. These guys had a way with torture. They were naturals. It's in their holy book apparently, cutting off hands, gouging out eyes, old ladies pulled apart by camels—that's what they told me, anyway."

I knew next to nothing about schemes for growing second-rate grapes in former war zones, but I knew all about the religious basis for torture.

"They did shit to us that *you* never dreamed of."

"Not necessarily true," I said. "I probably dreamed of it, but I chose not to do it."

"Well, doesn't that make you a saint.?"

"No," I said. "It probably makes me a government lackey, much like you."

He didn't want to hear that, obviously. He took a firmer hold on the gun. I could see that his hand was slick with sweat.

"So I expected to be tortured, OK? But I thought it wouldn't be so bad. I thought I knew how to deal with it. I thought you'd done a good job on me, taught me what I needed to know. But it turned out you hadn't. Turns out you'd done a really shitty, fucking awful job. I lasted about maybe two hours and then I told them *everything*: names, locations, supply lines, translators, sympathizers, informers, bribe takers. I told them every fucking thing I could. Some of it I just guessed at. Some I even made up. What did it matter? I expected them to kill me. I wish they had. They let me live and then they went and killed everybody I'd named."

"I'm sorry for what you went through," I said. "I don't know what else to say."

"I don't want you to *say* anything. All I want is for you to go through what I went through. I'm going to do to you what they did to me. It'll be an education for you. Is that clear?"

"More or less," I said. Again, I didn't know what else to say.

THIRTY-ONE

I knew there was no point brooding about what had or hadn't happened between Miranda and me. A kiss was just a kiss, as they say. It was a mistake, obviously, but a bigger mistake had been avoided. With luck we'd never have to think about it, much less talk about it. As for my "confession" that I was still in love with my ex-wife, well, I supposed that was no great revelation. At some level I'd known it all along, but it did feel strange and maybe a little too revealing to have said it aloud to Miranda in those circumstances. But what was there to be done? Once it was said, it was said, and what did it matter? Miranda and Carole occupied quite separate worlds.

Probably there was even less point brooding about the circumstances surrounding the whole business of the article in the *Informer*, about Dee and Yuri and Miranda, and I consoled myself in that department by assuming there'd be few consequences. The *Informer*'s circulation was surely negligible. I hoped my fifteen seconds of publicity (rather than fame) was already over. If only.

Maybe I shouldn't have been surprised when Big Paul said he'd seen my picture in the paper—that probably went along with being the eyes and ears of the neighborhood—and it turned out he hadn't actually read the article, only been told about it by Renée. Perhaps he'd been too busy with animalistic sex, up at the outlet mall.

Darrell also told me he'd seen it, hardly a surprise since he'd delivered a copy of the paper, though in his case he'd read it online. Again, I wasn't totally surprised that the paper had a website, but now I had to try to find consolation in thinking that the online readership probably wasn't much bigger than the readership in print.

It was far more of a surprise, and there was no consolation whatsoever, when I saw Butch over the rear garden fence and he yelled in my general direction, "Hey, he's walking there!" No doubt he might have shouted worse, and in other circumstances, from other people, this might have sounded friendly, but coming from Butch it did not.

And then Wendy Gershwin tried to get in on the act. She and her niece were out in their yard. The niece was perched on a rock, posing, draped in a yellow chiffon sheet, while the aunt was drawing her, on an outsize sketch pad, in charcoal.

Wendy Gershwin spotted me and called out, "Joe, my dear, I saw that piece in the *Informer*. It was dreadful. Shameful."

I didn't disagree.

"You have my complete sympathies. That boy who interviewed you knew absolutely nothing about anything."

"He didn't even really interview me," I said.

"See what I mean? He thought you were some lovable eccentric or something."

"I've never claimed to be lovable," I said.

"But at least that article was informative in one way," she went on. "And I should have realized much sooner; this walking you're doing—I've seen you walking around your yard, of course, but I didn't know you were so *serious* about it."

"I'm serious," I said.

"My fault, my naïveté. This walking you're doing, it's an art form, isn't it? You're an artist, Joe. You're a potentially *great* artist."

She said this as though she thought it should make me very, very happy.

"Am I really?" I said.

"Yes, you are. And the fact that you don't know it makes you even more special."

"I'm definitely not trying to be special."

"Exactly. But you are. You just are."

I tried to shrug that one off, but Wendy Gershwin wouldn't let it go so easily.

"And I wonder if you might do me the honor of letting me walk with you for a while."

"No," I said.

"Oh please."

"I don't think so."

"Please. Let me walk with you, even if just briefly. It's all I want in the whole world."

It seemed an absurd thing to want, but it also struck me that I might waste a good deal of time standing there arguing with her when I could be walking. Judging by the woman's size, her shape, her general bulk, it was reasonable to think she might not last many circuits, so I went along the path of least resistance.

"All right, just don't get in my way," I said.

"No, absolutely not. I'd never do that. This is so great."

A few moments later Wendy Gershwin was at my gate, then in my yard, then on my path. We started walking, but not quite together. Wendy fell in a few paces behind me, following me like some miserable, downtrodden spouse. More than that, even though I couldn't actually see her, since she was behind me, I could nevertheless feel that she was observing me far too intently, as if I were an exhibit in a living museum, or perhaps some rare specimen in a private zoo. It felt excruciatingly uncomfortable. I stopped walking after a single circuit completed in this manner.

"Look," I said, "I don't particularly want you to walk with me, but if we're going to do it, then we should at least do it as equals."

"Oh my," she said. "I'm honored to be considered an equal."

I thought this was going too far. I also thought it was bullshit. "Stop being honored," I said. "Just walk."

She bowed her head, moved up, and fell in step.

"This is a lovely yard," she said, "very picturesque, very wild, totally natural. Elegantly overgrown. It would make a fabulous setting, a location. Are those weeds over there hemlock?"

"For all I know."

"Very Socratic," she said.

I knew, of course, that Socrates was supposedly poisoned with hemlock, but that didn't mean I knew what hemlock actually looked like.

Wendy Gershwin said, "You realize you're part of a long, honorable tradition of people who walk as their art form?"

"No, I didn't realize that."

"There are a great many of them: Richard Long, Hamish Fulton, Bruce Nauman, Francis Alÿs . . . not enough women, alas."

"Are these friends of yours?" I asked.

She chuckled indulgently. "I wish," she said. "Well, I did once meet Richard Long at a gallery opening, but I couldn't say we were friends."

"Was it a good party?"

"It was awful actually."

"I'm not much of a party boy either," I said, and she seemed to like that answer.

"You're marvelous," she said. "So fresh. The simplicity, the ease, the lack of complication. And the fact that you're not trying to be an artist."

"Are you saying I'm an idiot savant?"

That threw her for a moment, but her composure soon eddied back around her. "No," she said. "The one thing we know about idiot savants is that they don't know the term 'idiot savant.'"

I wasn't sure that was true.

"So are you saying I'm a primitive?"

"Let's just say you're a *natural*."

It was a good, clever answer. Another, very different man might have been flattered by it. Who wouldn't want their walking to be natural? We walked a couple of laps in silence, which I liked, though I became aware that we were now being watched over the fence by Wendy Gershwin's niece, her face taut with hostility, which I liked less.

Then Wendy Gershwin said, "Look, what I'm proposing is this—"

"I didn't know you were proposing anything," I said. "I thought you were walking with me for the honor of it."

She chuckled again, and I think this one was meant to be conspiratorial.

"What I'd like to do," she said, "is film you as you're walking, in high-def, multiple cameras, multiple angles, for a solid eight hours, or however long it takes to complete your daily twenty-five miles. Or perhaps I'd film you for a longer period, perhaps much longer—days, weeks, months. We're talking about endurance, yes? Or maybe we could attach a GoPro to your head or you chest, record you in real time."

"Sounds like a boring film," I said.

"Not the way I'd do it. And the film would be only the starting point. Once I had the footage, then I'd collaborate with a choreographer and we'd get a group of dancers, and in some cases non-dancers, and we'd create a set of movements based on *your* walking style. And the group wouldn't just be men like yourself; obviously we'd have women too, and different races and ethnicities, and differently abled people, some with one leg or no legs, people on crutches, people with prosthetics, and we'd see how their walking—or non-walking—movements were similar to or different from yours."

"Really?" I said.

"And later, eventually there'd be live performances, in art galleries and nontraditional theatrical spaces, performances lasting the full eight hours, and some of the performers might not make it to the end, but that's fine, so there'd be further questions about duration and stamina and male performativity. You follow? How do you like the sound of that?"

"Sounds like you'd be the artist, not me," I said.

"No, no, it would be all about you. You'd be the prime mover, and you'd be there, in the gallery or nontraditional theatrical space or wherever, and of course we'd document it fully, and then we'd get grants and endowments and scholarships, and we'd be invited to *biennales* and festivals. Pretty cool, huh?"

I thought about Small Paul and his problematic thoughts about the coolness or otherwise of the Bataan Death March.

"I've never tried to be cool," I said.

"That's right. You don't have to try. That's the beauty of it. You're cool by nature, Joe."

"Is that an advantage?"

"In the art world it's essential. Look, I understand this is a lot to take in all at once, but will you at least think about my proposal?"

I thought about it there and then, for all of three seconds, and that was plenty. I knew right away it wasn't for me and knew I wouldn't change my mind at any time in the future. I thought Wendy Gershwin was an idiot, but for the sake of neighborliness I said OK, and pretended that this was a great imponderable that I might need a good deal of time to ponder.

"Here's another thing to think about," said Wendy Gershwin. "It's a quotation from Hamish Fulton. He said, 'An art work can artwork may be purchased but a walk cannot be sold.'"

I said I'd think about that too, and surprisingly enough I did, briefly. I was very glad not to be trying to sell anything.

THIRTY-TWO

On Day 75 Small Paul arrived again, unexpected, unbidden, though by no means unwelcome. I was almost glad to see him, though he was looking decidedly furtive.

"I have a question," he said.

I accepted that asking questions was a necessary part of the educational process, Peripatetic or otherwise.

"OK then, come on," I said. "You'll have to walk with me if you want me to answer questions."

Grudgingly—he'd known that was coming—he began walking with me.

"Is it a question about the Bataan Death March?" I asked.

"No, I think I know as much as I need to about that."

"What then?"

A hesitation, a pained look, and then he blurted out, "Do people walk in heaven?"

That was a bolt from the blue. And I didn't have an answer.

"I don't know, to be honest with you," I said immediately, and Small Paul looked very disappointed in me, once again. Perhaps I should have been flattered that he thought I was supposed to be the fount of all knowledge, but I wasn't, and I had never claimed

to be. "I never really thought about it," I said by way of explanation, but that only made things worse.

"You never thought about *heaven*?!" he said.

He sounded scandalized, outraged, as if I'd said I'd never
heard of Martin Luther King Jr. or Batman. And, of course, the
truth was I *had* thought about heaven once in a while, the way everybody does at some time or another, and it had always seemed
to be one of those things that the more you thought about it, the
more it slipped away from you, like thinking about time travel or democracy. In any case, I'd never thought about whether
heaven was a great walking venue. And so, adopting my best
pedagogic manner, I said, "What do *you* think, Paul?"

"Well," he said, tentative, though he'd obviously given the
matter some thought already, "if heaven is all clouds, then I
don't see how anybody could do any walking, because your feet
need something solid to walk on, don't they?"

"Haven't you heard the expression 'walking on air'?" I said.

Small Paul gave me a disapproving look: he thought I was
being flippant, not taking him seriously. He had a point.

"But maybe," he said, now more earnest than ever, "you
don't *need* to walk in heaven. Maybe everybody flies around, like
angels."

"But in that case," I said, improvising rapidly, "if you never used your legs, they'd atrophy. That doesn't sound right for
heaven, does it?"

"Atrophy?"

"Become weak and useless; it's what happens to people
who've been in a hospital bed for a long time."

"Oh, right," said Small Paul, "I think my grandma had that,
but she wasn't much of a walker to start with. And she's dead

now, and I don't know if she's in heaven or not, but if she is, I expect she wouldn't want to do any walking there either."

"Is this a big worry for you, Paul?" I asked, hoping I sounded genuinely concerned.

"Yes, because you see I don't like walking any more than my grandma did. And if heaven is supposed to be a paradise, then for me there wouldn't be any walking there."

"OK," I said.

"But then *you* really like walking, so for you it wouldn't be a paradise unless there was *lots* of walking up there."

I didn't want to get into the whole business of whether or not I thought I was going to heaven, nor whether I actually believed in the existence of such a place, nor the extent to which it struck me as a grotesque fantasy and an absurdity, so I said, "Well, maybe heaven is much like earth: you can walk if you want to, but you don't have to."

"So I could fly everywhere if I wanted to?"

"Why not?" I said.

"So I'd be able to fly around in the air and maybe I'd see you walking on the ground or in the clouds or whatever, and I'd give you a wave."

"I'd definitely wave back," I said. "Though of course there might not be anywhere to fly to. Or walk to. I imagine one bit of heaven is very much like every other bit of heaven."

"So maybe I'd have to fly around in circles, kind of like you're doing on foot."

"Maybe," I said.

"But wait," said Small Paul, "heaven can't be all the same, because it'd be boring, and if heaven's a paradise, then it can't be *boring*."

"Well, that's probably true . . ." I said.

"So there'd have to be oceans, because some people really like oceans, and there'd have to be mountains, because some people really like mountains, and there'd have to be rivers, because—"

"Yes, Paul, I understand your reasoning. And a lot of people like nightclubs too."

"So are there nightclubs in heaven?"

"The theologians are pretty quiet on that one, I think."

I was relieved when he didn't ask what a theologian was.

"But if there are nightclubs in heaven, do you think they'd let me in?" Small Paul asked.

"Well, it wouldn't be paradise if they didn't, would it, Paul?"

The boy settled into a thoughtful silence, perhaps contemplating the possibilities of a heavenly nightclub, but not for very long.

"And what about hell?" he said with a new, gloomy urgency.

"What about it?" I said, and I probably let some irritation show through.

"Is there walking in hell?"

"I honestly don't know," I said honestly.

"Because for you it'd be hell not being able to walk."

"I can think of far more hellish things."

"And for me hell would be being forced to walk more than I want to. And I'm already forced to walk more than I want to, right now, here on earth. So maybe I'm in hell already!"

He was understandably agitated by this thought, and he bristled with the terrible, cosmic unfairness of it all. It seemed a little extreme and hysterical, but by no means fake.

"You know, Paul," I said, struggling, doing my best, "people much smarter and wiser than you and me have been thinking about this heaven and hell stuff for thousands of years, and they still haven't been able to figure it out."

He considered this, and then he started to cry. I wasn't having much luck with the emotional stability of the people who came into my yard, but in this case I didn't put a hand on his shoulder. Things didn't seem to be getting any better when Renée's head suddenly appeared over the fence. I suppose some mothers would be alarmed to see their young son crying in a strange man's yard, but Renée was made of sterner stuff.

"What's he crying about this time?" she said.

"Heaven and hell," I explained.

"No," she said, "I reckon that's just displacement activity. Do you know what displacement activity is, Joe?"

"Yes, I think so."

"Course you do. You're a smart guy. The real reason he's crying is because his dad's left home."

"Oh," I said. This was bad news for Small Paul, no doubt, but not the biggest surprise. "That's always hard on kids,"

"It's hard on me too!" she said, and of course I hadn't suggested otherwise. "I'm devastated."

I must have looked unconvinced.

"I'm devastated on the *inside*," she said.

"Of course," I agreed.

"And it's not like he's gone very far," she said. "He's moved into a shared house with some of the people from the outlet mall. I think it's supposed to be a commune or some shit like that. God knows what he's getting up to. I think he's trying to regain his youth."

"That's always a problem," I said.

"But don't fret, Joe. I don't really hold you responsible."

I had no idea why she would, but I knew she'd be eager to explain.

"He eventually read that piece about you in the *Informer*. He said you were living your dream. So he went off to live his own dream. It's a real blow to my self-esteem," she said.

I decided to ignore the question of whether I was living my dream, but the therapist in me did have something to say about self-esteem. I said, "That's a very tricky business. Half the world has low self-esteem, and half the world has a wildly inflated sense of self-esteem. Knowing your own worth is the trick."

"And what's my worth, Joe?"

"Only you can determine that," I said.

"Dead right!" she agreed. "Anyway, I'm resilient. I'm trying to get on with things. Taking one day at a time. Putting one foot in front of the other."

"That's good," I said. "I'm sure that's the right thing to do."

I glanced over at Small Paul. He'd stopped crying and was looking at his mother with awe and fear.

"I've already started seeing somebody," Renée said proudly.

This didn't really surprise me.

"Good for you," I said. "Who's the lucky man?"

"Darrell," she said even more proudly.

"The mailman?"

"Is there any other Darrell in these parts? I'll probably be spending quite a bit of time over at his place from now on, so don't worry if you don't see me around."

"I'll try not to."

Darrell seemed to be an OK guy. I was sure Renée could have done much worse.

"And Darrell will be homeschooling Small Paul from now on."

That was fine by me too, but then I became aware that Renée was staring at me wistfully.

"It could so easily have been you, Joe," she said. "You could have had it all. And I'm not joking this time."

I said nothing. Renée wiped something—perhaps a tear, though not necessarily—from the corner of her eye.

"Come on, Paul, let's get you reeducated," she said.

THIRTY-THREE

At the risk of being prescriptive, I'd say that a man cannot—or at least should not—live a life based on regrets and resentment, and mostly I didn't, but there were certain things I couldn't quite put behind me.

Was I sorry that I'd missed my chance with Renée? No. I thought I could honestly say no, absolutely not.

Was I perhaps disappointed that Darrell was taking over as Small Paul's teacher? Well, you know, surprisingly, I think I may have been, just a little.

Was I still seriously pissed off about Miranda and the *Informer* business? Yes indeed. I didn't want to be; I wished I could put it behind me, but I couldn't, not completely.

Was I infuriated that Wendy Gershwin had condescended to think of me as some kind of outsider artist–cum–walking fool? You bet.

And the riffraff boys. Oh yeah, I still resented them like hell.

I realized, of course, that things were far from settled between them and me. I tried not to think about it too much, but that wasn't always easy. I could constantly hear them and their dogs and their music and their martial arts practices. On some days there'd be

more barbecues and bonfires, and on those occasions I could actually *smell* their presence. I knew that ignoring them was the best
option, but I also knew I wouldn't be able to ignore them forever.

The issue was apparently on Miranda's mind too. When she
next came to do her duties at the house, she made a cocktail that
she called the Conflict Resolution, which was some distant relation of the Truth and Reconciliation, and not much more attrac-
tive. And she started talking about "conflict resolution counseling." Maybe I'd inspired her to read some self-help book, though I
didn't think that was anything to be proud of. When she suggested I might like to try some of this counseling with the riffraff boys,
I knew something was seriously amiss.

"Conflict resolution is a very fine thing," she said. "You can
increase your understanding both of each other and yourself. You
can avoid negativity and reproach. There'll be opportunities for
growth and communication on both sides."

"I know what conflict resolution is," I said.

"I'm sure you do," she said. "So do you want to try it with the
riffraff boys?"

"No," I said. "I really don't."

"You sure?"

"Totally."

"You disappoint me sometimes, Mr. J."

"Sometimes I disappoint myself."

"Well, in that case, if you really won't try reconciliation," she
said, "you'd better watch your back. And your front."

"I always do," I said.

"And actually you'd better watch your feet. They're planning to
come over with hammers and smash your feet, so you can't walk."

"How do you know that?"

"It's a small world. I go to bars, and I continue to make bad choices about the company I keep."

"You've been hanging out with the riffraff boys?" I said.

"Kind of thing. You should be grateful. Forewarned is forearmed."

I felt many things, and gratitude toward Miranda may have been among them, but it was low on the list.

"Wouldn't you say that this talk of hammers and broken feet probably means it's too late for conflict resolution?"

Miranda's shrug signaled that she thought I was right and that she'd known this all along.

"I thought it was worth a try," she said.

I tried not to brood about it, and yet I couldn't quite prevent thoughts of broken tarsals and metatarsals, smashed phalanxes and taluses and calcaneus bones, rolling through my mind as I walked my daily twenty-five miles. It started to get me down. It took up a lot of mental space and I had other, better uses for that space. I needed to *reclaim* that space. And on the night of Day 80 I did just that.

I've no doubt forgotten quite a few things my trainer Duncan taught me, but the one that's stuck is this: when in doubt, overreact. I kept it simple. I didn't intend to kill anybody, although there are always risks with these procedures. Late in the evening, when the riffraff boys had turned in for the night, and after I'd given them an hour or two to bed down and fall asleep, I began by tossing some ketamine-laced ground beef over the fence for the outdoor dogs. Yes, I had some ketamine stored away for emergencies, and if a drug is good enough to tranquillize a horse, I reckoned it would be good enough to knock out a trio of hounds.

Then, once the dogs were out of commission, I very quietly climbed over the fence and set about building several small piles of flammable material at strategic points around the outside of the riffraff house. It wasn't hard. The whole yard was littered with combustible trash, not least a large number of discarded spray paint cans. Yes, they'd been discarded, but that didn't mean they were completely empty. I figured there'd still be enough xylene, toluene, and acetone in them to create some flames and possibly a big bang or two. Once the trash was in place, I sealed the locks of the house with Krazy Glue, rolled up a few newspapers to act as fuses, lit them, then climbed back over the fence into my own yard to wait for results.

I understand there's quite a science to the classification of domestic fires, but in layman's terms I think you'd say this was a small- to medium-size fire. It wasn't a mighty conflagration or a raging inferno, though I'm sure that when you're trapped inside a burning building with your pals and three of your dogs—as the riffraff boys were—then matters of classification aren't uppermost in your thoughts.

Be that as it may, when the fire trucks arrived you could tell that the firemen weren't initially very impressed. They thought the fire looked like small potatoes, but they perked up considerably when they realized that the doors of the house were stuck and there were people trapped inside. This meant they could put on respirators, and wield axes and bolt cutters, and smash doors and windows. By the time they'd done that and then doused everything in water and foam, it seemed that putting out the fire had done at least as much damage as the fire itself. That was fine by me.

But the firemen did perhaps save some lives, both human and canine. The riffraff boys and their three indoor dogs looked in pretty bad shape as they were finally led or dragged from the burning house. They staggered around in the driveway, choking, gasping, and sprawling against the wrecked, graffiti-streaked cars, but then an ambulance arrived and ferried the boys away. I'd have guessed they were suffering from smoke inhalation, but I really didn't need or care to guess.

It took a little longer for a team to arrive from animal control, and it took a good deal longer still to wrangle the dogs into the van. The unconscious ones in the yard weren't much of a problem, but the ones who'd been in the house were downright frantic. But eventually order was restored: the riffraff inhabitants were gone, the fire was out, the house smoldered gently, there was smoke without fire, and the rest of the night passed very quietly indeed.

On the morning of Day 81, pale pigeon-gray smoke still drifted over the fence from the riffraff property, though I didn't let that get in the way of my walking, obviously. I could see that the house wasn't completely and utterly destroyed, though it was definitely now uninhabitable. To my admittedly untrained eye it looked as though it would be more trouble to repair and restore it than it would be to tear it down and start again from scratch. I hoped the owner had insurance, but on balance it seemed to me that landlords who rent out their property to riffraff deserve everything they get.

The fire was the talk of the neighborhood, naturally, or at least the small part of the neighborhood I knew about. In due course there was even an article in the *Informer*, though I didn't see it myself: it wasn't a paper I ever wanted to look at again. Darrell, whom I now looked at through considerably different eyes, even stopped to discuss it when he delivered the mail. He thought it was obvious what had happened.

"Look," he said, "they were young guys, drunk or stoned or whatever, and they were smoking—maybe they were smoking crack, or freebasing, or whatever these guys get up to—and maybe they'd had a sex orgy and afterward they all fell asleep, and a cigarette or a joint was left burning in an ashtray. Old story. Sad in a way, but also inevitable. Karma, right?"

"That all sounds perfectly plausible," I said, and it did. I was going to ask him how things were going with him and Renée and Small Paul, but I thought better of it: we didn't have that kind of relationship.

When I talked to Wendy Gershwin a couple of days after that, she told me she'd seen a pair of plainclothes cops looking at the fire-damaged house. I didn't understand why I hadn't seen them myself, and I didn't understand how she could know they were cops if they were in plainclothes. But whoever they were, and even if they thought a crime might have been committed, they obviously didn't think it was worth investigating: they didn't even bother asking questions of the nearest neighbor, me.

"Anyway, those riffraff boys got what they deserved," Wendy Gershwin said.

"Ah, Wendy," I said. "'Use every man after his desert, and who should 'scape whipping?'"

I'm not sure she knew what I was talking about, but she agreed nevertheless. "You can say that again," she said.

But I saw no need to.

"Anyway, at least I managed to shoot some footage of the fire," she said. "Maybe my niece and I will be able to use it as the basis of an art project, about the elements or alchemy or something like that."

I didn't rise to that one.

"You're still thinking over my walking proposal, aren't you?"

I said I was, though of course I wasn't.

"Good," she said, "I'd hate to be forced to start the project without you."

THIRTY-FOUR

Another day, Day 85, another twenty-five miles: not easy miles—the day was hot and muggy—but not the hardest. My rhythm was pretty good, my body felt up to the task, the hours and the miles passed quickly. It did no harm that the riffraff boys had gone, I presumed for good. Renée and the two Pauls might be gone only temporarily and/or intermittently, but for now things were very quiet in that direction too. I was trying to keep well out of the way of Wendy Gershwin, apparently with some success. I hoped she and her niece were engrossed in their art. And in the evening another call from Carole, which I now welcomed.

"Things are looking up, eh, Joe?" she said.

I had no idea what she meant by that, so I said, "I'm not sure things were ever looking down."

"But you've been applying for jobs?"

I had no idea why she'd think that, but I didn't immediately see anything sinister in it. I said, "I honestly don't think I'll ever have another job as long as I live."

Carole laughed in a way that she probably thought was light-hearted and full of understanding. I was not wholly averse to her understanding me, but I saw no cause for light-heartedness.

"Oh, come on, you don't have to pretend with me," Carole said.

That still wasn't altogether true, but I said, "I'm not pretending."

"OK, have it your way. But I know you're up to something."

"Do you really?"

"Yes, I do, and I maybe shouldn't even be telling you this, but a couple of people came to see me about you. They said they were considering you for an 'important post' and the visit was standard procedure, as part of the background checks, to ask the spouse a few questions."

I said and did nothing dramatic. I didn't swear, didn't yell, didn't drop the phone.

"The ex-spouse," I said, but that really wasn't the issue.

"I know what we are to each other, Joe," Carole said.

I liked that. It was a good thing to have said, though it was hardly relevant in the circumstances.

"Who were these people?" I said.

"They said they were from the agency."

"Which agency? Collection agency?" I suggested.

"No," said Carole, a little defensively now, "I don't know, the recruitment agency I suppose, or maybe the government. This is another government job, right?"

"You tell me."

"Don't be so mysterious, Joe. They said you were pretty much a shoo-in, and this was just a formality. Your security clearance was fine, but they needed to do a final screening. That's all."

I saw no point explaining that I hadn't applied for any job with any "agency," much less the government. I tried to stay calm. I tried to be neither alarmed nor alarmist, but it was a hard act to sustain.

"Did they maybe say they were from the Team?"

"No. What team?"

"It doesn't matter. They came to the house?"

"Yes."

"A pity you didn't call me while they were there," I said.

"They said I shouldn't. Confidentiality issues. I'm starting to think I shouldn't be calling you now."

"It's OK," I said, trying to persuade myself as well as Carole. "Just tell me, what did they want to know?"

"Nothing out of the ordinary. It was basic stuff. Obvious stuff. Had you ever done anything illegal? What were your hobbies? Were you addicted to drink and drugs? Did you have weird sexual quirks?"

"And you said?"

"I told the truth. I said you were a good guy, Joe, because you are. And I didn't mention Albert Speer."

"Did these people have names?"

"Well, I have the card of one of them—the woman. She was the one who did all the talking. The guy just sat there. I've got her card somewhere here. Hold on."

"Christine Vargas, yes?"

"That's right," said Carole. "So you *do* know all about this. Oh, come on, Joe, admit that you want a new job. Accept that you're probably going to get one."

I was ready to accept a great many things, but a job wasn't one of them.

"Did they ask you where I live?"

"Yes, but only to confirm the address. I assumed they knew that from your application."

What could I possibly have said to her that would have made the situation any better? Carole hadn't done anything wrong, hadn't said anything she shouldn't have said, probably hadn't said anything that most people couldn't have guessed just by looking at me. And of course Christine Vargas, in some respects, already knew more about me than Carole did.

"I understand," said Carole, with no understanding. "I can see that getting back into to work might be a shock to the system."

"That's one way of putting it."

"I can tell you're nervous. But I don't really know why. You've always been good at what you do."

Now she was sweet-talking me. It wasn't the worst thing she could have done, but it didn't help me much.

"Look, why don't I come and see you?" Carole said. "Soon. Like we discussed. We could talk. You could tell me your troubles, more than you ever did before. You know, I've been thinking about it, and I think maybe that was one of our problems: we weren't open enough with each other, we didn't talk enough."

There was no denying that, and in many ways she was saying the right things, just at completely the wrong time.

"Not right now," I said. "This would be a bad time to come visit. But later, for sure."

She decided to accept that. "All right," she said. "You're the expert. You know what you need, but I said it before, and I'll say it again, don't be afraid to ask for help."

"I won't," I said, but at that moment I didn't know whom I could possibly have asked for anything, least of all help.

THIRTY-FIVE

I suppose I might have said to Sylvester, when he came for me in the Black Kettle State Forest, that torture is universal and traditional, though of course there are local variations. Arabs have been known to favor *bisat al-rih* (the flying carpet), in which the victim is strapped faceup on a hinged wooden board, the two ends of which can be moved toward each other, bringing the head toward the feet and causing agony in the lower back and the core of the body. Then there's the *shabeh*, which involves being bound in a variety of stress positions, sometimes strapped to a chair, sometimes hung up by the wrists until the arms pop out of their sockets. To be fair, the Jews have favored the *shabeh* as much as the Arabs.

Given that this character Sylvester seemed to be carrying no great amount of equipment with him, no board or chair, I assumed that his captors had favored simpler, more down-home, improvised methods. The fact is you can put somebody through hell with a pastry fork if you've a mind to.

"You got a cell phone in your backpack?"

"Yes," I said. "But there's no reception here."

"Get it out."

"Sure," I said.

I'd have preferred to keep it, of course, but it wasn't something I was willing to get shot for. We're constantly told that any bullet wound can be fatal. Admittedly, if he killed me he wouldn't have the pleasure of torturing me, but even a nonlethal bullet can inflict all kinds of permanent damage even without killing you. It seemed, on balance, that it was best to give him my cell phone.

"Put it on the ground."

I put the phone on the ground. He stamped on it and kicked away the fragments.

"And now take down your pants. And the underpants."

"Oh please."

"You want a bullet through your knee?"

The same logic applied as with the cell phone. I lowered my pants and underpants. I still had my boots on, so the clothes pooled at my feet, like fabric ankle cuffs. In other circumstances I would have felt humiliated and ridiculous, but I had bigger problems. And so, frankly, did Sylvester.

There are several difficulties facing the solitary would-be torturer, even one with a gun in his hand, perhaps especially one with a gun in his hand. Before the process can start, the victim always has to be immobilized in some way: roped, chained, shackled, whatever. And that's not an easy thing for one man to do when he's holding a gun. Failing that, you need the victim to acquiesce to his own captivity, you need to scare him so badly that he submits, gets in the trunk of the car, or steps into the box or concrete bunker, more or less willingly.

Of course we had no car trunk or box or bunker: we had boulders and trees. You can't tell a man to tie himself to a tree. Sylvester hadn't thought this through. A rookie mistake. Nevertheless he seemed to believe I was scared of him, which was another mistake.

He reached inside his camouflage jacket and produced a section of broom handle, maybe fifteen inches long.

"You know where this is going, right?" he said.

I did, of course.

"And while they shoved the broom handle up my ass," he said, "they attached battery cables to my balls."

He reached inside his jacket again. He clearly didn't have a car battery in there, but he produced a Taser, a serviceable approximation. It was an interesting moment, one of those moments when you know you're going to learn a lot about yourself, one way or another. I'd spent a good part of my life involved with what some people call the "talking cure." I didn't doubt that I could say any number of things that would confuse and anger Sylvester.

"Go ahead," I said. "The sooner you start, the sooner you finish."

This is not strictly true in most cases of torture, but he obviously didn't know that. And maybe I sounded impatient, which must have been unsettling for him. Nobody likes to be hurried at a time like that.

"Move over there," he said.

There was a rounded granite boulder, about the size of a compact refrigerator turned on its side. My role was clear. I shuffled across and bent over the boulder. The rock was rough on my cock and belly and thighs; the air was rough on my ass. Sylvester came closer.

There's another difficulty facing the solitary, novice would-be torturer: some people find it surprisingly hard to administer torture. It doesn't always come naturally. Sylvester hesitated. I did not.

"Go on," I said. "It's what you've been waiting for. Get your revenge. Show me what a big man you are."

That made him angry, naturally, but it also unsettled him, slowed him down even more. Talking was having a certain amount of effect, but something told me it wouldn't enough.

As I bent over the boulder, my hand reached down to the ground and my fingers settled around a rock about the size of a grapefruit. Sylvester might have thought about that beforehand. When he took another step—as he concentrated on what he had to do, as he juggled the gun and the Taser, as the broom handle made first contact with my flesh—I whipped around and belted him in the temple with the rock. The broom handle went flying, the gun too, though it didn't go off. I don't know what happened to the Taser. And I heard myself yelling, "You fucking *amateur*." I had no idea where that came from.

Did I mean to kill him? I've asked myself that a lot of times, and I still don't honestly know the answer. Obviously if you smash somebody in the head with a rock, you know that death is a possibility. If you hit him again, and again after that, as I did—if you overreact—then you definitely know the odds are stacking up against him, and maybe later you question your own motives. But only later. At the time, in the moment, you do what you do: bash the fat, stupid fucker's head in. Only later do you start feeling ethical.

Sylvester lay on the ground, face and skull pulped, arms and legs twitching, so I suppose he was, in some sense, still alive at that point, but by the time I'd searched him, gone through his pockets—no ID, no cell phone, no car keys, no cash—he'd stopped moving, and I knew it was all over for him.

I was then, and I still am, enough of an existentialist to believe that very, very few people are born killers. And I certainly believe that nobody's a killer until the moment he or she kills somebody.

On the other hand, if somebody tells me they could never possibly, in any circumstances, kill another human being, I'm always inclined to say, "Well, let's devise a little experiment to test that out, shall we?" I had been faced with such an "experiment," and the result had not come as much of a surprise to me.

I wanted to get out of there, of course, but I didn't want to do anything too quickly. I knew there was nothing to be gained by rushing. In one sense it seemed I had all the time in the world, time enough to think things through, and I spent a short while wondering whether I could find any use for Sylvester's body, but in the end I didn't see how, so I kicked it off the ledge. It fell a long, long way, then rolled arrhythmically, in fits and starts, down the steep slope. There was no walking trail down there, no dirt road. There wouldn't be any hikers coming along to find the body, but there would be coyotes, hawks, maybe even the occasional bear. I threw the broom handle and the Taser after him, and despite my distrust of guns, I put Sylvester's pistol in my waistband, just in case.

I knew I had a difficult journey ahead of me. Even going the shortest route, it would take a few hours for me to get back to my Jeep, time for somebody to catch up with me if there was anybody out there. Sylvester had said this was just between him and me, and although I was inclined to believe him, I didn't know exactly what that meant. He'd also talked about "us," and I considered it perfectly possible that he might have a partner, possibly more than one, who could be watching me, waiting for the right moment, lining up a rifle shot. If that were the case, the gun I'd taken from Sylvester wouldn't do me much good anyway.

I put on my backpack and started walking. I saw there were blood splatters on my T-shirt, but I did nothing about them. If I encountered another hiker, I could always take the shirt off and walk bare-chested; there was nothing so unusual about that, but the likelihood was that I wouldn't meet another soul.

And at first, as I continued to think about all the many variables and imponderables of my situation, it seemed conceivable there would be no consequences whatsoever. Sometimes that happens. A man dies in the forest and nobody's there to acknowledge it. I would get back to my Jeep; I would drive home, change my clothes, burn the old ones. Carole wouldn't ask me any questions when I got back, because she was barely talking to me. I'd go back to my life, get on with things as though nothing had happened. This was, of course, way too optimistic and glib of me.

I'd walked maybe a mile before I felt myself shivering. That didn't seem right. The day wasn't cold and I was exerting myself; if anything I should have been sweating. And then the shivering took on a life of its own, became uncontrollable. It seemed over-dramatic, something involuntary and showy, and something completely separate from me. I knew, theoretically, what dissociation was, but this was something brand new in my own experience. And then I had an even more involuntary and even less controllable reaction: I started to cry. Tears streamed down my cheeks and my nose started to run. I wiped away the tears and the snot, but there was plenty more where they'd come from. Before long I was blubbering like a child.

My eyes were blurred and I had trouble seeing where I was going, but I kept walking as best I could. If anything I pressed on harder and faster, trying to shake it off, to walk it off. But before long that wasn't a possibility. I found myself sobbing harder than I'd ever sobbed in my life. My whole body was convulsing: it no longer felt as though it belonged to me. I'd been seized by some elemental, though all too human, force. I knew I couldn't continue walking. I knew I'd lost it.

I had to sit down before I fell down, and I slumped to the ground, sitting with my back and my head against the sharp, ridged trunk of a pine tree. I did the things you're supposed to do: breathe slowly and regularly but not too deep, try to focus on some nearby point, tell myself this was OK, I wasn't dying, I was just having a panic attack—behavioral therapy, right?

And a part of my mind was still functioning perfectly well, telling me this really wasn't all that surprising. I'd just killed a man, for god's sake, and whether he deserved it or not, whether I'd acted in self-defense or not, the fact is very few people can do a thing like that and just shrug it off. And in the end that may even be construed as a *good* thing. It's only right that there should be an emotional and psychological cost. This was a reasonable response, proof that I was human.

It was a response that might have left me inert and paralyzed, but even in the worst possible circumstances, human beings do continue to function. Despite it all, people survive and endure, and they do what they have to do. I knew I couldn't stay there forever, leaning against that pine tree. I knew that sooner or later I would have to go on, and maybe that would be a good thing too. Maybe the simple act of walking would bring me back to myself.

So I got to my feet and I walked, not thinking, not rationalizing, and I pressed on for maybe fifteen minutes, maybe a little more, covering maybe half a mile, and only then did I stop, look up and around me, and at that point I realized I didn't have the slightest fucking clue where I was. If I'd lost it metaphorically and emotionally before, I'd now lost it quite literally and geographically.

THIRTY-SIX

Back in the present, in the here and now, in my own yard, I kept walking of course, hour after hour, mile after mile, day after day. What else was there to do? I worried about many things, but I kept on walking. Then, on the afternoon of Day 95, I happened to look over the rear fence and see a man standing in the burned-out remains of what had been the riffraff house. I had no idea how long he'd been there. It could have been a good while, and I got the sense that he might have been watching me for some time.

At first I didn't recognize him. He looked unfamiliar. His back was bent, his posture hesitant, and he was using an ornate metal walking stick with an etched shaft. His scalp was tufted with coarse, patchy black hair, and he was wearing a foam collar around his neck, which hid his tattoos.

"Butch," I said at last, "is that you?"

"You fucking know it is."

By then, of course, I did, but the voice sounded unfamiliarly deep and smoky.

"How's it going?" I asked.

"It's been better," he croaked.

"Where are you living these days?"

"Mind your own fucking business." He poked at a piece of charred, crumbled timber by his foot.

"Looking for something specific?" I asked. I supposed that even riffraff had keepsakes and personal possessions they cared about. Or maybe he'd come back to look for souvenirs.

"An explanation," he said.

I didn't think it was incumbent on me to explain anything, but I said, "These things happen."

There was no denying that, and Butch didn't.

"You've won this one," he said, "but you can't win 'em all."

That was debatable, of course, but I said, "Maybe it's not only about winning and losing."

He considered this, but not for long. "Yeah, it is," he said. "It's always about fucking winning and fucking losing. That's all it's ever about."

I didn't contradict him, because I wasn't sure he was wrong.

Butch had never struck me as a very wordy person, but he obviously had things he wanted to say, to get off his chest.

"You bother me," he said at last. "I don't know who or what the fuck you are. And I don't like that."

"I never asked you to like me, Butch."

"That's not what I'm talking about. Whatever you are, it's not what you seem to be, and that's what I don't like."

He brought the walking stick down on a pane of smoke-blackened glass that was lying in the weeds. A star of silver splinters exploded from the point of impact.

"I'm going now," he said. "But I'll see you again."

"I'm not hard to see."

"I'll see you somewhere else, in different circumstances."

That sounded perfectly possible. The older I get the more the world seems to be full of coincidences that aren't really coincidences at all, full of unlikely and uncanny events and encounters that in fact appear ever less unlikely, ever more "canny." You can call it synchronicity if you like. People turn up at unexpected times, at just the right moment or just the wrong moment, in places and circumstances you would never dream of. It was easy to imagine that Butch might sooner or later fall into this category.

"Things will be different next time," Butch added.

"No doubt," I said. "Things change all the time, from moment to moment."

I hoped it didn't sound too much like something Darrell might have said, but Butch seemed to agree, or at least he grunted in vague assent.

"And maybe next time we won't even be on opposite sides," I said.

Butch grunted again, though this time in disagreement: whatever side I was on, he wanted to be on the opposite.

"People change," I said. "They become different people. They change sides; they change allegiances. Old enemies become new allies."

"Fuck off," Butch said.

But he was the one who left. He limped away through the black and gray rubble, pushing himself to move as fast as he could, which was not very fast. I had time to get a better look at the walking stick he was using. It was very fancy, very stylish, possibly even made of silver. Perhaps he really did need it in order to walk, but it still seemed like an affectation; either way, it also looked like something that could be used as a weapon if necessary. Butch struck me as the kind of man who would enjoy finding it necessary, but I was glad that, at least for the moment, he knew better than to try to use it on me.

THIRTY-SEVEN

Day 96: a hot morning, a gusty allergy-laden wind, a vague threat of rain in the evening, and I saw a pickup truck arrive at Wendy Gershwin's house. The back of the truck was heavy with gardening equipment, and I saw the words VERDANT SPACES were stenciled on the truck door. There was just one man in the cab.

I knew that Wendy Gershwin wasn't any kind of gardener. Her yard was nearly as much of a mess as my own. It didn't seem surprising that she might have decided to get a little professional help. Those blighted apple trees of hers looked especially in need of attention, but the guy in the pickup truck didn't look like anybody's idea of a gardener.

I had to peer hard through the overgrown bushes to get a good look at him, but in any other context I might have thought he was a fitness instructor: supple, alert, buff. And he didn't look like the kind of man who wanted to get his hands, or any other part of him, dirty. His boots, gloves, and overalls were all suspiciously spotless.

I kept half an eye on him as I walked, and I saw he was doing some very slow, very amateurish, very perfunctory cutting back and weeding, stopping at regular intervals to make phone calls and consult a laptop. Do gardeners use laptops these days? Well, no doubt some do.

In the course of the day I saw Wendy Gershwin and her niece come out several times to deliver coffee and sponge cake to this gardener. Wendy Gershwin waved at me over the fence, and I waved gently back, but her gardener pretended not to see me. He hadn't gotten much done by the end of his shift, but it didn't seem to bother him. He behaved as though he had all the time in the world and left well before the rain arrived. He was back the next morning doing even less of the same.

I almost wished Big Paul was still around so I could gauge his opinion of this guy and then come to a different one. As it was, I had to wait for Miranda's arrival that afternoon. Having a suspicious gardener to talk about would be a distraction from other matters.

"I don't like the look of that gardener," she said straightaway, without me having to prompt her.

"No?"

"For one thing, he's not doing any work, is he?"

"Not much," I agreed.

"He's just hanging out in the yard. Whatever she's paying him, it's not worth it. And I bet he's charging her plenty."

I had no idea how much gardeners charged, but no doubt I'd have considered it way too much.

"Or maybe he's not really a gardener at all," Miranda said. "Maybe he's a crook and he's going to get inside the house, go through Wendy Gershwin's stuff, take anything he likes. Maybe steal some art."

"You think so?" I said.

"I'd love to be proved wrong."

I suspected she didn't really mean that.

"I could go over there and talk to him," Miranda said. "Ask him what he's up to."

"No," I said, "better if he doesn't know we're onto him yet. We don't go to him. He comes to us."

Miranda looked at me with an odd mixture of admiration and bafflement. "Well, you're the boss, Joe."

I didn't think that for a moment.

"Ready for a cocktail?"

It so happened, I was.

I didn't have to wait long at all to encounter the gardener. True, he didn't in the literal sense come to me, but in the late afternoon, once Miranda had gone, Wendy Gershwin forced us into a kind of proximity. She appeared at the fence with a tray, carrying more tea and cake for her gardener and me. I stopped walking and took mine with a gratitude that was only partially feigned. The gardener didn't seem grateful at all, but he was happy enough to stop what little work he was doing.

Wendy Gershwin lingered by the fence, and, with no particular plan in mind, I lingered too, and I said, "I hope this guy isn't charging you by the hour, Wendy. You'll have a heck of a bill if he is."

"Oh no," Wendy replied, "he's not charging me anything. He's from a charity. They help out old folks like me who can't cope with their gardening anymore. He's a volunteer."

I had not known how old Wendy Gershwin was, but she hardly struck me as too old to "cope," and in any case she had a young and at least somewhat able-bodied niece, though I could perfectly well understand why she wanted to get work done for free.

"Looks like slow progress," I said to her.

"Oh yes," she agreed. "It's a big job."

"In fact to the untrained eye it doesn't look like any progress whatsoever," I said. I thought that might provoke some reaction from the gardener, but again there was nothing. "But don't you think it's a little over-symbolic?" I said to him directly. "The garden, the spoiled Eden, the blighted apple trees? And what am I in this scheme of things? Adam? The serpent? Come on, you can tell me."

Perhaps he could have, but he didn't. And Wendy Gershwin gave me an indulgent but warning look. She didn't want me driving him away.

I said, "Well, when this guy finishes with your garden, maybe he can keep going and come into mine."

That surely had to provoke him one way or another.

"Oh, but you're not *old folks*," Wendy said. "They only work for old folks."

I don't believe, however old I get, that I will ever use the term "old folks" to describe myself. Still, I said, "Well, they don't have to check IDs, do they?"

Wendy Gershwin giggled. And finally the gardener acknowledged my existence. He said, "We *do* have to check IDs actually, but for you we might make an exception."

It sounded only partially like a threat.

THIRTY-EIGHT

On the afternoon of the next day, Day 98, I became aware of Wendy Gershwin again trying to attract my attention over the fence. I also saw that her niece was silently, meticulously, resentfully loading up their car with luggage.

"We're going away for a few days," Wendy Gershwin told me. "Road trip. My niece has been under the weather lately. She needs a getaway to recharge her creative batteries."

It was true that the niece looked even more drained than usual, but this didn't sound like anything I needed to know about. On the other hand I was glad to be talking about this rather than about the gardener, even gladder not to be talking about Wendy Gershwin's (and arguably my) walking art project.

"Well, have a good time," I said.

"There is just one thing," Wendy Gershwin said. "The gardener's going to keep working while we're away. I'm sure he's trustworthy, but you know, I'd appreciate it if you can keep an eye on him."

I said I would—isn't that what good neighbors are for?—though of course in this case I had my own, perhaps paranoid reasons for keeping an eye on the gardener. I watched Wendy Gershwin drive away, her niece sitting in the passenger seat looking like a spoiled, sulky, and very possibly sedated child.

Next morning, Day 99, I heard the gardener's truck pull into the Gershwin driveway as I was starting my day's walk. In a sense I'd been waiting for him, and in that sense I was glad when he arrived. I heard him kill the engine, get out, and slam the truck door. He wrangled some tools out of the back, went into the yard, and then things went very quiet.

I peered over the fence once in a while as I walked, but I couldn't see any sign of him or hear anything. That was just a little bit odd. I expected at least to hear some footsteps on the gravel or the sounds of hacking or raking or sawing or even his talking on his cell phone. I guessed he must be around the other side of the house, out of sight, and taking it even easier than usual since he knew Wendy Gershwin was away, although if he was just going to laze around and do nothing all day, then why had he even bothered to come? Perhaps he had other reasons for being there.

I seemed to be obsessing about this damned gardener, and I more or less welcomed the distraction when my phone rang, welcomed it even more when I found it was Carole on the other end.

But she immediately demanded, "What's going on *now*?" which did not sound welcoming.

"Not much," I said, trying to sound innocent. I was hardly going to tell her about my gardener obsession.

"Well, something's definitely going on. With you."

Was it something in the sound of my voice? Could she hear my anxiety? Or was she being intuitive? Psychic? Making a lucky, though perhaps pretty obvious, guess?

"Sounds like you know more than I do," I bluffed.

"Maybe I do. I was googling you."

"Why the hell were you doing that?"

"I don't know exactly. Maybe because of those people who came to the house to do the background check. The weird way you reacted. Maybe something to do with still having...feelings for you."

"As opposed to, say, just spying on me?" I said.

"That wasn't my intention, but apparently it's somebody else's."

This was getting all too inscrutable. I said, "Just tell me what you mean."

"OK, somebody *is* spying on you," Carole said, "but it isn't me."

I tried to stay calm, not that it would make a difference. "What are we talking about?" I said.

"There's a website."

"What kind of website?"

"About you. Featuring you."

"What do you mean a website? What the fuck?"

"What the fuck, indeed, Joe. It's called Walking Still. And there you are, walking."

"Are you serious?"

"You think I'd make this up?"

"No, I don't suppose you would."

"The site is really simple. It just shows you walking—in your yard, I suppose, not that I know what that looks like—and that's all, there's not much else to it, just a man walking around and around a circular path, sometimes disappearing behind his house, although every now and then some kind of arty quotation gets superimposed over the image."

"'An artwork may be purchased but a walk cannot be sold,'" I said.

"That kind of thing."

"Wendy fucking Gershwin," I said.

"Who?"

"My neighbor. She's an artist, or so she says. She wanted to film me. I said no. Well, actually I didn't say much of anything, but it seems she went right ahead and turned me into her art project anyway."

"Why would she do that?"

"Isn't that the kind of shit that artists do?"

"But you know," said Carole, "I'm pretty sure this isn't film or video. I mean I've been watching it for a day and a half now. I couldn't believe it at first. But as far as I can tell it goes on twenty-four/seven. It goes on whether you're walking or not. I mean it's just a camera trained on your house and yard. The camera's static, it doesn't move. There's only one angle. It goes dark at night except for the lights on in the house. It gets light when the sun comes up in the morning. So I think it must be live, a webcam trained on your house all the time, like a security camera. When you walk, anybody can see you. I can see you now."

"You can see me?"

"Yeah. I'm watching you now. You're talking on your phone, obviously, and now you've stopped walking, now you're raising your hand to your face. You're scratching your chin. I see you've grown a beard."

All this was true, of course. She was describing exactly what I was doing.

"Now you're looking straight into the camera."

"I am?"

As far as I was concerned I was staring into the trees on Wendy Gershwin's property, and now I saw, not too far above head height, and easily visible once you knew it was there, one of those camouflaged wildlife stealth cameras that people set up in their backyards to photograph wandering deer or raccoons.

"And now you've picked up a rock," said Carole.

"Damn right," I agreed. "Hold on."

I put the cell phone in my pocket and pitched the rock at the camera. It missed, and so did the next one, but with the third I got a bull's-eye. It smashed the camera, so that thin plastic and metal shards tumbled down from the tree. Job done. I took my phone out of my pocket.

"Nice throw," said Carole. "That did it. It did something anyway. The screen's gone black. I can't see you. You still don't want to tell me what's going on? Is this something to do with that government job?"

"No. I don't know what's going on. Honestly I don't, Carole. I'd tell you if I did."

"Would you?"

"Yes."

"I'd like to believe that, Joe. I'd like to believe that you don't lie to me."

I said, "You ask a lot," but I didn't say she asked too much.

"I think I should come to see you, Joe."

"Don't do that."

"I need to see you. I really do. I want to know what's going on. And despite whatever you say, and maybe despite what you believe, I think you need to see me too."

I knew there was no point reasoning with her, so I tried pleading. "Please, please don't do that," I said. "Please. Not now."

"If not now, when? It's no good, Joe. Once upon a time maybe you could tell me what to do, but not anymore."

I thought that was ridiculous and wildly inaccurate. There had never, ever, at any stage of our relationship, been a time when I could tell Carole what to do.

"I'll be there," she said. "Soon. And I'll bring a razor. That beard of yours really looks like crap."

THIRTY-NINE

Being lost in the Black Kettle State Forest struck me as downright absurd and infuriating. I was not the kind of man who got lost when he went out walking. I just wasn't. Only fools and amateurs and children in fairy tales did that kind of thing. But lost I very definitely was.

I'm not the biggest fan of Kübler-Ross's five stages of grief, and yet as I wandered aimlessly and disoriented, I certainly went through some of her designated stages: denial and anger, for sure, and then a certain amount of depression. That was perhaps inevitable. But I'm pleased to say I never entered the bargaining stage. I didn't think God or anyone or anything else was going to get me out of trouble if I promised to behave myself in the future, and I definitely never reached the final stage, that of acceptance. I thought there was a real possibility I might die out there, but I never accepted it.

What I did instead was spend the next three days and three nights—yes, all that stupid amount of time—in the Black Kettle State Forest, utterly lost, walking in the hours of daylight, sleeping when it was too dark to walk. Sometimes I felt I knew where I was and where I was going. I thought I could tell east from west, north from south, but that didn't help. Sometimes I was pretty sure I recognized certain rock formations or trails or clusters of trees, places I'd walked before, but that never did me any good either.

I found a certain amount of water (not good and not enough), and I ate bugs and moss and leaves. And I walked hopelessly, increasingly randomly, in physical and emotional pain, without direction. At times there was, I admit, a certain exhilaration in being so in touch with my animal survival instincts, but at other times there was a hideous, bottomless terror.

Anyway, look . . . this isn't a mystery story. You know I survived, because otherwise I wouldn't be here describing the walk and the struggle for survival. It was tough, as tough as anything I'd experienced until that moment, maybe even worse than the institutional torture I'd received before I joined the Team. My suffering would surely have made Sylvester very happy. And maybe I didn't deserve to survive; maybe natural justice would have had me die in the forest. But I did survive, of course. My salvation was gloriously, humiliatingly banal and undramatic.

I had covered a lot of ground, most of it in various wrong directions, and some of the time I must have been literally walking in circles, but one way or another, slowly, by dumb luck, by an insanely long detour, and completely without knowing it, I'd gotten to the edge of the forest. And there, on the fourth day, on what I could see was one of the tamest, shortest, easiest trails in the whole forest, nothing more than a "hiking loop," I ran into an elderly couple out for the gentlest, least strenuous of afternoon strolls.

I'm sure I looked and acted like a crazy person. Somewhere along the line I'd lost the gun, which was no doubt a good thing. There was still blood on my T-shirt, but I suppose it looked like my own. In any case, the old couple weren't alarmed, weren't even particularly surprised to see me. They seemed, incredibly, to have been looking for me in a half-hearted way. A park ranger had told them to keep an eye out for a lost hiker, but they never expected to find him. Stuff like that never happened to them, they said.

I was dehydrated, barely able to speak, close to hallucinating. I know I did a lot of sobbing. The old couple called the ranger on their cell phone, and he arrived minutes later, seeming oddly relieved to see me. He said he'd found my Jeep a couple of days back. It had been vandalized: windows smashed, tires slashed. There were some bad, sick people out there, he told me. Still, he thought at first it might just have been dumped—they got a certain amount of that in the forest—so he hadn't called out a search party for a missing hiker. They had a protocol for these things, and the circumstances didn't merit one. But something had nagged at him, told him things weren't quite right, that there was more to this than a dumped vehicle. He seemed moderately pleased that I was alive, but he was far more pleased to be right, to have it confirmed that his instincts were solid.

I spent a night in the hospital having fluids, salt, and sugar pumped into me. Nobody asked many questions, least of all the important one: "Did you happen to kill somebody while you were out walking?" The nurses had trouble deciding whether I was an idiot for getting lost or a hero for surviving. I wasn't able to solve that for them.

As I lay in the hospital bed, flipping channels on the TV, I understandably spent a lot of time thinking about Sylvester and what had happened, and I came up with something that I might have thought of much earlier. If the rangers had found my vehicle out in the forest, why hadn't they found Sylvester's? He must have had one. He couldn't have come all that way on foot. He couldn't have parachuted in, could he? He must have gotten there in a vehicle, and he'd have needed it to get out again after he'd concluded his business with me. So where was that vehicle now? Perhaps he'd hidden it incredibly well; conceivably it might even have been stolen, but that didn't seem very likely to me. It seemed far more likely that Sylvester had an accomplice, perhaps more than one, or at the very least a driver, someone he'd left behind in the vehicle because he wanted to confront me alone, because this was, as he said, just between him and me.

I imagined the driver waiting at some appointed spot to which Sylvester would return after he'd completed his business, maybe right beside my own Jeep. Maybe the two of them had destroyed it together when they first saw it, or maybe the driver had done it after it became clear there was no longer any likelihood of Sylvester coming back. And if Sylvester wasn't getting out of there, neither was I.

And then at some point—who knows when exactly, maybe after twenty-four or forty-eight hours—the driver must have realized something had gone wrong. And really, how many possibilities are there when your buddy fails to come back from the wilderness, and you know he was going out there to torture somebody? How many explanations are there? Obviously the other guy won. What would you do next? Calling the rangers or the cops, asking them to send out a search party, wasn't an option, even if it had fitted the protocol. Going out alone to search for Sylvester even less so. In the end, the driver must have simply driven away, gone home to plan the next move, and that too wasn't exactly hard to fathom. I figured that somebody, perhaps several people, perhaps with reinforcements, would come looking for me sooner or later, come looking for revenge: the friends of Sylvester.

The hospital had called Carole, and she came to pick me up the next day. I didn't expect it to be a warm and loving reunion, and it definitely wasn't. It was far more complicated than that. She told me I was impossible, and I didn't disagree. She was furious about what I'd "put her through," and I didn't bother to defend myself. If I'd asked for forgiveness, if I'd sobbed with her the way I'd done in the forest and with the elderly couple, then maybe things would have been OK. But I didn't. Sure, I said I was sorry, but I probably didn't sound very sorry, and then I said the marriage was over, that I couldn't see any way of going on. Things would have to change completely. I would quit my job and we'd get divorced. We'd start new, separate lives, become new people.

Carole gave me no argument; I guess we really were past arguing. She seemed relieved in a way, accepting and eerily calm, maybe just emotionally exhausted. She didn't demand a detailed explanation, which was just as well. What could I have said? How do you explain that you're divorcing somebody you love because you think that may be the best way of saving her life? If we stayed together we both might be killed. This way it might only be me.

That was the last time I went walking in the Black Kettle State Forest, and in fact it was pretty much the last time I went walking anywhere, except around the world in my own yard.

FORTY

It would be ridiculous to say I felt in any way "good" about what was happening around me, with Wendy Gershwin and the camera and the website, and the gardener, and Carole's visit from Christine Vargas, because for one thing I hadn't any idea what actually *was* happening, what any of these things meant. Even so, I did have some sense that things were changing, progressing, even perhaps edging toward a conclusion, and that was surely to be welcomed. I thought again about the gardener. Surely throwing rocks into the garden where he was working should have produced some kind of reaction from him. Was he asleep over there? Was he dead? Was he in a drug-induced coma? I decided to find out.

Reluctantly, because it was an interruption to my walking, and stealthily, because I didn't know what I was about to find, I went to the fence and took a good look into Wendy Gershwin's yard. There wasn't much to see, certainly no sign of the gardener, though his truck was still in the driveway. I climbed over the fence and lowered myself into a patch of ivy and nettles, shrugged them off, and moved toward the house.

I circled past the truck, perused the tools in the back, concluded that a garden shovel offered me the widest range of options for both attack and defense, selected one, then continued with my expedition to the other side of the house. I moved as silently and unobtrusively as I could, but it wouldn't have made much difference. The gardener was otherwise engaged. He'd made a little grotto for himself, assembled from a woodpile, a deck chair, and a wheelbarrow. He had a can of beer in one hand and his cell phone in the other. He was watching something on the phone—it looked like wrestling—and he had his earbuds in place so he didn't hear me even when I was standing right behind him. I could have knocked his brains out, but I didn't.

Instead, I grabbed either end of the shovel's shaft and hooked it over his head like a yoke and pulled back hard across his throat, so I could compress his windpipe as much or as little as I saw fit. He struggled at first, naturally. His arms and legs flailed, and he tried to stand up so he could shake me off. He couldn't. I pulled harder on the wooden shaft.

"The more you fight, the more you'll get hurt," I said.

That settled him down a little.

"Who are you?" I asked, and I released the pressure so he could speak, but he didn't even understand what kind of question I was asking.

"My name's Marco," he said.

"And what are you, Marco?"

"I'm a gardener, man. I'm a fucking gardener."

"You don't look like much of a gardener to me," I said.

"Hey, man, I don't tell you how to do your job."

I tugged sharply on the spade. "You a friend of Sylvester's?" I demanded.

He stuttered. He wanted to give me the "right" answer, but he didn't know what that was, whether it was good or bad to be a friend of Sylvester's, and whether it was better to lie or tell the truth.

"I'm everybody's friend," he said

"You're not my friend," I said.

"Well, you're fucking crazy, man."

I didn't like that. I yanked hard on the spade again. He choked and strained for breath.

"I decide who's crazy and who's not."

"OK, man, OK, so you're not crazy."

"I didn't say I wasn't, only that *you* don't get to decide."

"OK, whatever you say. My name's Marco. I'm a gardener, and OK, I'm a lazy son of a bitch, and I don't know...whatever this guy's name is."

"Sylvester," I repeated.

"I never even heard of anybody called Sylvester. I'm not lying. Why would I lie?"

"I don't know if you're lying or not. But you're finished here, OK? You get in your truck, you drive away, and if you're lucky you never see me again."

I could feel relief run through the man's body.

"Fine," he said. "You know, I've been fired before. Doesn't have to be this hard. You could have just told me to pack up my tools and go. And it's not like I'm charging the old bitch anything."

I let him have that one. Then I let him get up. He rubbed his throat and spat, though well away from me.

"That hurt, man," he said.

"Yeah," I agreed. It did not come as news.

He walked away toward his truck. I followed him, a shovel's length behind him. I saw him stare into the pickup bed and I wondered if he was going to grab another shovel, or maybe a machete, and we were going to have to fight this out like real men. I think we were both relieved when he decided against it, got into the truck and started it up.

"Can I have my shovel?" he said.

"You can have it in your head," I replied.

He didn't like that, but I hadn't expected him to. I held on to the shovel. He put the truck in gear and started to move away.

"You tell your friend Sylvester he can go fuck himself," he yelled out the window.

It was a stupid thing to say, and I shouted back, "No, he can't do that," but I don't think he heard me over the rattle of the engine.

FORTY-ONE

I was now ready—more than ready—for Sylvester's friends or buddies or brothers in arms, or whatever the hell they might call themselves. Naturally I didn't know how many there would be, how they would arrive, how loyal they were, or how dangerous, nor whether Marco the gardener or, for that matter, Christine Vargas was included in the cohort. Neither did I know whether my appearance in the *Informer* and then online in Wendy Gershwin's fucking art project had accelerated matters. Maybe those things were nothing more than static and background hiss, but sometimes you can still hear a message through the white noise and interference. It's a message for you, not exactly coded because you know the gist already, what it says and what it means, even if it's lacking certain crucial details of time and location and personnel. All that seemed to be in place.

Walking away from the situation had never been an option, and so, after I'd chased off the gardener, I returned to my yard and walked on in the same old fashion, continuing with the grand project, which was perhaps now seeming less grand than it once had. I completed my twenty-five miles for the day and then went into the house. I realized—had known it all along—that this was Day 99. Tomorrow would be Day 100: a landmark of a sort, though only a minor one for a man who's planning to walk for a thousand days and twenty-five thousand miles.

It was a long evening and nothing felt right. I had been unsettled by the gardener's presence; now I was fretting about his absence. Was he coming back? Alone? With others? No doubt the same could be said for Butch and the riffraff boys. That empty, burned-out lot now seemed all too full of threatening possibilities. I'd never been exactly troubled, or indeed reassured, by the presence of Renée and the two sizes of Paul, but Big Paul seemed to have gone for good, and this was evidently another of those nights that mother and son spent over at Darrell's place. I felt their absence too.

Above all I felt very alone. I had always been perfectly comfortable being alone, but now things were different. I thought of calling Carole, but that seemed too alarmist. I thought of calling Miranda, but that would have been even worse. I didn't crave company, but I did want something that was no longer available to me: call it peace of mind.

I had never been an insomniac. I could probably count on one and a half hands the number of sleepless nights I'd had in my entire life, but this was one of them. I wasn't frightened exactly, but I felt horribly isolated, hobbled, a solitary individual at the center of his own constricted, circular universe, but maybe that's what everybody always is. What was so special about me? On the other hand, unlike so many people—and this may be a contradiction or it may not—I did feel utterly, exhilaratingly *ready.*

Somehow I got at least a couple of hours' sleep, and when I woke up very early the next morning the world was still in one piece and recognizable enough. And so was I. It was a Sunday. Week-days and weekends were all pretty much the same as far as I was concerned, but Sunday mornings were always the quietest times in the neighborhood. This day, Day 100, was starting out quieter than ever. I would have hesitated to say the day felt grave-like, but others would have had no such hesitation, I'm sure. Still, what else was there to do but get up and start walking? And that's what I did, covering the miles and the hours.

I didn't for a moment expect Miranda to come to the house that day. She rarely came more than once a week, only ever on weekdays, and she never arrived unannounced. And yet, in late afternoon, as I was approaching the end of my daily mileage, I heard the unmistakable sound of her truck arriving. I felt extreme-ly ambivalent about this. Should I tell her about the camera in the trees, the website, my trouble with the gardener, my troubles with Sylvester and his potential friends? Well no, I thought not.

Should I tell her this was Day 100, a cause for a small celebra-tion? And again, no, in the circumstances that didn't seem right either. I decided I'd get rid of her as quickly as possible. But as it turned out I didn't have the opportunity to say or do much of anything. She took charge. She strode up the path carrying a small, chunky picnic cooler. She looked all business, serious, very deter-mined, and pleased with herself, as pleased as I'd ever seen her.

"I've got it," she called to me. "I've had my eureka moment. I've got the Miranda cocktail."

Timing is never the whole story, but it's always part of the story, and this seemed, in one sense, the worst of all possible times to be talking about cocktails, much less drinking them, however new and wonderful they might be. On the other hand there was some pleasant synchronicity in her coming up with the cocktail on my hundredth day of walking. And maybe both bad timing and good timing work in much the same way. Both involve a jolt to the system, a change of perspective, something unexpected that may or may not be relevant or welcome. Maybe I could use that. So I made the best of it, stopped walking and decided that a late-afternoon drink could do no harm. It might even fortify me for those last few circuits.

"So tell me about the Miranda cocktail," I said.

"No need to tell you, I've got most of what I need right here." Miranda gestured toward the cooler. "But I need a couple of other ingredients that I keep inside the globe. You carry on with your walking while I go inside and do my magic."

A couple of circuits later I saw Miranda come out to the porch carrying a shaker and a single conical glass. I left the path, went into the porch, and sat down on one of the rattan chairs in the usual way.

"You're not drinking with me?" I said.

"I had one before I came out. And I had a bunch of them last night. It's really good, but I don't want to get bagged. Again."

"What's in it?" I asked.

"Taste it first."

I took a mouthful of pale, dense orange liquid. I don't know what I was expecting—too much, no doubt. It didn't taste bad, but it wasn't exactly startling. It was strong, simultaneously very sweet and very sour; there was citrus in there, maybe whisky, maybe Pernod, maybe some kind of sticky liqueur that tasted of vanilla or, conceivably, violets. But it was potent. After a couple of swigs I was already feeling light-headed.

"It's got quite a kick," I said.

"That's the idea," Miranda said.

As ideas went it didn't seem such a bad one. I had only a few more circuits to do that day: they could wait a little while. I took another sip, and the drink continued to do its work. The world was a much pleasanter place than it had been just a few minutes earlier: more distant, which is rarely a bad thing, and softer, and considerably less threatening, although I knew that might not be a strictly accurate perception. And after a while, not only did my head feel light, but my whole body started to feel light too, and elastic and uncoordinated. The idea of going back to walking suddenly seemed a very tricky and perhaps rather absurd proposition.

I felt suddenly, inexplicably content, more so than a single drink would usually account for, and even as I enjoyed the feeling, I knew there was something illusory, something too good to be true, about this contentment, and I wasn't wholly surprised when the sky suddenly seemed overcast. Things had been going much too well; some late-afternoon rain was only to be expected. But I looked out through the glass of the porch, up at the clouds, and they still seemed perfectly bright, not at all like rain clouds, which didn't make sense, and then the clouds seemed to be flashing, pulsing, getting lighter and darker in a complex and inscrutable sequence.

Of course I knew something was wrong, that something was happening to me. I didn't know precisely what a stroke or a heart attack or a seizure felt like, but something told me this wasn't any of those things. I struggled, but I couldn't fight it or shake it off. I definitely couldn't stand up. It was hard enough just to remain upright in the rattan chair. My arms, my legs, my spine, even my skull seemed to have been transformed into the softest, most pliable rubber.

I turned to Miranda. Her face was set in an expression I couldn't fathom. It appeared quizzical, determined, sinister, though I was well aware that I could have been misreading all those things. And then her face started to fade away, and the whole world went with it, in erratic stages, as if it were on a faulty dimmer switch, and then I wasn't aware of much of anything except the coarse, woolly sensation of making a long, slow, inelegant slide from the rattan chair onto the bare wooden boards of the porch.

FORTY-TWO

I don't know how long I was passed out. I don't suppose it could have been so very long, but it was long enough for a few surprising things to happen around me, or maybe just fall into place. In due course it was easy to see that these were things that had been on their way for a good long time, though I couldn't have said I'd exactly been expecting them.

I floated back to myself, slowly and patchily, and I arrived with that dislocated post-anesthetic uncertainty, where some things appeared perfectly clear, other things utterly perplexing. I was in the living room of my own house, and that seemed to be a positive thing. The curtains were drawn—it had gone dark while I was unconscious—and the space was lit by just a couple of low, pale lamps. I saw the familiar walls and floor, the couch, the footlocker with the notebooks full of hash marks, the cocktail cabinet in the shape of a globe, the statue of the Buddha. These things appeared quite ordinary, quite reassuring, but then, gradually, belatedly, I became aware of other things in the room that weren't ordinary by any means.

For one thing I realized I was tied up, tied to a straight-backed chair, barefoot, my ankles hitched to the chair legs, a rope around my abdomen, my wrists lashed together behind my back. There was no auspicious explanation for this, although there were other, bigger things that needed explaining.

For one thing, the room seemed oddly crowded. There was a woman standing over me, shadowy, heavy, somehow metallic. It took me a surprising amount of time to realize this had to be Miranda. For some reason she was hard to recognize. Maybe it was because her face was set in the kind of hard, mean, hostile scowl I'd never seen there before, although that didn't seem to be a complete explanation. And she had a claw hammer tucked in the side of her belt. At first this struck me as oddly comical, and then a lot less so.

There was somebody else in the room. A man was standing by the front door that led out to the porch, although he seemed very, very far away, shadowy, big, and formless, wearing a wrestling mask—shiny metallic red, the mouth and eyeholes edged with yellow—which also seemed comical, though no less threatening for that, and he was holding a chunky semiautomatic pistol, which didn't seem amusing in the least.

There were one or two things I wanted to say, and many more that I wanted to ask, but my mouth wasn't working very well: it felt like something constructed out of polystyrene and chicken wire, and I had to reassemble it into working condition before I could speak. Nevertheless, eventually I found myself saying to Miranda, slowly, clumsily, in a voice that didn't sound much like mine, "Am I missing something here?"

I was dimly aware that she had the metal cocktail shaker in her hand. She drew it back and slammed it into my face with sudden, vehement force. It hurt a lot, and the contents of my skull rattled like ice cubes, though that seemed to be the least of my problems.

The masked man left his place by the door, crossed the room, and, not wanting to be left out of the action, delivered a couple of well-directed kicks: a low one to my knee, a high one to my face. These blows had a strangely tonic and sobering effect on me.

"Miranda," I said slowly, deliberately, when I could dredge up a few more words, "I may not have been the very best employer, but this seems a little extreme."

That only annoyed her, which may have been what I intended, though I couldn't be sure.

"You piece of shit," she said. "You murderous piece of shit."

"How's that?"

"You killed my husband."

It sounded rehearsed, like something she'd wanted to say to me for a very long time. I was surprised by it, of course, but since I'd only ever killed one man in my life, there wasn't much doubt about whom she meant.

"Really?" I said. "You were married to Sylvester? Girl, you really do make some bad choices."

She hit me again, which I'd been expecting, with her hand this time, but she didn't contradict me.

"Just how much do you know about Sylvester and me?" I said. She obviously couldn't know the whole story.

"I know enough," she said. "I know what he told me. And he told me a lot. I helped him track you down."

"OK," I said. Maybe I was starting to get it. "You were with him when he came after me in the Black Kettle Forest. You were the driver? Is that right?"

She grunted reluctant consent. I knew more than she thought I did. And, of course, I knew quite a few things that she didn't. Through the wisps of steadying consciousness, parts of the situation were becoming clearer. I had been right about certain things, made some correct deductions. That was good to know, though I wasn't sure how much it mattered. Yes, I'd known there had to be a driver, and I'd certainly had enough imagination to think it might be a woman, but I hadn't thought of it being a wife, much less Miranda. That was a big mistake on my part. And now I supposed she had to be the one who'd wrecked my Jeep. Well, why not? It probably, briefly, made her feel better. I could also understand that after that she might want revenge for her husband's disappearance and death—and yes, I was having trouble thinking of Miranda as a married woman, even more as a widow—but those weren't the only gaps in the narrative.

I wondered, for one thing, if Miranda knew what Sylvester had had in mind to do to me. There was no reason he should have told her his exact plans. Perhaps his plans were never very exact in the first place, though I'd have thought she might have noticed that he was carrying a broom handle, a Taser, and a gun. These weren't exactly weapons of mass destruction, but they were very much the means by which you might kill somebody. But maybe that didn't matter to her.

"And now you're going to kill me?" I said.

"That would be fair, wouldn't it?" said Miranda.

"Sure," I said, though I assumed that fairness wasn't going to be much of an issue.

My instinct was to play for time, though I didn't know whether time was on my side.

"But fair or not," I said, "I don't think you're a killer, are you, Miranda? Otherwise you'd have done it by now, wouldn't you? Let's see if I've got this right. After you lost Sylvester, and after you worked out that I must have killed him, you came looking for me again, on your own this time, and you found me here, and I suppose you wanted to kill me, but you weren't going to hide in the woods and shoot me like a sniper. You needed to be at close range. Or maybe you don't like guns. Maybe you thought you could poison me. Slow poison? Is that what the whole Miranda cocktail business was all about? The poison in the martini glass—classic, old school. But when it came to it, you couldn't do it that way either. You had to settle for the Mickey Finn. You knocked me out. You tied me up, and here we are. And you needed an accomplice, and so you've got this clown here to help you. You can take the wrestling mask off, Paul, it makes you look like a dick."

Big Paul made a muffled, irate, primitive grunt beneath the slick fabric, but there was no point in him denying his identity.

"Fuck," he said, and he hit me across the face with the butt of his gun, very hard, very effectively. The man wasn't completely without ability. Then he tore off the wrestling mask. "I knew this was a lousy idea."

I wasn't sure if he was referring only to the mask, and apparently neither was Miranda. She decided he needed reassurance, and she walked over to him and delivered a thick, wet French kiss. If I'd still been capable of surprise, maybe that would have surprised me. Big Paul seemed to enjoy it, though I couldn't help thinking it was done for my benefit rather than his.

"You're right, of course, Joe," Miranda said, peeling herself away from Big Paul. "I'm not a murderer."7

Was I supposed to feel relieved? I didn't. I looked at the gun. I looked at the hammer. I wondered how much of a psycho Big Paul was, whether he was going to do the job for her.

"So you're 'just' planning to torture me?"

"Not much gets past you, does it, Joe?"

She walked over to the globe and flipped open the upper hemisphere. She took out the bottles with their multicolored liquids, removed a kind of false floor from the globe, and revealed a metal object nestled in the bottom of the sphere, a device that she'd been hiding in there, I wondered for how long. It wasn't a wholly unfamiliar thing. I'd seen a couple of them before, though never outside of a museum. I'd certainly never seen one in use.

It was a version of the torture instrument known as the Spanish or Malay boot, whether a genuine antique or a modern replica, I couldn't have said. It was a hollow, clunky, foot-shaped metal form constructed from movable plates, with a complex arrangement of bolts, flanges and hinges, and a geared hand crank, much like a corkscrew, that could bring all the moving parts into excruciating, contracting proximity.

Miranda knelt in front of me, and then in an act of bizarre, studied, paradoxical supplication, she assembled the boot around my bare right foot.

FORTY-THREE

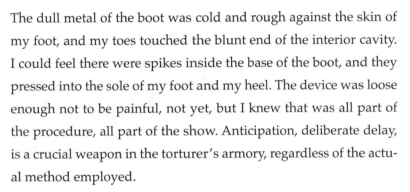

The dull metal of the boot was cold and rough against the skin of my foot, and my toes touched the blunt end of the interior cavity. I could feel there were spikes inside the base of the boot, and they pressed into the sole of my foot and my heel. The device was loose enough not to be painful, not yet, but I knew that was all part of the procedure, all part of the show. Anticipation, deliberate delay, is a crucial weapon in the torturer's armory, regardless of the actual method employed.

"I know what you're thinking," said Miranda, which I doubted. "You're thinking that this is a waste of time. We all know that you can withstand pain. You're trained for it. You've trained others for it. I know that's what you're good at."

She wasn't altogether wrong.

"Well then?" I said.

"But that's not the point."

I wasn't so foolish as to ask her what the point was.

A great many people who have no interest in psychology, and have never heard the name Stanley Milgram, are nevertheless familiar with the Milgram experiments conducted at Yale in 1961, part of his investigations into the psychology of the Holocaust, to determine whether the "just obeying orders" defense actually held water.

His eighteenth experiment, referred to as "shock administration," is the one everybody knows about, or thinks they do. Under the auspices of an experiment apparently to test memory, participants were encouraged to give increasingly powerful electric shocks to fellow participants every time they gave a wrong answer. Various authority figures egged them on, "authorized" the use of dangerously high voltage, told them they were relieved of responsibility. Most of, though in fact not all, the participants were content to administer "lethal" electric shocks. Significantly, or not, there were no women involved in this experiment.

Milgram concluded, "The extreme willingness of adults to go to almost any lengths on the command of an authority figure constitutes the chief finding of the study and the fact most urgently demanding explanation." But frankly, who needs to have this explained to them? Who can seriously doubt that people will do the most terrible things when they think they're "permitted" to? And it's by no means only about somebody in a white coat or a military uniform taking responsibility. Sometimes it's about believing that circumstances demand it: the old ticking time bomb justification.

In some other cases a different kind of permission and justification comes into play. The mother attacks the schoolteacher because he's laid hands on her precious child. The man beats up the guy in the bar because his girlfriend has been insulted. The motivation is real enough, and it's not done for "no reason," but sometimes it seems that the protagonist is looking not for a reason but an *excuse*.

I wondered where Miranda fell on this spectrum. Did she feel at that moment entitled to do whatever she liked to me because I was such a *bad guy*? Could she do it on Sylvester's behalf, as an act of defensible posthumous justice and revenge? Whether she was a genuine pathological, diagnosable sadist—an Elizabeth Báthory or an Eichmann in the making—I had no idea. As for Big Paul's role in the proceedings, was he the muscle, the insurance policy, the guardian angel? Or did he have needs and desires of his own that he was now about to indulge?

It will hardly surprise you if I say that torture is a form of self-expression. The methodology reveals the man or woman. In my job with the Team, I was bound by certain strict guidelines, but even so there was always scope for improvisation, for personal idiosyncrasies. Clearly Miranda was not bound by any guidelines whatsoever; nevertheless she obeyed a set of her own imperatives, had her own *style*. It would take me a while to experience her complete repertoire, to understand the full extent of her capabilities, but my immediate impression had her down as a—that word again—*natural*.

Miranda began her work. She grimaced at some private thought, and then, with care rather than exuberance, she turned the crank on the front of the metal boot. The process began, the coming together of the mechanical and the organic, the mute indifference of the device, the human imperatives it could articulate. A shot of sudden, hot pain fired up from my foot, through my leg, and deep into my core. It was thrilling in its sharpness and intensity. I gave a low, involuntary cry, and it seemed to me I could detect a phantom smell of wet paper and stale vegetables.

Of course threats are a part of any torture. You threaten to kill the victim (though Miranda had apparently lost that option), or you threaten to kill the victim's mother or sister. Only some of these threats are entirely real, but only some of them are entirely empty.

Torture is, or can be, a subtle art. You don't rush. You keep the victim waiting and guessing. You don't immediately turn up the pain to full power. You don't even turn it up gradually in a steady progression. No, as with any performance there's a need for dynamics, for light and shade, tension and release. Miranda seemed instinctively to know all this. She tightened the screw again. A clear, constricted spasm pulsed through me. My body tightened. I started to pour sweat.

"How much does that hurt?" Miranda asked. "On a scale from one to ten? Do you think the scale only goes up to ten? I don't, Mr. J, I really don't."

I didn't reply, didn't speak. I tried to appear impassive as the agony flashed through me, keeping my face as blank as I could, trying to fake stoicism and absence. I tried not to give Miranda the satisfaction of knowing how much I was suffering. Simultaneously I knew this was probably a pointless exercise and that it wouldn't last long. What good does it do to pretend you're not in pain when all concerned know that you are? Maybe it only forces them to raise the stakes.

Miranda gave the crank another twist and I heard Big Paul laugh. He was not directly involved, but I'd have said he was not quite impassive. I wouldn't have claimed to know all that was going on in his head, but I'd have said he was enjoying this spectacle way too much.

There was one element in the current procedure that was very much the same as that experienced by my volunteers. As I've said before, torture is often done, and perhaps done best, for some clear purpose, with a specific end in mind: to get the subject to reveal names, dates, the location of the ticking time bomb. Questions are asked; answers are sought. When the victim coughs up the information, then the torture stops.

But, as when I dealt with my volunteers, here was a situation where none of this applied. It seemed to me that I had nothing Miranda wanted, nothing that she couldn't have obtained by other methods, just as the volunteers had nothing that I wanted. And this meant that now, in the living room of my own house, there was nothing I could do to bring this torture to an end, except perhaps dying, and we seemed to have established that wasn't the intention. Miranda simply wanted to hurt me, to have me suffer. It was a question of how much and for how long. And Miranda, I discovered, had considered that too.

"You know," she said, "I've been thinking about the whole 'that which doesn't kill us makes us stronger' thing. I think it's kind of lame. I don't think being killed and being stronger are really exact opposites, do you, Joe?"

I assumed she didn't expect me to reply, and I didn't.

"In any case," she continued, "you're right, I'm not a murderer. I'm not planning to kill you. Good news, right? But obviously I don't want to make you stronger either. So the plan is this: I'm just going to fuck you up for the rest of your life. By the time I'm finished you won't ever walk again."

FORTY-FOUR

It's said that the human body, or I suppose more correctly the human mind, has a bad memory for pain. Having been tortured twice in my life, I can confirm that this is in some limited sense true, but having a bad memory is not the same as having amnesia. Therefore, I am not simply reconstructing events from scratch when I say that I was in complete agony for the next many hours, as Miranda and I mapped the neural pathways, the pain and nerve centers and receptors, of my body. It seemed that my foot, this distant part of the empire, was constantly sending back messages, dispatches from the front line, from the war zone, and reporting with extraordinary detail and vividness, making this distant conflict real for every other part of my being.

It seemed to me that my foot, anybody's foot, was an absurdly, needlessly complex piece of equipment, so vulnerable, so fragile, so temperamentally unsuited to its crude, practical purpose. And as these pulses and wavelengths of agony traveled through me, it seemed that I was getting to know my own body better than I had ever known it before. I understood how the blood flowed, how the oxygen pumped, how the bones fitted and ground together, how the viscera moved around and against one another. Perhaps this was worth knowing.

Miranda did a fine, economical job. The smallest act on her part, the simple, casual turn of the crank on the metal boot, was amplified and enlarged through my whole body. But even so, as I could have told her, or Big Paul, or anyone else, inflicting pain on another human being for a sustained period of time is not a simple business, either physically or mentally. Remaining fresh and focused is difficult, and now Miranda, a natural though she might be, was learning this for herself. By the middle of the evening she looked exhausted, and she slumped down on my couch swigging a beer—no fancy cocktails, no mixology at this point. Big Paul sat beside her, adjacent yet far away, looking serious, stupid, infinitely dangerous.

Pain continued to ripple and twang and reverberate through my body even though the boot had been temporarily partly loosened. For now I was experiencing a milder agony, inhabiting a point in the world that was suddenly static and falsely calm. I knew better than to allow myself to feel relief.

Then there was a noise outside the house, a car pulling up by the garden gate. We all heard it, and in other circumstances I expect none of us would have thought anything of it, considered it to be just random background noise, but as it was, both Miranda and Big Paul leaped to their feet, newly alert, poised, ready for some urgent, necessary, though undefined, action. And then there was the sound of the car door opening, someone getting out, the car door slamming shut. There was a rattle at the gate, then footsteps on the path leading up to the porch and the front door.

"I'll take care of it," Miranda said, even before the knock came. "You two be very quiet."

Big Paul was resentful at being given the same instruction and status as me, but he didn't argue about it.

Miranda stepped out onto the porch and closed the front door behind her, but I knew I'd be able to hear most of whatever was happening outside. God knows I didn't get many visitors, and never any on Sunday evenings, and I didn't know if this unexpected arrival was likely to be a good or a bad thing.

I heard Miranda open the glass door at the front of the porch, and then there was a quiet, though urgent, conversation, two women's voices, and I couldn't hear what was being said, until the second voice, belonging to the new arrival, suddenly said, very loudly and very clearly, "This is bullshit, I'm here to see Joe."

I recognized the voice now. It was Carole's. She'd been as good as her word. She'd come to see me. Timing is everything. I knew things could now only get worse.

I heard Miranda say, "I told you, he's not here," and I wanted Carole to believe her, but I knew she wouldn't.

"Don't be ridiculous," said Carole. "Of course he's here. He never goes anywhere, does he? If he's not walking in the yard— and I can see he's not—then he's got to be inside the house."

"All right," said Miranda, trying to remain calm and placatory, "yes, he's inside, but he's sleeping. He's been sick. Flu."

Nobody could have thought that sounded convincing.

I heard Carole say, "I'm going in."

"You shouldn't do that. Really," said Miranda.

And obviously, in every conceivable way, she shouldn't have, but Carole wasn't the kind of woman who took no for an answer. She interpreted Miranda's words as a challenge. This did not, in any way, surprise me. There were the sounds of what might have been a scuffle on the porch, though not much of one, and then Carole threw open the front door of the house and stepped into the living room.

I can't imagine what she expected to find, but not this, never this: her ex-husband tied to a chair with his foot inside a torture device, and a man sitting on a couch, holding a gun that he now raised and cocked and pointed at her. She stopped dead, looked at Big Paul, looked over at me. We made brief, painful, confused eye contact, and then Miranda clubbed the hammer down on the back of Carole's head. Carole went down fast and hard, hit the couch with her flank, then slid to the floor.

"What the fuck?" said Miranda to Big Paul. "You were going to shoot her?"

"No," he said, "I wasn't going to do that."

But neither of us entirely believed him.

Torturing one person in order to make another person suffer is a well-known tactic. In the case of civilians it works best when it involves members of the same family, particularly parents and children. In other circumstances it also works surprisingly well with members of the armed forces or a militia who perhaps like to see themselves as a band of brothers. When it comes to spouses, things can get trickier and less predictable. Certain husbands and wives can be remarkably sanguine about seeing their "loved one" suffer. I suspected that Miranda didn't know this.

My sense of reality was alarmingly fluid by then, and I didn't entirely trust my senses, but I was aware of Carole being dragged across the room and tied to a straight-backed chair much like the one I was on, though unlike me her mouth was bound with silver duct tape and her feet were not bare, and neither of them was inside a metal boot.

Carole's arrival had made Miranda angry, and I wasn't surprised by that, but I didn't like it. An angry torturer can be dangerously volatile. The arrival also energized her, and I was the recipient of this new energy. She ramped up her performance, even as I tried to tamp down my own reactions even further. Nonsensically, absurdly, I didn't want Carole to see how much I was suffering. My body trembled and shivered. Gold and black amoebas burst deep inside my eyeballs. I tried to absent myself. I pictured planets, volcanoes, pilgrims walking across the desert, an empty classroom with maps on the walls, and geometrical diagrams drawn on a whiteboard.

It was a long night. I made further eye contact with Carole once in a while, but I said nothing. If my eyes were communicating anything to her, it was probably something crass and bogusly inspirational: *Hang in there, kid. We're survivors. It isn't over till it's over.* I would also have liked to convey that I was sorry and that I loved her, but I don't know if that got across. In turn, her eyes seemed to be saying, or at least I interpreted them as saying, *What the fuck did you do to get me into this?*

I could have told her, but not right then.

Time passed, but not quickly, in an incomprehensible show reel of pain, interspersed with trailers, clip shows, bloopers, cliffhangers, repeats. There was torment, the occasional relief from torment, which would then start again and mutate into a different, though intimately related, species.

I felt the many broken components of my foot grinding and splintering against one another. I knew the foot was damaged beyond all reason and perhaps beyond all repair, and it scarcely felt as though it belonged to me. I didn't want it to; I didn't want to be forced to claim ownership, to have the terrible responsibility.

I had the profound sense that I wanted to be rid of it, rid of my own weak body. I wondered if Miranda had really known what she was talking about when she said she wanted to fuck me up for life. I wondered if I'd ever, in any sense, be able to walk away from this.

FORTY-FIVE

When I heard the furious banging at the glass door of the porch, I thought I could be imagining it. I thought it might be my own heartbeat or a pounding headache or just wishful thinking, a deranged dream that somebody might be coming to save me. But Miranda and Big Paul and Carole obviously heard the noise too. And there was nothing remotely dreamlike about the voice calling my name.

"Come out here, Johnson. Come out, you fucker. Let's settle this once and for all."

It was not imaginary. It was Butch's voice, wild, drunk, angry, barely in control. He'd come back to complete some unfinished business he imagined he had with me, or perhaps to prolong it.

"I know that voice," Big Paul said unnecessarily.

"Of course you do," said Miranda. "He was your neighbor. Butch."

"That little jerk," said Big Paul. "I'll go out and shut him up."

"No," said Miranda very calmly, and expecting to be obeyed. "Don't do that. I'll go. I'll get rid of him. I can handle him."

I wondered if she could. It seemed to me she hadn't handled Carole all that skillfully. I knew there had to be some kind of history between her and Butch, otherwise she wouldn't have known when and how the riffraff boys were going to attack my house and me, but that hardly constituted a bond. I thought Butch would still take a lot of handling.

For my own part I could suddenly see some small room for optimism here. Was that reasonable? Maybe reason had nothing to do with it. Was I an idiot to see some sign of hope in Butch's arrival? Maybe I was, but at least it meant that Miranda was again not going to have things her own way. Her plan, whatever it had been, was going to have to change. Random factors were coming into play, and a certain amount of chaos always guarantees, if nothing else, unpredictable and unexpected outcomes. I hoped I could benefit from that.

Did I think Butch was, in any sense, on my side? No. His yelling certainly suggested not, although I didn't think he was on Big Paul's side either. In other circumstances, all things being equal, in a straight fight between Butch and Big Paul, my money would have been on Butch. His violence and anger seemed to come from a deeper, more intuitive place. But things are never exactly equal—Big Paul had the gun. Or maybe it would never come to that. Maybe Miranda would sweet-talk Butch and send him quietly on his way. I hoped not. I wanted the chaos.

I could hear them on the porch talking quietly at first: Miranda's presence had calmed Butch down. But soon they were shouting at each other. There seemed to be some kind of dispute, an escalation of volume and vehemence. It seemed to me, from what I could hear, that there were accusations from Butch about what Miranda was doing in my house in the middle of the night. The inference was opaque, and it wasn't immediately clear to me why Butch would care. Did Miranda owe him something? And then it became perfectly clear. Of course she knew about Butch and the riffraff boys' activities, because Butch had been another of her bad choices. The argument outside now sounded as though it was a lovers' quarrel and I was being cast as the "other man." Even in my desperate state I could tell there was something absurd about that.

And then Butch changed tack, started to play the role of the aggrieved party, and after what sounded like a rougher struggle than Miranda had had with Carole, Butch too threw open the front door of the house and stepped into the living room.

He saw me, saw Carole, saw Big Paul still sitting on the couch nursing a gun, and he too stopped dead. Butch was not a complete idiot. He knew he'd walked into the wrong room at the wrong time. Miranda was right behind him, though this time she wasn't brandishing a hammer. She shoved him deeper into the room and closed the front door.

"Oh fuck," Butch said. "This is, I don't . . ."

Big Paul didn't stir from the couch, but he raised the gun, straightened his arm, and without hesitation let off three shots. The walls reverberated with the noise, and the smell of oil and carbon wafted through the room. At least two of the shots hit Butch in the chest, and he was thrown backward as though on bungee cords. If any gunshot can be fatal, then it was hard to believe that these could be anything but. He clutched his torso, as though feeling around for something—his wallet, his heart—then twisted around to look at Miranda.

His face was all hurt and confusion, but then the confusion eased and slipped away. He didn't have to think about anything anymore, and his features were smoothed into quiet, though painful, acceptance. He looked suddenly young and untroubled, like a blissed-out schoolboy. He fell with a thick crash onto the footlocker in front of the couch, his head pointing precisely between the globe and the Buddha.

"Now see what you made me do," Big Paul said, then looked down at Butch. "Fucking pantywaist."

FORTY-SIX

The corpse on the floor of the interrogation room is not the worst ploy for an entry-level torturer. The proximity of death—its look, its ontological resonance, and eventually its smell—concentrates the mind of the victim considerably, though I knew it would be a day or two yet before the putrefaction and stench began. I wondered if we'd all be around that long.

I know that more time must have passed, because I know that's what time always does, but it didn't seem to. Right then, in my living room, it felt as though certain laws of nature and physics had been bent and buckled, ceased their standard operating procedures, and we were living in a hellish eternal present.

I know I didn't sleep, so there's no way I could have been dreaming, but I don't think I was exactly hallucinating either. Nevertheless my mind and my imagination were full of images that came from somewhere other than the real world. The best of them offered a kind of escape: a man who both was and wasn't me, walking in a garden of giant mushrooms that towered over his head like massive alien umbrellas; a man walking on water, but then the water turned to quicksand, and he sank into nothingness; a man in a prison cell, pacing back and forth like a caged zoo animal, trying to log his progress in a tiny notebook the size of a thumbnail.

And then I started doing math in my head, an attempt to make myself absent, envisaging the parameters of my grand project, its line and length, its coordinates. I saw a world, or maybe just a globe, divided into segments like an orange, or I suppose more correctly (because Earth is ellipsoid) a grapefruit, and I could see the distances, set out like a textbook figure: the circumference, the radius, the diameter. I tried to cut the world into twenty-five-mile fragments. I tried to add up the days, the distances, the years; divide them; multiply them. This helped just a little.

And so the night passed too, a broken, ramshackle, ruined thing, its end signaled only by the eventual seep of light around the edges of the drawn living room curtains. For a second, in my bewilderment, I thought it would soon be time to start walking again, and then I remembered who and where I was, the situation I was in, and suddenly that situation seemed the saddest thing in the world, a sorrow rather than a torment. And then the actual torment returned as Miranda came back into action and cranked the handle on the metal boot. I heard something snap and crumble inside me.

Carole and I had stopped looking at each other. Of course we had no choice but to stay where we were, but Miranda came and went, mostly in silence, doing a little more work on me from time to time, as and when she thought necessary. Big Paul sat around, a brooding but largely inert presence. Killing Butch had had a settling effect on him. Maybe it had satisfied something in him.

My perceptions weren't exactly trustworthy, but it did seem to me that the gaps between Miranda's periods of activity were growing longer. I might almost have thought she was losing her taste for torturing me, though I didn't dare to believe that. She was looking worse and worse, more tired, more frazzled, though I wasn't naive enough to think this should necessarily give me any cause for hope. A weary torturer can get sloppy, and a sloppy torturer can be much worse than a fastidious one.

Then out of nowhere I heard Miranda say, "Oh, fuck it. What is this? Somebody *else* is coming in the gate."

Big Paul stirred himself, out of duty rather than enthusiasm. "Who?" he demanded, reasonably enough.

"It's the mailman," Miranda said. "Darrell."

It was by no means unknown for Darrell to come in through the gate and up to the house, whether to deliver a package, junk mail, or even a bit of Zen wisdom. I thought he was much earlier than usual, but my sense of time was in tatters, and I didn't read much into it. Maybe his courtship of Renée was putting a spring in his step and he was getting through his work that much quicker. Did Big Paul know about him and Renée? Would he care?

"Leave it," Big Paul said. "He's just delivering mail. He'll be gone in a minute."

"I don't know," said Miranda. "He's not in his uniform. And he's got a fucking kid with him."

Big Paul got up, crossed the room to the window, and peered around the edge of the curtain. "Hey, that's *my* fucking kid," he said. "I'll handle it."

"Try not to kill anybody this time," said Miranda.

It seemed to me that Big Paul didn't much care whether he killed anybody, but he tucked the gun into the back of his waistband so it wouldn't be seen as he faced the new arrivals. Apart from that, it seemed to me he was being very reckless or careless or stupid. He left the front door of the house open, and we could clearly hear what was being said to Darrell, and Darrell, if he chose, could quite easily have seen into the house.

"Hello, son," I heard Big Paul say.

Small Paul mumbled a grudging hello.

If Darrell was surprised to find Big Paul there, and surely he must have been, he kept his reactions in check.

"I'm bringing him back," he said. "So Joe can go on with his homeschooling. It's not been working out with him and me."

That didn't sound right at all. Obviously he knew my first name from having read it on various pieces of mail, but I didn't think I'd ever heard him use it before. It was an odd time to start getting familiar.

"OK," said Big Paul, "leave the kid here and I'll take care of it. You can go."

It seemed that Darrell was about to leave, but then, making it sound like an afterthought, he said, "Is Joe around? I need to talk to him about something."

"No, he's not around," said Big Paul, a remark that was obviously going to raise more questions than it answered.

"Thing is, I need my statue back," Darrell said.

"Statue?"

"The Buddha. I think he keeps it in the living room. Maybe you've seen it."

This all sounded utterly unlikely.

"You need it right now?" Big Paul said.

"Yeah, I've found a better home for it."

I wondered if he maybe intended to regift it to Renée. That made a kind of mangled sense. I guess when you took on Darrell you took on the whole package, though I was oddly offended that he was taking back what he'd given me. Had he decided I wasn't worthy of it?

"Well, I can't start giving the guy's stuff away when he's not around, can I?" said Big Paul.

That sounded plausible as far as it went, but it didn't go far enough for Darrell. "It's not his stuff, it's mine," he said.

"Does it have to be right now?"

"Yeah, it does."

"OK," said Big Paul smoothly, "you stay here, I'll bring it out to you."

"You'll need help," said Darrell. "It's heavy."

Now, we both knew *that* wasn't true.

"I can handle it," said Big Paul.

"And it's fragile. And valuable."

Neither of those things was true either, as far as I knew. It seemed that Darrell, just like Carole and Butch, really wanted to get inside the house. I wondered why he wanted that.

"Look, I'm not going to stand out here *debating* with you about it," Darrell said. "I'm going into the house to get what's mine."

I wondered if they'd fight. I wondered if Big Paul would shoot him. He didn't. Maybe the boy's presence deterred him. I hoped that was the reason. Or maybe he was just obeying Miranda's order not to do any more killing. And so Darrell, like the others before him, pushed his way into the house, with Small Paul trailing after him, and Big Paul behind them both. But unlike Carole and Butch, Darrell was quite unfazed by what he found in the living room.

"Having a party?" he said to nobody in particular.

He turned to look at Big Paul, who was now pointing the gun at him.

"You sit down," Big Paul said to his son, "keep out of trouble," and somewhat to my surprise the boy sat down in the middle of the couch, his eyes wide, as though he'd strayed into a live wax-works and had gotten a prime seat in the chamber of horrors. His eyes flicked back and forth between Butch's splayed corpse and the metal monstrosity at the end of my foot. He seemed too shy to look at Carole.

"And you stay right where you are," Big Paul said to Darrell.

"This is your idea of 'dealing' with it?" said Miranda.

"Hey, I'm not here to cause trouble," said Darrell evenly, and he sounded like he meant it, and he didn't sound at all scared. Maybe he was used to dead bodies and tied-up people and having guns pointed at him.

"Pat him down," Big Paul said to Miranda, "see if he's carrying a weapon."

Miranda patted him down, grudgingly it seemed to me, and found nothing.

"I don't usually pack heat this early in the day," said Darrell.

"Maybe you should," said Miranda.

"Look, guys," said Darrell, "if you all have got into some kind of sex thing here, I'm not going to interfere. I'll just take my Buddha and you can get on with it."

I didn't believe that Darrell honestly thought he was seeing any kind of consensual group S&M scene, and Miranda obviously didn't believe it either.

"I don't think so," she said. "If I let you leave you'll run straight to the cops."

Darrell looked deeply hurt. "You don't know me," he said. "Maybe you haven't noticed, but I'm a black man. That kind of distorts my feelings about the cops."

Who would have doubted him?

"And I never liked this smug white motherfucker Johnson very much either," he added.

Again, it wasn't something I was in a position to feel sensitive about, but I did wonder why everybody seemed to hate me so much.

"Sit down on the couch," Miranda said to Darrell. "Next to the kid. And keep your hands where we can all see them. We're going to have to figure this out."

Darrell took his place on the couch beside Small Paul, adjacent to the statue of the Buddha. His arms were relaxed, his hands cupped over his knees. He looked at me, at Carole, at Butch's body on the floor, and his face remained expressionless. I couldn't say he'd reached a state of Zen tranquillity and transcendence, but he definitely looked a lot more at ease than most people ever would in that situation.

"I've got nothing against you, Darrell," Miranda said. "I know you're just a mailman."

"Ain't that the truth?" said Darrell, though personally I was no longer so sure.

We all stayed where we were, in silence, for a good long while. I, of course, and Carole too, and Butch in his own way, had no choice in the matter. Small Paul was restless and twitchy, but he did his best to be still. The seriousness of the situation was seeping into him.

At first I thought Miranda was genuinely trying to think of a course of action, a way out of this. That would have been quite an achievement, maybe an impossible one, but it seemed to me that before long she'd completely stopped thinking, and we were all just sitting there, doing nothing whatsoever. Nothing was happening, and nothing seemed likely to happen. I wasn't even being tortured, though the pain still hung around my body like a burning towel.

Darrell stretched himself a little and spoke gently. "You know what the Buddha said? He said, 'Do not dwell in the past, do not dream of the future, concentrate the mind on the present moment.'"

It didn't sound like bad advice, in general terms, but I'd have been surprised if Miranda, or in fact any of us, had found it to be any practical help in the circumstances.

Darrell continued: "The Buddha also said that he didn't believe in a fate that fell on men regardless of how they acted. He believed in a fate that fell on them *unless* they acted."

"What the fuck does that mean?" Big Paul demanded. He was suddenly very angry. I thought he might shoot Darrell there and then, out of sheer irritation, but Darrell remained unruffled.

"The Buddha also said, 'Holding on to anger is like grasping a hot coal with the intent of throwing it at somebody else; you're the one who gets burned.'"

Big Paul laughed without humor and said, "So this guy lived before gloves were invented?"

Darrell smiled serenely, smugly, infuriatingly.

The Buddha, I'm sure, said a lot of things that are very hard to disagree with, and given time, I expect that even Big Paul would have recognized the self-destructive nature of anger, but in that moment the idea didn't make him any less angry.

He said to Darrell, "One more word and somebody dies. And it's probably you."

I wondered if Miranda would have gone along with that—it seemed she really didn't want anyone to die—but by now she didn't have much control over things. Darrell smiled again, beatif-ically this time.

Buddhists, as I understand it, don't believe in hell, and most of the time I'm pretty sure that I don't either, but the next mo-ment, in a metaphorical sense anyway, all hell broke loose in the living room of my house. Darrell had never struck me as especially graceful or catlike, but he suddenly broke into elegant, fluid, fe-line motion, dreadlocks trailing behind him. Or maybe it wasn't so much sudden as inevitable, and not so much sweeping into action as becoming the action itself. He grabbed Small Paul by the shoulder, pulled him off the couch, then cast him aside so the kid ended up on the floor, facedown, out of harm's way, although pressed against the footlocker and Butch's dead body, and then Darrell continued with the movement, diving toward the statue of the Buddha.

At first, absurdly, impossibly, I thought he was trying to hide behind it, but that would have been downright idiotic. Darrell knew better than anybody that the figure was only made of bam-boo: it would scarcely have protected him from birdshot. And then even more improbably, he drew back his fist, as if he was going to punch the Buddha in the back, and then he did exactly that.

I wondered why he was doing it, if maybe he thought his holy man had let him down, though that didn't seem very plausi-ble. The punch was fierce and precise, and Darrell's fist smashed straight through the smooth lacquered surface, splintering it as it went into the cavity of the body and reached for something hidden inside, and then the fist reemerged and I saw—we all saw—there was now a gun in Darrell's hand.

Big Paul was surprisingly quick to understand what was go-ing on, much quicker than I was, though admittedly I wasn't at my most alert and perceptive right then. Or perhaps it wasn't a matter of understanding, and maybe Big Paul started shooting only because he didn't know what else to do. And maybe there was nothing else he *could* have done, not really. And maybe it was simply luck or chance, or something that some people might call fate, that one of the shots, one of half a dozen fired quickly and without much premeditation, certainly without much aim, hit Darrell in the hollow of his neck, right under the Adam's apple. Darrell coughed and gurgled, looking clownishly amazed as a thick cravat of blood formed around his neck, and he fell back onto the couch, his dead eyes fixed on a crack in the ceiling.

Miranda hissed, "What the fuck are you doing? What the fuck is going on?" and although she was obviously saying it specifically to Big Paul, I had the sense that she was asking a much broader, much more general, maybe even cosmic question. Big Paul didn't choose to explain his actions even if he could have, but at least he didn't blame Miranda this time.

"It was self-defense," he said, and I suppose there possibly was an argument to be had about that.

"Oh, you fucking idiot," Miranda said.

I felt weary and I felt sick. I had a terrible sense that this could go on forever, that all these arrivals, all this killing, really amounted to nothing. They made no difference. I was still in the most terrible pain, I was still tied to a chair, still being tortured; my ex-wife was still a hostage. And it seemed unlikely I would ever again walk normally or with pleasure. The last of these seemed by far the worst. Was this selfish of me? Oh yes. Self-absorption is never an appealing trait. And maybe that's why I stopped paying attention to what was going on in the room.

I hadn't been keeping much of an eye on Small Paul. I was glad enough that Darrell had pushed him to the floor, to safety, but after that the kid hadn't been uppermost in my thoughts. By the same token I didn't know what had happened to Darrell's gun either. If I *had* thought about it, I'd have assumed it must have dropped onto the floor when he was shot and that maybe it had slid behind the Buddha or under the couch. And I'd have been right about it dropping to the floor, but it hadn't fallen behind or under anything.

It had landed very close to Small Paul's right hand, and of course if anybody had been aware of that, we'd no doubt have told the kid not to touch it, but I guess we all had other, apparently more pressing things to worry about. But now I looked up and saw that Small Paul had picked up Darrell's gun and was holding it loosely, clumsily, but with an extraordinary calmness. And I think I may have said, or at least started to say, "Be careful with that thing, Paul," and Big Paul certainly said, "Put it down, you little fucking idiot," but this time Small Paul didn't do what he was told, and he got to his feet and stumbled toward his father.

I didn't know what he was up to, and neither did Big Paul. Was he in need of a fatherly hug? That seemed perfectly possible. And by the time any of us realized, it was way too late, and the kid was pumping bullets into his father. The shots might have gone anywhere, and some definitely went into the floor and the wall, and one hit the globe and shattered it, but a significant, crucial number went into Big Paul's stomach and groin.

Small Paul's homeschooling had taken a sudden, unexpected, and no doubt revelatory turn. And even in that moment as Big Paul belly-flopped onto the floor, dead as a roll of carpet, I thought, "There's a kid who's going to need an awful lot of therapy in the years ahead." And then he raised the gun and pointed it at me.

FORTY-SEVEN

Sometimes you save yourself, sometimes you don't. Sometimes you can't. Sometimes somebody else has to do it for you, but Miranda and Carole were in no position to help me. And if you're tied to a chair, you really can't do much of anything, but at least I could talk. I said, in what I hoped was my best, calmest, most reassuring therapist's voice, "Hey, Paul, why don't you put that gun down and then untie me?"

He didn't want to do that.

"OK, Paul, let's take it a step at a time. Why don't you at least stop pointing the gun at me?"

"I don't know."

"You don't want to kill me, do you?"

He only had to think for a few seconds before saying, "No," but it was a long few seconds.

"And this is Carole, my ex-wife, you don't want to kill her, do you?"

"I don't know her."

"Well, you wouldn't want to kill somebody you don't know, would you?"

I didn't wait for his reply to that one.

"And you don't want to kill Miranda."

"No."

I wasn't sure what I wanted him to do to Miranda, but I was glad when he pointed the gun at the floor, and that was enough for her. She ran from the room and out of the house. I wondered where she could be running to. I wondered if Small Paul would chase after her, but he didn't.

"I only wanted to kill my father," he said.

"And you've done that. Now you can take it easy."

Without having to be asked again, he put the gun down very deliberately, very carefully, on top of the footlocker.

"And now, Paul, would you be kind enough to untie both of us, maybe Carole first?"

He didn't say anything, but he moved over behind Carole's chair and, after a lot of ham-fisted fiddling, managed to free her hands. Then he returned to the couch, threw himself down, and hid his face in the upholstery, sobbing. Carole could do the rest herself. She pulled the silver duct tape from her mouth, balled it up and threw it across the room, then untied her own feet. She got up, looked as though she might fall down, but steadied herself, went over to the footlocker, picked up the gun so Small Paul couldn't reach it, then came over to me. It did cross my mind that she might shoot me in the face. I'd have more or less understood if she had, but she didn't. She kissed me on the forehead, then slapped me across the face, then kissed me again. It was as good as I could have hoped for.

She tucked the gun away, undid my ropes, but that was the easy part. Together we had to remove the metal boot. I can't say that Carole helped lovingly or even very willingly, but she did it. The process was agonizing enough in itself—the pain doesn't stop just because the torturer has run away—and the thing that emerged from its metal container, the thing that had once been a foot, my foot, no longer resembled anything quite human, anything mine. It was a piece of crushed, pounded meat, dripping with blood and fat, fragments of bone and gristle poking out through the shredded purple-and-red skin. Seeing it now, clearly and fully, made it hurt in a brand-new way, even as the old hurt persisted.

When it was done, while I still sat on the upright chair, Carole leaned over and put her arms around me. That didn't feel especially loving either, but I was prepared to settle for it.

I said, "Would it help if I said I was sorry?"

"Couldn't do any harm, could it?" Carole said.

"How's your head?"

"It hurts."

"I love you," I said, and I wasn't sure if that was likely to do harm or good.

"Yes, we love each other," said Carole. "So fucking what?"

Like Miranda, I too had to get out of the house, out of that room, though I wasn't even sure if I could stand. Somehow I managed it by draping myself around Carole, and together we supported and dragged each other out of the living room, across the porch, into the yard, and at last onto the stone bench with its resting lions. Small Paul remained in the house with the bodies, and I knew I should have cared more about him than I did.

Carole and I sat together silently for what seemed a very long time. There was nothing more to say and nothing to do. We were passive, powerless, waiting for the next thing to happen. I could hear my own breathing and also, of course, Carole's: loud, regular, desperate, and deep. And then I heard a car pulling up outside, the tires heavy on the road surface. Another arrival. My first thought was it might be the cops coming to the right place at the wrong time, or maybe the opposite. Conceivably it might have been Renée or Wendy Gershwin and her niece. Whoever it was, I could see that a great deal would need to be explained, and I didn't think I had the strength for that.

And then the garden gate opened and two men came in, followed at a distance by a woman. The men—one broad, one lean; one black, one white; both exceptionally tall—had guns drawn, had unnecessary sunglasses, and wore leather jackets that flapped open to show the empty holsters beneath. They looked around the yard as though it might get up and attack them. The woman, who had no sunglasses or gun, was somebody I recognized, and I supposed Carole did too: Christine Vargas. The men moved into the house while she remained outside.

She took a few paces along the circular path as far as the stone bench and said by way of greeting, "Mr. Johnson, how the heck are you?"

The question was so ludicrous, so deliberately so, that I wanted to laugh, but that was not an option.

"I've been better," I said.

"Of course. But you've also been worse."

"I'm sure."

"And, Mrs. Johnson, nice to see you again."

"Fuck you," said Carole.

"Of course," said Christine Vargas, who now also looked around the yard, though unlike her colleagues, she seemed to find it fascinating rather than threatening.

"All the real mess is in there," I said, nodding toward the house.

"Don't worry," she said, and it really honestly sounded as though she didn't want me to worry. "My boys will deal with whatever needs to be dealt with."

"Darrell was one of yours, yeah?" I said.

"Sure. So was the gardener. Not two of the brightest and the best, obviously, but yes, on the payroll. Temporarily."

"The gardener was one of yours?"

"I think you should say one of *ours*, Mr. Johnson. One of the Team. You're one of ours too."

"So these guys were trying to *protect* me?" I said.

"Well, to keep an eye on you. And protect our interests. We knew someone was coming to get you, but we didn't know who and we didn't know when or how any more than you did. I gotta say I wasn't expecting it to be the girl who bought your groceries."

"No," I agreed.

"We had to wait for her to make the first move."

"And her second and third," I said. "And she got away."

"She won't get far now that we know who she is," said Christine Vargas. "The police will pick her up. The courts will deal with her."

"And what, charge her with assault? It's not even attempted murder, is it? She'll get a couple of years and then probation?"

"We don't make the laws, Mr. Johnson, we just bend them."

I may have snorted in exaggerated derision.

One of the leather-jacketed goons came out of the house, nudging Small Paul in front of him. The guy looked beseechingly at his boss. He didn't know what the hell he was supposed to do, and he looked relieved when the kid ran over and threw his arms around me. I put just one of my arms around him in return: it was the least and the most I could do.

"We'll locate his mother," said Christine Vargas.

"Great. That'll solve everything."

"It'll do no harm, will it, Mr. Johnson?"

I saw that Small Paul, and for that matter Christine Vargas and Carole, kept staring at the butchered remains hanging at the end of my leg.

"That doesn't look good," Christine Vargas said.

"You think?"

"Spanish boot?"

I nodded. Say what you liked about the woman, she could recognize torture when she saw it.

"I'm afraid that's going to put an end to your walking project," she said.

I didn't even bother to answer.

"And that may not be such a bad thing," she added. "You know, some of us have been thinking that you must be ready to come back to work for the Team."

I didn't want to contemplate who the "us" were who'd been doing this thinking.

"Because it all worked out so well last time?"

"It worked as well as could be expected, Mr. Johnson. Sylvester was our only significant failure. And of course, as you see, the small failures are always infinitely more trouble than the big successes."

"I can't go back to what I was doing before," I said.

"No, we wouldn't expect that. It wouldn't be the same job, though it would be the same skill set. Training."

"Training who?"

"Our staff. Training our interrogators."

"To do what?"

"To interrogate, of course. Are you being deliberately difficult, Mr. Johnson?"

I didn't think I was being difficult at all. "Training them to be torturers?" I asked.

"I never said that, Mr. Johnson. I never said anything remotely like that."

That was perhaps because she didn't need to.

"The terms would be better, the hours shorter. It would leave you plenty of time to tend your garden."

"I think you can see I never did any tending. I just walked in it."

"What you do in the privacy of your own backyard is entirely your business, Mr. Johnson . . ."

I could feel Carole stirring beside me, as if she was about to utter some grand condemnation and denunciation, but the words wouldn't quite come out.

"You and your wife should discuss it, obviously," said Christine Vargas.

I tried to get to my feet.

"I'm no medical expert, Mr. Johnson, but I'd think that walking on that foot of yours is a very bad idea. There's an ambulance on its way."

I did my best to ignore her, and yet I wanted to explain myself. I said, "While I was being tortured I did some thinking."

"It probably wasn't your *best* thinking, Mr. Johnson."

"Call it calculating then. I realized that whatever happened I wasn't going to be able to complete the grand project. I know I'm not ever going to be able to walk twenty-five thousand miles."

"It does look that way," said Christine Vargas.

"But you see, here's the mathematics of it. They got me at the very end of Day 100. I'd walked twenty-five miles a day for ninety-nine days. I'd very nearly completed twenty-five miles on the last day."

"It's very impressive, nobody's denying that."

"I'm not trying to impress you. I'm saying I would have completed one hundred days, twenty-five hundred miles, if Miranda hadn't drugged and tortured me."

I took out the small notebook that had remained in my back pocket throughout this ordeal, opened it, showed Christine Vargas all the orderly hash marks. I could tell she didn't care.

I said, "So I may not be able to walk around the world, but ten more circuits and I'll have walked a tenth of the way, about the same as walking across America."

"If you say so," said Christine Vargas.

"I do. And any damn fool can walk ten circuits," I said.

"That's right," Small Paul agreed. "I can help."

He offered me his hand and shoulder for support. Carole raised herself up and took the other side of me.

"It's going to hurt like fuck," I said, "but I'm going to do it."

"Yes, Mr. Johnson, I believe you are," said Christine Vargas.

I started walking.

ABOUT THE AUTHOR

Geoff Nicholson is the acclaimed author of *The City Under the Skin, Bleeding London, Bedlam Burning*, and the cult classic *Footsucker*, among many others. His journalism has appeared in many periodicals as varied as GQ, The New York Times, Bookforum, Art Review, the London Daily Telegraph, the Guardian, and McSweeney's. *The Miranda* is his most recent novel.